Luna Sea

KIM ROBERTS

ISBN 978-0-9885868-0-2

Dedication

To Blain: I cannot express it as well as Brandi Carlile's lyrics in her song "The Story," but, thank you. This is what happens when our stories collide.

Acknowledgments

Good friends offer you their time and talent when you need it most. I thank my writing partners Marlene Thomasson and Brian McGregor for the many hours of shared reading, writing and laughter. I offer special thanks to my friend and editor Barb Aue for finding time when there was none. Thanks to Tammy Jones Harding for the nudge to publish. Thanks to Delores Zelepuza for introducing me to the songs of Brandi Carlile. And always—I thank Blain for believing.

Lunacy: 1. insanity, mental disorder. 2. intermittent insanity, formerly believed to be related to phases of the moon. 3. extreme foolishness or an instance of it. 4. unsoundness of mind sufficient to incapacitate one for civil transactions.

Webster's Encyclopedic Unabridged Dictionary of the English Language

Chapter One

Surfing off Lahaina is like having sex with your ex-husband. It's almost always available, and although it might not be the biggest you've ever seen, you can usually out-compete the twelve-year-olds, if not the nineteen-year-olds. Plus, once in awhile, you get the kind of ride that you reflect on late at night and almost feel wet again. At least that's what I'd heard.

Three hundred yards off the Lahaina Harbor breakwater, close enough to see people waving and hear a dog barking, I wondered if I still had the body to wear a bikini as I tugged the royal blue bottoms of my swimsuit out of my butt crack. My oldest sister Liebe and I had just paddled out to surf the break on the south side of the Roadstead—an area known for its excellent anchorage and average surfing. A cruise ship was anchored a half-mile away from us and there were maybe half a dozen other surfers, who looked to be in about fourth grade, competing for the waves. It was not the North Shore. As we paddled, we could see the ship's tenders shuttling tourists into town like ants carrying sugar. Again, I reached around and gave the boy-short bottoms of my swimsuit a tug. This time Liebe noticed.

"Aloha, what's on your ass?" Liebe, an Air Force lifer, interrogated me in her usual blunt tone.

I pretended not to hear her. Since leaving the Coast Guard with a full disability due to a tiny accident with underwater explosives, I was one ear away from total deafness. The three bones in my inner ear had punctured my eardrum causing an injury to the vestibular area that also affected my balance mechanism. Technically, I could count relearning to surf as therapy.

"A. J.!" she shouted this time. "Really, what's on your ass?"

This time I tried to pull the waist of my Lycra surf shirt down over my rump. I kept paddling, held my breath, and ducked my head as a small wave broke over the tip of my board. I had my hair pulled back in a tight bun wrapped in a scrunchie. Blonde bangs slicked back by saltwater left freckles my most prominent feature.

On the other side of the wave she shouted. "Ha! I knew you could hear me. You're such an ass." Then she grabbed my board—all waxed up for a better grip—and held tight. She slipped into the water and yoinked on my bottoms. For a woman who'd had a double mastectomy within the past year, she'd rebuilt a lot of her arm and chest strength. Surfing was her therapy too.

"You've got a tat' on your ass!" She had set a new record for using the word ass in consecutive sentences.

"Really? I had no idea," I replied, narrowing my eyes at her and paddling away. Ten feet below us, a school of green sergeant majors with black vertical stripes skittered through a sand channel and into the muted green reef. A silver-bullet-shaped barracuda followed in hot pursuit, dodging the hard corals and lava ridges.

"Wait! What's it say?" Back on her board, Liebe paddled next to me, sat up and read the words, "Once Bitten—Twice Shy" inked above my not-so-young, but oh-so-bare lower back. Then she laughed like the lunatic she was until she was flat on her board slapping it and kicking her feet. "How long have you had that?"

"Since Basic," I said. Liebe had earned her wings by the time I got the tattoo. Over the years, she hadn't had a chance to see its canvas. Her interest reeked of amusement.

I ignored her hysterics, sat up, straddled my board, and watched for a wave worth surfing. The ocean was too calm, but it was only my second week living on Maui and I wanted to reacquire my skills. May as well start small.

"Ever hear from him anymore?" Liebe had turned toward shore and was paddling fast to catch a little roller. She hopped to her feet and rode it out, splitting the difference between where she started next to me and the Lahaina Harbor channel, sparing me having to answer. I didn't want to talk about Snake. And watching her tall, lithe figure finesse the wave was a bonus.

One of the cruise ship tenders was chugging down the channel, forcing a bulky catamaran heading out on the evening booze cruise to wait inside the breakwater. The cat's crew blared beach music at a decibel level so high even I could hear the chorus to "Margaritaville."

I looked away from Liebe, the boats and the harbor, just in time to see a wave set coming in with my name written on it. Paddling like I meant it, I felt the tip of my board lift and I hopped up to find my balance. Right away, my visual senses began compensating for my blown equilibrium. For a modest wave, it had a steep drop that turned into a nice shoulder. I rode in just a little past Liebe before I let the board scoot out from under me. I tried to slide into the water like a seal so I didn't scrape on the shallow coral.

When I pierced the surface, I paddled over to my board and hung my arms over it for a moment. That's when I noticed someone snorkeling between the harbor's breakwater and the green can buoy on the opposite side of the narrow channel.

The catamaran I'd seen waiting to leave the harbor was cutting through the channel's ruffled surface, picking up speed as she turned the corner. I noticed the name *Awiwi* painted on the starboard bow and I thought it sounded like a dopey name. Nevertheless, for a gigantic floating party platform, the scow was quick. She plowed ahead and I willed the snorkeler to swim faster. He didn't. I began waving my arms to warn the boat off and the revelers aboard dutifully waved back. I could see—if not hear—them mouth the word "Alooooo-ha!" I hadn't technically learned to read lips, but since the accident, I realized I'd already started to use my sight to compensate for my hearing loss. I didn't know them and they didn't know me, so it surprised me to see my name shouted by strangers. Meaning hello, love, and goodbye in Hawaiian, my name's definition could also be a summary of my personal life. Still, none of this helped slow the boat.

From my vantage, it looked like the snorkeler—his face in the water—might get lucky enough to split the difference and swim between the cat's twin hulls. The captain, outfitted in navy shorts and an epaulette-laden white shirt, posed with one hand casually on the huge wheel. He had his other arm around a middle-aged woman in a floral printed muumuu, while a man—I assumed to be her husband—in a shirt matching her muumuu, video-recorded the event. Then the boat swung to port just enough to bob up and splat down on the snorkeler's back.

"Liebe!" I yelled to my overachieving sister. She was already halfway out to sea, paddling for her spot in the line-up. I gave her the international water distress signal by waving both arms. She immediately turned her board and began paddling toward me like a tiger shark after a whale calf. Sometimes, her intensity is scary.

I threw a leg over my board, went flat on my belly and began paddling to where I'd seen the snorkeler get hit. The prop wash from the *Awiwi* swirled around me as I slid off my board and free dove into the water made murky by the harbor traffic. In my rush, I hadn't removed my surf leash and my free dive was halted by my board's buoyancy. I popped back up to the surface just as Liebe paddled in, peeled the Velcro leash off my leg and threw it to her. She was busy waving an inbound dive boat away from us. I refilled my lungs and kicked myself underwater. I felt incredible pain in my bad ear as I swam down and remembered that diving of any kind was one of the things I'd been warned not to pursue. I kicked harder and scanned the water as best I could without a mask or goggles. In the gloom, bobbing toward me I saw the snorkeler. I grabbed his arm and swam to the surface, exhaling as I rose.

Breaking into the warm Hawaiian air, I gulped a breath of water and proceeded to hack up a lung while wrapping my arm around his chest to keep his face up. Liebe was yelling at me. I was choking. The guy wasn't moving. I was getting really whipped.

"Aloha! It's too late." Liebe, now off her board, pushed my board toward me.

Shit she's bossy. No wonder she'd made rank early, I thought. "Never too late." I gasped between coughs.

She said, "He's stiff." She'd know. Since she'd had her bout with cancer followed by a divorce, she'd been playing the field with the vengeance normally afforded a professional athlete. She knew stiff when she saw it.

As the oldest of the six sisters, her role had traditionally been "crew chief" as my retired Air Force father liked to say. Now, post-mastectomy, she was acting like her hormones had gone to boot camp and her scruples were AWOL.

Of course, I was thinking all this as I struggled to get the snorkeler's face clear of the water. That's when I realized his arms extended into the air. Plus, he wasn't wearing a mask or snorkel. The *Awiwi* had hit a floater. Liebe was correct. He was stiff.

The *Awiwi*'s captain had spun the boat around and tacked back into the channel. Above us, one of his crew tossed a life-ring while the rest of the crew along with fifty or a hundred borderline drunks, leaned over the stainless steel rail for a better look. I had already wound my surf leash around the man's waist and was using my board to keep him afloat—albeit face down—so I ignored the ring.

"Is he okay?" The captain, with a soul patch on his chin and an apparent abhorrence for underwear, called down to us, his personal equipment visible, untethered and unremarkable from our vantage point in the water.

Liebe, the same person who had asked me if I knew I had a tattoo, hastened to reply, "No, he's not okay. He's dead. And did you know your nuts are shaved?"

Somehow I thought he knew.

"I'll call the harbormaster," he said, seeming to ignore her last comment.

As he turned to reach for his radio mike, I yelled, "Don't bother!"

"No, I'm calling him. You two are crazy." I noticed he didn't say we were nuts. I also noted that he had some kind of quasi-British accent going.

I was swimming my cargo toward the harbor during this exchange and yelled back. "You can't call the harbormaster."

"You bet your ass I can," he said, up for the challenge. Liebe had that kind of glassy look in her eyes. I realized he'd just used her favorite word, plus, I could tell she liked the idea that he was going commando under his shorts. She is such a pervert.

"No you can't!" I yelled back, beginning to get annoyed. "Just call the cops and tell them to meet us at the loading dock."

"Jesus, lady, who made you boss of this harbor?" His crew had gone aft to put out rubber bumpers in preparation for tying off to the concrete loading dock, and to herd the passengers away from the floater—never a good encounter on a booze cruise. It was just the four of us involved in the conversation: Captain Smooth Sacks, me, Liebe, and the dead guy.

In answer to his question I said, "Max Yake." Just then, I could almost see a dim light go on over his head.

"You're the new harbormaster?" he asked, as I heard a grinding screech off his port bow. He had gotten a little out of the channel and run the boat down the side of the green can buoy. Instinct took over and he slammed the throttle into reverse. The water off the stern swimstep churned as he scraped the buoy back along the fiberglass hull.

"Yep!" I yelled, even though I was pretty sure he wasn't listening anymore. Liebe and I and our corpse kept swimming, as the boat's crew raced to find a way to cut the line from where it was hung up on the buoy. One by one, I could hear the cat's metal stanchions popping as the captain tried to pull the boat away from the can buoy, which had become a large and immobile anchor. Finally the line parted with a loud snap. The boat idled and I could see him making the call, cell phone in one hand, the other on the wheel. He slowly spun the boat around and motored out of the channel to regroup. His port railing bowed like a cheap metal coat hanger.

We kept swimming. By the time we were twenty feet from the loading dock, a big Maui cop sauntered over to us, waving tourists aside.

"You no swim here." He flicked us away with his hand. "We got boating accident coming in." From the water he looked like he was about eight feet tall and half that wide. He had a buzz hair cut, and a big gun on what looked to be a thirty-inch belt under a fifty-inch gut.

"But officer…" I tried to draw his attention to the guy next to me.

It worked. Kind of. He looked at the man and said, "*Ho brah*, you no swim here. We got boating accident." The dead guy didn't look up. I could tell it pissed off the cop. He looked at me, yelled, "*Aznuts!*" and waved his giant paw. I took it to mean he thought we were nuts and no great loss if we got an Evinrude haircut.

Just then, Liebe decided to outrank him. "Hey you ass. Don't you want this dead guy?" Then she rolled our floater over. His arms reached up like he was looking for a hug. The Maui cop didn't seem to mind. I was straight-armed on the side of the monolithic loading dock, ready to climb out when he said, "You push him up here."

I kept climbing. "No, you pull him up." We had an impasse. Then I looked over at the fish hoist and raised an eyebrow. The not-quite-big-enough-for-Sumo cop looked at the dead guy, then looked at the hoist, then looked back at the dead guy. I could tell he was thinking about it. Lucky for all of us that while he pondered, the paramedics arrived and hefted the body onto the dock where it teetered for a minute on fingertips before rolling over, arms in the air. The tourists waiting to board the cruise ship tender on the other side of the dock gave a group gasp.

Thinking things couldn't get any worse, I retrieved my board just as Liebe tried to boost herself out of the water and onto the dock. That's when one of her double-D prostheses popped out of her suit and bobbed nipple-side-up next to her in the water.

The big cop choked so hard he doubled over trying to look like he was coughing, but I think he might have been giggling. I know I was. Liebe grabbed her bobbing boob and chucked it onto the dock. The cruise ship crowd gasped again. Then she climbed out of the water, shook out what was left of her chemo-thinned hair, and popped the prosthesis back into her suit.

"Alrighty then ..." she looked around, hiked both breasts into place and said, "What?" The word unflappable came to mind.

We leaned our surfboards against a concrete planter next to my tiny office building. My fingers trembled as I tried to unlock the door. "Wuss," Liebe whispered as she pushed past me to grab her towel where she'd left it on the counter for easy access.

"Flasher," I responded, as I grabbed my towel off my desk and wrapped it around me like a skirt. Man, she was one tough broad. We took turns doing a quick change in the negligible bathroom and went back out to the melee on the dock.

By that time, one tender had left and another was docking. The paramedics had the dead guy in the ambulance where he was making a tent with his arms. I grimaced at the thought of his rigid wave and turned to look for Liebe when I swear I heard the corpse call my name. The hair on my arms stood up. Then I felt a hand on my shoulder. I about wet myself.

"Jones, what the hell's going on here?" My Harbors Division boss, Max Yake, kept his hand on my shoulder a moment longer than I would have liked. I'm not much of a toucher, so his lingering fingers were unwelcome in an instant. Next to him stood his subordinate, Gil Mangas, the marine patrol officer out of the Kahului office. He wasn't my superior, but during my training, he'd acted as if he owned the whole damn ocean. Gil was to Max what Yogi was to Boo-Boo Bear: Big, brown, hairy and outwardly gregarious versus little, hairy, morose, and blue in an old white guy kind of way. Both were dressed in their civvies. Gil didn't have on a Yogi tie, but he was wearing the hat. Max had apparently opted out of the bow tie.

Man, I loved that cartoon.

"How'd you get here so soon?" I shook off my heebie-jeebies when I realized his was the voice I'd heard call my name. Whew!

"Whadya mean? Gil and I were out on the cruise ship having cocktails with the captain. We just got off that tender." Max pointed across the dock where the cruisers—exhausted from a day of shopping in Old Lahainatown—shuffled on board. You could almost hear their wallets heaving a sigh.

Just then, I heard a shriek. "Oh! My! God!" A woman ran from the cruise ship queue toward the big local cop. "Awiwi!" she cooed as she rushed up, attempting to wrap a hug around his ample chest. Three of her friends took off after her, pulling cameras from their bags as she yelled, "Oh, take my picture with Awiwi."

"Awiwi?" I asked. "Like the boat?" Max just shrugged.

Another voice over my shoulder said, "His name, it means fast."

I turned to see a guy who looked like a sepia-toned Amish Rastafarian. His dreadlocks dangled almost to his waist. He wore a beige gauzy Mexican-style shirt with black cotton slacks, and black leather Topsiders. What I mistook for suspenders were long-strapped bags over each shoulder. One looked like it held a guitar and the other, maybe a ukulele.

"Huh?" I said, demonstrating my usual flair for witty repartee.

"Officer Lono there. His name's Awiwi. It means fast in Hawaiian."

He punched a series of numbers into his cell phone and turned away. Definitely not Amish, probably not even Rastafarian. In fact, he wore a large silver cross hanging from one ear, reminiscent of a pirate. Overall, I judged by his dark skin and large muscular build, although not as big as the cop he called Awiwi, that he was at least part Samoan or Tongan.

And what kind of name was Awiwi? It made sense for the catamaran, but I didn't get why anybody would drop that name on a little kid. Good thing Liebe was back at my side. "Whadya mean fast? He's not fast. He's not even half-assed." She smiled at managing an old joke with her favorite word in it.

My boss tried to step away from her, assuming she was a tourist. He was the type—one of the white minority on the island—to disassociate himself from *haoles*. I decided not to introduce them. I heard Amish Dreadlocks ask a couple questions before he flipped his phone shut. Then he walked over to Awiwi. They did some kind of high-five jive-hula handshake—well maybe they just knocked knuckles—but it had the same effect. The tourist ladies then had their picture taken with Dreadlocks. These gals really needed to get a life. My boss interrupted my musing.

"Know who that is?" he asked.

Duh, no. I left that unsaid and just shook my head.

"Koni Ke," Max said this as though I should immediately jump up and down or sing hallelujah. "Deaf Lesbians?" he said.

I smacked my good ear with my hand. Did he just call me a deaf lesbian? A girl shows up for a job, she's not married, she surfs with another woman, doesn't know Koni Ke, and he immediately assumes I'm gay. Oh, this was rich.

"Never mind." He shrugged and walked over to Gil, who knew I was deaf in one ear, but looked like he thought I was dumb, too.

"Blow me, jerk," I muttered. He turned and squinted at me. I smiled and even though it was nearly six, I said, "Goin' to work?"

He nodded. "Got a meeting tonight." Seemed like everyone had something to do or someone to confab with except me. Excellent.

"Liebe, let's go." I said.

No answer.

Instead of next to me where she'd been a minute ago, she was on the face of the loading dock making nice to the *Awiwi*'s captain. Yeah, the naked-nuts navigator. Damn, I needed to put a bell on her. The whole scene was starting to resemble a circus. And there I was without an animal act or oompah music.

Just then, a dog that looked like a yellow lab on steroids—wearing a red bandana—ran onto the loading dock and began barking at the ambulance as it pulled away. He followed it a few yards before turning back and following his nose. The scent he tracked seemed to be the path of the corpse, since he homed in on the spot on the dock where the dead guy had teetered. After a thorough recon of that area, he lifted his head for an air scent and came at me in a rush. It looked like he was going to jump and hit me in the chest, so I braced for it. It didn't help. I hit the deck with a "whoomph" and I might have tooted. Flat on my back, he snorted around my bad ear with his nose. I just lay there praying he wasn't hungry. About then, the band in the Pioneer Inn's bar burst into a calypso edition of *Aloha 'Oe. Oy* indeed. I opened my eyes and realized I was in the center ring of the biggest circus in town.

Chapter Two

"The priest said he's got transference," Liebe said, referring to the gi-normous yellow pooch who had stalked us from the loading dock across the street, into the Pioneer Inn's bar. While she munched on roasted macadamia nuts, the dog—who looked like a yellow lab crossed with a pony—did some kind of Stevie Wonder impersonation. He had his mouth open, his eyes closed and his head swung from side to side in sync with Liebe's handful of mac nuts. Liebe must have noticed the resemblance, as she started singing *My Cherie Amour*, using the nut can she'd smuggled in, as her microphone. If three sheets to the wind means drunk, she was hoisting a fourth sail.

"First off, he's not necessarily a priest. He's a police chaplain." I raised my three middle fingers to go through my points of contention. "Second," I dropped my ring finger, "What's a chaplain know about dog psychology? And third," I kept my second-most-used finger up, "He's the singer on a booze cruise. He's probably not even ordained."

I stirred my Mai Tai with my straw and stabbed the maraschino cherry. After I sucked the rum off and swallowed it, I counted the whole thing toward one fruit for the day. After she got cancer and before the dead guy, Liebe had adopted a healthy whole food diet. Ever since, she'd been pressuring me about better eating.

Trying not to overdo a good thing, I gave the pineapple wedge to the pooch. I knew from having had a dog of my own that mac nuts were off-limits, even to what I assumed was a dead guy's dog.

I shuddered. Swimming with a dead guy was a gruesome sport. One

I never wanted to experience again.

Liebe handled the incident in her own way. Apparently it was goodbye to whole foods and hello to whole-grain alcohol. She had pretzeled her lanky frame into a chair in the darkest corner of the Pioneer Inn's bar, feet off the ground, drink in hand, panties exposed. This left me with my back exposed. Better than my panties. Fortunately, the bar wasn't crowded. Its usual mélange of bikers, boaters and tourists were in short supply. The dark green walls featured photos and memorabilia so obscure even those reprobates didn't want to steal them. Half were askew—the frames and the customers. They drove me crazy. Already in my short tenure on Maui, I'd decided that the P.I. probably wasn't my first choice for relaxation. Even though it was most convenient, it catered to a couple of my least favorite sub-groups.

"Priest or not," she waved my points away. "He's still a star." She followed her assessment with a long slurp from her fourth Cosmopolitan and another handful of mac nuts.

"Liebe, the essence of being a star is that you're recognizable. Therefore: no recognition; not a star." I grabbed the can and looked at the label. "Did you know there are two hundred calories in a quarter cup?"

"They're chock full of Omega 9," she said. "And the cranberry juice is a natural detoxifier." She looked at her empty glass and then to the bartender, and swirled her finger in a circle, requesting another round.

"L.J. we need to have something besides cocktails and mac nuts for dinner."

She ignored me and handed the server a twenty while changing the subject. "A.J., he was the lead singer for the Deaf Lesbians. He's famous."

I just shook my head. The band had had one hit, and the dumbest band name on earth. Their romantic ballad played on all the booze cruises once the sun set and the real stars came out. It probably helped sell a lot of watered-down cocktails.

"Plus, he's a flippin' hotty and I think he likes you." Liebe said, while she fluffed up her wisps of new hair and dabbed on Blistex in lieu of lipstick. She was still cross-legged in the chair. At a glance it looked like she had a Christmas theme going with green and red-striped undies, even though we were closing on Valentine's Day.

I needed another drink.

I had just fished a dead guy from the harbor, and was looking forward to my second week on a new job, so I wasn't thinking straight. The afternoon tradewinds had slacked to a light breeze laced with the jasmine scent of plumeria. A stereo blared Oakie beach music in the background, and my stomach was sending me a message about food.

After the body recovery, I had changed from my swimsuit to a loose gauzy sundress and sandals. Liebe had done the same. We looked more like tourists than former military—discounting Jumbo-lina lying on my feet. He might have been a clue that we were practically local. I saw Liebe raise an eyebrow and then smile. I assumed she was still pondering the hot chaplain's intentions.

"He's not that hot. I mean it's not like he's... he's... " And I tried to think of something wrong with him. He was nearly a cliché of tall, dark, and handsome. He could sing. He volunteered for a worthy cause. And the dog seemed to like him. I had nothing.

"What kind of name is Koni anyway?" I asked.

"Means Tony in Hawaiian," he said from behind me. Then he added, "I guess not everyone can be called 'Love'."

I guess he knew what Liebe's name meant, as well as mine.

She stood and hugged the chaplain. Next to him the *Awiwi*'s captain waited for his hug from her. Maybe more, since he said, "Merry Christmas." The dog rolled off my foot and inverted on his back, his tail wagging, his jowls hanging slack, and his equipment on display for God and everyone. I looked away. He and Liebe had a lot in common.

Liebe introduced us. "Aloha, this is *Captain* Nigel DeBarros." She made it sound like he flew the Millennium Falcon. Then, she blinded him with her billion mega-watt smile. It was almost sad. He was a goner and he didn't even know it yet. "Nigel, this is my little sister, Aloha Jones."

"*Aloha!* Aloha," he said with just enough of an English accent that I wondered if Liebe hadn't met a formidable opponent. She was a sucker for an accent. Then he kissed my hand and the gesture seemed somehow appropriate. Don't ask me why. Oh yeah, she was doomed. He was wearing his little captain's get-up. Despite her years in the military, Liebe still had uniform issues; issues that made her pant.

Liebe took charge like the Air Force commander she had been. Within minutes of ordering our next round, she had us seated with Koni and Nigel around a carved table in the Inn's dining room. We tried small talk for about a second and a half, but we were all thinking about the dead guy.

Liebe broke the tension with a toast. "Here's to the guy who brought us together. May he have the ultimate snorkel adventure on that great reef in the sky?" She tinkled her glass against Nigel's, held a mac nut between a thumb and finger, tossed back the drink, fed Nigel the nut, and dropped face first onto her plate. She never could hold her Triple Sec.

These guys were seasoned. They didn't even wince at her face plant.

When the waitress came to our table, Nigel asked for Liebe's meal in a doggie-bag. The pooch's tail did a "thump-thump-thump" beat that probably registered on a seismograph somewhere. Liebe sat up once, moved the dinner roll basket to her plate and put her head back down on the doughy cushion. Nigel waved to the waitress and ordered more drinks and another basket of rolls. They were sweet and dark and I appreciated his thought process. I asked for extra butter.

"I guess she thought he was snorkeling," Nigel said, referring to my sister's not so apropos toast.

"Wasn't he?" I asked.

"Did you see a snorkel or fins?"

Duh. "So what happened? I mean I know he'd been in the water awhile, what with him being stiff and all."

Koni looked uncomfortable, as if he was having some inner debate between a bearded guy in a white caftan sitting on one shoulder and another guy in cut-offs, flip-flops and sunglasses dancing on the other. The second guy might be holding a beer, but I wasn't sure.

Nigel noticed it too. "Geez, Koni, it doesn't all have to be a secret, just tell us what you can."

Nigel had said what I'd been thinking.

"Dude, I'm the chaplain. I took an oath."

It was like talking to the freaking Pope. Well, if he was really, really hot and Polynesian and sitting in a restaurant in Lahaina. Other than that, I was sure this was exactly like talking to the Pope. Except in English. I was ready to kiss something, but not his ring.

Then Koni said, "Besides, didn't you recognize Colley?"

Wow! Nigel the Englishman—as I had decided to call him instead of Captain Smooth Sacks—could blow vodka out his nose. What a talent. Looked like it hurt.

"Who's Colley?" I asked, as I tried to shift one numb foot out from under the upside-down pooch. I'd removed his bandana after my second drink and his self-esteem seemed to soar. I wondered how Koni would feel about getting stripped.

"He runs the water taxi," Nigel said. "Total a-hole."

"Out of Lahaina?" I asked, embarrassed that I didn't have a mental picture of the boat.

"Well, yes and no. His permit is to moor it off Kaanapali, but he's got some deal on a mooring in the Roadstead right now, probably so he can use the wharf," Nigel said.

The dog gave a little woof then looked up and cocked his head to one side. *Tres* cute.

"Nigel, he's dead!" Koni didn't seem to like the a-hole comment. Good thing he hadn't had much time with Liebe awake. She'd have given him a-hole tremors. Then I realized that *haole* and a-hole had the same letters. Hmm...

"So, okay, let's just say he's a jerk. What happened to him?" I asked.

Koni just shook his head. "Can't say. But he wasn't snorkeling."

"He still shacked up with Zhen?" Nigel asked.

"Roger that." Koni said in radio-speak. "Girlfriend's off island. Honolulu chaplain's doing the death notification."

"Does Tan still have a hard-on for her?"

Really! Nigel needed to tone it down a little in front of the chaplain. Still, I couldn't resist asking, "Who's Tan?"

"Tan Ringo. He's the drummer in our band," Koni said.

"The Deaf Lesbians?" I was puzzled. "Isn't having the name Ringo kind of a cliché?"

"No more Deaf Lesbians. Ringo's his real last name, so our band's called Ringo's. We play on the *Awiwi*."

No wonder Koni-the-chaplain had arrived on scene so fast. He'd been on the boat that hit the victim. How convenient.

"Tan's been in love with Colley's girlfriend since he met her at a gallery on Front Street," Nigel said. "He bought some medallion she designed and then had her sign his chest. She's got this Earth Mother thing going that some guys are into." He wiggled and swished his fingers in the air, signifying an aura. "You have to wonder about anyone who'd hook up with Colley. I mean, he wasn't exactly the epitome of cosmic harmony."

"So what killed Colley?" I asked. I can be a little bit pit bull when I want info. Still, it felt weird to quiz two guys who were basically strangers to me. I knew their names and their jobs, but I didn't know if they were serial killers, cross-dressers or what.

I'd experienced this before in the Coast Guard when immersed in an emergency. Everyone bonded instantly over their common trauma. It was like belonging to an exclusive club with a creepy initiation.

Koni just shook his head and said, "Looked like he'd been in the water awhile."

"I'm just glad I didn't do it." Nigel knocked back the last of his martini and looked for a waitress, didn't see one, then instead grabbed Liebe's abandoned Cosmopolitan. After he guzzled it, he shook his head and said, "Not that he didn't deserve it."

"You need to talk I'm here for ya, Brah." Koni was not good at the chaplain thing. He had the subtlety of a guy on a scooter at a Harley ride. But what do you expect from a man who plays beach music on a booze cruise and moonlights with the cops?

It was probably a good thing our food came right then. Nigel had braised leg-of-lamb. How British. Koni had a huge slab of grilled Mahi Mahi that the waitress said was fresh. It looked pretty fresh to me. I had ordered teriyaki chicken and brown rice to appease Liebe. Even passed out, she had that older sister hold on me. The brown rice was denied when our server told me I could have the chicken with white sticky rice or sticky white rice. I got the white sticky rice. Koni said a prayer for our food and bounty, blah, blah, blah. I was too hungry to pray.

"Mahi fresh?" I queried Koni, trying to avoid watching Nigel carve his lamb as though it was some kind of science experiment. Maybe it was a good thing Liebe was still face down. Maybe I should ask him about serial killers.

In response, Koni just closed his eyes and savored the fish. I took that to mean *yes* on the freshness. Then he said, "I hear this is your first week on the job."

"Well, starting the second actually. The first was training."

"You like it?"

I finished chewing a mouthful of teriyaki chicken and rice. It was good sticky white rice. I took a moment to think about my answer. "It's okay." I paused. "It's different. I guess I'm more used to the military: Chain-of-command, order, belonging, knowing what comes next. Everything here's ... " I searched for the right phrase and couldn't find it.

"Hawaiian style," Nigel said. "It's the Polynesian way." He glanced at Koni, "Sorry Brah, but you know what I mean. The clocks run a little slower, there's an unspoken element of racism and well, you stop to smell the *pikake*. It's like living in a potluck. Little bit of everything, no big hurry, and everyone's related unless they're white." Somehow when spoken in that high society accent, he sounded intelligent. Plus, he'd nailed my thoughts.

Koni asked, "How'd you get the harbormaster gig?"

Gig? How musical. "I joined the Coast Guard out of high school, they paid my way through college, I was theirs for over ten years, and then, one day I blew my ear out," I tapped my hearing aid. "And as a result, blew out my career, too."

Ike was appalled." I switched to a deep, stern voice with my chin tucked in. "Joneses don't *do* disability. Joneses do full military retirement." Then I dropped my Ike-speak and added, "I took my Civil Service test, scored high, and came to Maui. I wanted to live where I could surf without a wetsuit and not worry about snakes."

"Ike?" Koni raised an eyebrow.

"My dad." I explained, "See Liebe? She did the right thing. Twenty years in the Air Force and on to a second career in the private sector flying for United."

Nigel choked. "She's a bloody pilot?"

I looked at my sister, face down in a basket of whole-grain dinner rolls. "Builds confidence doesn't she?"

Liebe didn't stir, but the dog growled in his sleep. 'Nough said.

Koni changed tacks. "So, Aloha, I told you what my name means.

What were *your* parents thinking?" he asked, as he forked up a bite of his grilled Mahi.

"Eve chose our first names, all meaning 'Love' in the country or state where we were born." I grabbed for a roll, thought of the bikini, and went back to the chicken and rice. "Dad chose our middle names. Mine is Hickam, since that's the base where he was stationed when I was born. Liebe got Ramstein. Amoré's middle name is Aviano. Sarang's is Osan. Love's is Lakenheath, and Viva's is Nellis. Viva was born in Vegas. Guess they couldn't find a word for love in Vegas-ese."

"Eve?" Koni was good with the one-word questions.

"She had us call her Eve instead of Mom since she wanted us to feel equal, not subservient to her." I continued to blather on. "We called our dad Sir, except on special occasions then we'd call him Ike. My mom was the perfect Yin to his Yang."

"Six girls? Your dad must have been lonely." Nigel didn't say what most people said. Your dad must have been disappointed.

"He says it doesn't matter if we were boys or girls as long as we made officer."

"You're all military?"

"Yep." Then I paused, "Well, mostly. I told you about Liebe. Our next sister, Amoré, retired from the Navy and has some top-secret civilian job at a base in Washington state." I started listing us off on my fingers. "Then there's Sarang. She's a jarhead, and you know what they say? 'Once a Marine, always a Marine.' I'm the rebel. I blew off the Army and became a Coastie. That left my next sister in line for the Army of one. Perfect for Love, since she marches to her own drum roll. Maybe she'd like to meet Tan."

Koni and Nigel looked up.

"She's lead snare with their marching band," I said. "You know—the drum connection?"

They nodded. Then Nigel said, "That's only five."

"Our youngest sister, Viva, joined the Peace Corps. She just loves to piss off my dad." I smiled. "Other than Love, we were like the Von Trapp children without the talent."

Then I realized Koni was better at the chaplain thing than I thought. He'd just quizzed the bejeebers out of me and I'd spilled my guts like a sorority girl after an all-you-can-eat buffet.

Chapter Three

"Did you sleep with him?" Liebe asked at the breakfast table. Like she was one to talk, ever since her divorce, she seemed like a different person. Nigel and Koni had helped me load her in my Harbors Division truck and then followed us to the guesthouse—called an *ohana*—I was renting part way up the side of the West Maui mountains off Lahainaluna Road in an area called Little Manila. They'd help me unload her too. I couldn't speak for anyone else, but I'd gotten no sleep. Liebe looked ... perky.

"What if I did? He's sweet, cute and lonely." I justified my actions, still unprepared for the consequences.

"What if you did? I'll tell you what. What if he gets attached? What if he moves in? What if he eats you out of house and home?" She pointed at the big yellow dog lying on the floor, his front legs wrapped around a mixing bowl full of kibble, looking like an inmate guarding his plate. "You stopped and bought him food. Geez, Aloha, you're one step from putting that bandana back on him."

The microwave dinged and she stopped her anti-dog diatribe long enough to make herself some green tea and I-don't-know-what concoction that she said was full of antioxidants. I popped a handful of chocolate chips and got the same results. She looked back over her shoulder just in time to see me turn down my hearing aid. She narrowed her eyes.

Then the dog burped and got a look on his face as though he was remembering good times. Liebe burst out laughing. "Do you realize he looks just like ... " She stopped mid-sentence when she saw my face. "Oh, I guess you did." Then she turned away to add water to her cup and stir her potion. I could see her shoulders shaking with laughter. All innocent-like she turned back and said, "You never answered my question yesterday. You ever hear from him anymore?"

The him, whom she referred was her ex-brother-in-law, or if you had to get technical about it, my former husband. "Been awhile," I said.

"Bet you're glad you got that tat'," she said.

There's a word for girls like her, but my mom told me not to use it on my sisters or female dogs. What could I use for an argument? At least my husband left me right away instead of waiting around until I got breast cancer like yours did. No, that was best left unsaid.

"At least your husband left right away instead of waiting around like mine did until I got breast cancer, and then bailed," Liebe said.

Did I mention that she's one tough broad?

"Yeah right," I said, "Snake's a saint." I looked out the window and watched my landlord squire a new landscaper around the grounds. I could tell he was giving him special instructions on how to trim the trees. I hoped they'd chop down the mango tree next to my place. Every time one of the ripe fruits let loose, it sounded like a mortar hitting the galvanized metal roof. Plus, those things started to reek in about a day. Then wasps and myna birds feasted on them like maggots on a corpse, making a mango, both in the air and on the ground, an altogether unpleasant experience.

"Why do you still call him Snake?" Liebe asked. "You don't know that he's still playing outlaw biker." She referred to his jump from motocross in high school to Hell's Angel wannabe when I went to boot camp. I got the matching tattoo before I shipped out. Funny what great decisions you make when you're young. Our marriage failed faster than it took me to get my first base assignment.

"Last time I saw him he had a stringy blonde ponytail, a Yosemite Sam moustache, several new tats, and a Harley with some kind of skull painted on the fuel tank." I didn't mention that he looked buff to the hilt and hotter than smoke. Instead, I got down on the floor and rubbed the dog's belly. He stretched like Under Dog in flight. Maybe I'd watched too many cartoons as a kid.

"Don't really care what he looked like," Liebe said, rubbing sunscreen on her legs, clearly her greatest asset. "What'd he say?"

"He said he wanted to talk. I told him I didn't. Said it would be a cold day in Lahaina before I had anything to say to him."

Liebe stopped slathering. "You saw him recently?"

"Yeah, about a month before I left the mainland. Doesn't matter, it's not like I care." Then I got up and went to the tiny bedroom to get dressed. The dog followed me and hopped up on the bed. I paused to rub below his ear with one hand and below mine with the other. I really did have a headache. I didn't know if it was from the Mai Tais, the new job, Liebe's questions, or from free diving for the dead guy. I decided to call an audiologist once I got into the office. I was due for a check-up on my hearing aid anyway. Might as well get it over with this week.

I slipped on a pair of khaki cargo shorts and pulled a white wife-beater tank top over my red sports bra. I then, slid my feet into some checkered Vans. Now, where were my Serpico-inspired sunglasses? I looked in my fanny pack, on the desk, and even in the dirty clothes basket.

When I came out, Liebe had magically turned the bed back into a couch and was packing her shoulder bag. "Want to meet again this afternoon to surf?" I asked, looking around the room for my sunglasses.

"Yeah, I'll stop by your office when I get back."

"Back? Back from where?"

"Nigel invited me out on the boat today for a snorkel charter. Okay if I catch a ride to the harbor with you?" I just shook my head as I locked up the house. How she had wrangled a date while passed out, I'll never know; but I admired her nonetheless. Koni and I had exchanged numbers, but I was so out of the dating scene I didn't know if this meant something or not.

I rifled around in my bag some more then gave up looking for my shades. If they cost me a buck I could keep them for years. As soon as I got the good ones, they lasted about three minutes. I should have known better. Now I'd need to buy some new cheap ones. If they were truly hideous, they'd last me the rest of my life. Liebe dug around in her bag and pulled out my sunglasses. When I gave her my best stink-eye she handed them to me and pulled out a pair of Oakleys for herself that looked exactly like the pair I'd lost on our last vacation together.

In my new office, I spent the morning shuffling paperwork. I also called headquarters with questions only to be shut down by my boss's assistant, and took fees from two couples on sailboats who had moored in the Roadstead the night before. The sailors were spending their retirement money cruising the Pacific. The leg from L.A. to Lahaina was their first big sail, so they were just beginning to live the dream. They had apparently done their homework since they asked for Junior, the previous harbormaster, by name—or at least by his diminutive nickname. When I explained that he'd retired a week earlier, they seemed surprised.

On my way to the office I had noticed a different giant white floating hotel had cruised in and now lay at anchor offshore. Little tender boats shuttled the newlyweds and nearly-deads into town. I could see already that the tenders used about half the loading dock's time and space, which left the regular harbor users backed up and more than a little testy.

Several cruise ship passengers had tried to finagle me into letting them use the restroom in my office despite the sign on the door that said "No Public Restroom." One lady claimed an emergency so I gave into her. Big mistake. For the next twenty minutes, I had to explain to thirty others that there were as of that moment, *no exceptions!* Threatened with everything from lawsuits to wet floors, they did little to change my mind. Yep, Liebe was right, great assignment.

As I sorted through the various files and reports on my desk, I could see from the records that the cruise ship traffic had been steady for the past year, with an average of two ships a week documented to use the harbor. I'd only been working two days and it seemed like we'd had two already. I didn't look up the next time the door opened. I just said, "Sorry, no public restrooms. Try the library." The room seemed to darken. Awiwi, the big Maui cop I'd semi-met the day before, had stepped in front of the windows. He was followed by an older guy.

"Better not let my mom hear you say that," Awiwi said.

"Or what, she'll threaten me with a lawsuit or pee on the floor?" I said. "I've heard it all before." I gave him a flip of my wrist.

"No, boss, she da librarian," he said.

Across a well-worn lawn—next to the Pioneer Inn sat the Lahaina Library like the last bastion of civilization before the touristy shops of Front Street. Busted. I'd been shoving my problems out my door and into someone else's. Not cool.

"Sorry. I'll stop it. What can I do ya for?" It was a classic Ike-ism designed to ameliorate problems. I hoped it would work.

Awiwi wore his cop uniform, and stood with his hands crossed in front of his huge belly. As I looked closer, I could see that he was not fat so much as big and muscle-bound under his body armor. His round face simply made him seem overweight, while his passive countenance made him appear simple. Now, looking him in the eye, I sensed he used both to his advantage. His whole look said, "I'm huge, so don't fight me and I'm easy-going, so you don't have to." Hmm, interesting.

Then I checked out his sidekick, another cop, but maybe twice Awiwi's age. Same buzz cut, pleated slacks with a rumpled crease, ubiquitous aloha shirt of a vintage well before my time, and a huge semi-auto—probably a

Glock—in a holster on his belt. He looked like he might be what they call *hapa hoale*—half-white. As Nigel had said, Hawaii's like a potluck, little bit of this, little bit of that.

The smaller guy broke the silence. "*Aloha* Jones?" he said, with a huge question mark in his tone like, what's your *real* name?

"Yep." I said, while I thought, *here we go again.* Time for the questions about the name. Sometimes I wanted to find a way to get even with Eve. Maybe send her a lifetime membership in the NRA or a donation in her name to the Republican Party. Something that would grate at her Sierra Club-PETA-Ralph-Nader-loving psyche.

He didn't digress. "Detective Killingsworth," he said, as he handed me a business card. It said his first name was Ho. No wonder he didn't want to talk names.

"Hi, Ho, nice to meet you." *Hi ho?* What next? *Off to work I go¼?* I mentally smacked my forehead. Awiwi was smiling his huge smile. I narrowed my eyes at him. He kept smiling. No, he wasn't simple at all.

"Heard you found a floater yesterday," Ho said. "You doin' okay?"

"Yeah," I did a little down-turned smile intended to say, "No big deal."

"Want to tell me about it?" Ho was leaning on the counter at this point. Awiwi wandered the miniscule customer area, which amounted to pacing, as he looked at the photos on the walls. I told Ho what I know—oops, knew, and waited for the next question. He surprised me. "What happened to the last harbormaster?"

"Well, I don't really know. I heard he retired and moved to the mainland—Colorado or Wyoming or one of those four-corner states."

"How'd you get the job?"

"Just lucky I guess."

"Don't be smart. It doesn't suit you."

"Can't help it."

"Seem kind of young to retire."

"Really," I said, "I didn't know him. What do you care?"

"Just a curious guy. Thought maybe you had some kind of *in* to get this job." He gazed around the office while he spoke, taking in all the details. It seemed like he was just killing time. Very Hawaiian-style. Then he said, "So, you ever meet Colley?"

"Not till yesterday," I said. I was losing interest in the conversation, so I pulled another file I wanted to review. My hearing aid was picking up static from Awiwi's radio and it wasn't helping my headache.

"Well, we're trying to figure out what he was doing down here. I mean, his boat's from Kaanapali. I guess he could've been getting fuel. Or maybe just cruising around Mala Wharf."

"Woof," the dog said from his spot under my desk.

Awiwi and Ho both leaned over the counter and peered under it for a look. Ho said, "Where'd you get the pooch?"

I told him. He and Awiwi shared a shifty glance.

"Been looking for the pooch," Awiwi said.

"You the dog catcher, too?" I was just bantering for sport, nothing personal.

Awiwi grinned.

Ho pulled out a little notebook. "You have some next of kin?"

I frowned. "Why?"

"Hey, Colley was murdered," he said, telling me this wasn't any accidental drowning. "The dog was always with him. Now you got the dog. Maybe you killed him or maybe whoever killed him will want to get rid of the pooch. You know, eliminate witnesses. Thought someone with your people skills could get into trouble and end up floating too. Just wanted to know who to contact if things go bad."

My people skills! I think I'd just been insulted. I looked around for Awiwi. Apparently, he was fast *and* quiet. I could see him outside talking to the *touristas* and posing for more photos. What was it with that guy?

"Yeah, right," I said, "Maybe you're just trying to pull that Hawaii Five-O-style interrogation technique on me where I get scared and confess, or worse . . . ." I paused, "need a shoulder to cry on." I continued to shuffle files, one ear deaf and the other not really listening. Maybe my handicap would be a blessing in disguise. The dog shifted at my feet. I reached down to pet him and felt the fur standing up along his rough as he quivered. When I looked down, I could see him making a snarly face. Ho had moved around the counter and was squatting next to me looking at the dog. I had a large personal bubble and he was inbounds.

"You don't look like you scare easy," he said.

Ho was so close I could see tiny wrinkles at the corners of his eyes and I could smell cleaning fluids on his gun. So could the dog. I pushed off with my feet and rolled my chair back to the file cabinet. To make sure it looked legit, I pawed around and said, "Aw, there it is," when I pulled the file.

He said, "Hmm, maybe I was wrong." Then he said, "Worf" and the dog barked. I jumped.

"You think he's Klingon?" I said, referring to the Enterprise's security officer. I loved Star Trek almost as much as I loved old cartoons.

Ho looked confused. "It's his name, Wharf, you know, like Mala Wharf. I heard that's where Colley found him."

I thought Worf seemed more appropriate, but I didn't say so. People seem to think Trekkies are geeks. Yeah, right. It's not like I had an Enterprise uniform in my closet. Well . . . bad example. I mean, it's only for Halloween and that doesn't really count, right? And the walkie-talkies that look like tri-corders? Those are practically collector's items. Nope, I'm no Star Trek geek.

"You gonna keep him or give him back to the missus?" Detective Killingsworth asked as he leaned back against my desk, his arms and legs crossed, ignoring the still rumbling pooch. "Seems like she's lost enough already."

I didn't know. I rather liked the dog and he seemed to like me. More than I could say for Ho. "I didn't think they were married," I said by way of not answering his question. Ho rubbed his wedding ring finger. I could see a slight tan line. I wondered if he was trying to pass or just divorced. I hadn't had time for a tan line.

"Maybe, maybe not, but from what I hear he treated her like she was his property. Some girls like that you know. *Haole* girl hooks up with a local *moke*, he smacks her around once in awhile, she knows she's wanted." He shrugged.

"*Moke*?"

"Big guy—like Awiwi—but not as smart."

"Colley didn't look..." Was it politically correct to say local, or Hawaiian? Did that imply only locals hit their women? Did it mean he was born here? Yikes! As usual, my face betrayed my thought process.

Ho said, "Don't matter what color, he still a *moke*. Maybe that why she hook up with him." He'd begun dropping the past tense in his speech. How local would he go?

"Are you saying he hit her and she liked it?" I wondered if that was why Ho wasn't wearing a wedding ring. Maybe he empathized a little *too* much.

"No, I say some *wahine*s like 'dat," Ho opined in pidgin.

"No wonder Nigel said he's an a-hole." I was talking to myself more than Ho.

He perked up. "Nigel DeBarros?" All the pidgin accent absent from his speech.

Oops.

"Yeah, my sister and I were..." I didn't want to say out to dinner. "... talking to him and the chaplain, and Nigel said Colley was a... jerk," I said for wont of a better word.

"Nigel might be a little prejudiced. He and Colley have some history," Killingsworth said. He didn't elaborate.

"So you're telling me Nigel's boat ran over Colley, and you're sitting here questioning me? How about questioning him?" I said. Then I realized Nigel was on a charter—with my sister. I grabbed the mike on the VHF radio that came with the office.

Ho grabbed it away from me. "What are you doing?"

"I'm going to call the boat and tell them to get in here for you to question him."

"You *lolo*?" he asked.

Hunh?

"You stupid?" He dropped his local boy pidgin. "You're the freaking harbormaster. You can't call a boat to come in. You don't have any authority. You sure can't speak for me. You got a lot to learn, lady." He put the mike back in the clip and walked to the door.

"What about my sister?"

"What about her?"

"She's on the boat with him. What if he's a killer?"

"Nigel's no killer." Ho shook his head.

"How can you be so sure?"

Of course, as I thought about it, I realized that Nigel had been as shocked as anyone when Koni told him the victim was Colley. Unless he was a great actor. Moreover, he had no reason to kill my sister. If he had killed Colley, his problems were over. All he had to do is be lucky and be smart. Of course, I thought to myself, if he wanted Liebe, he'd better be both.

Before Ho could answer my question, another tourist opened the office door and asked to use the bathroom. Ho sneaked out while I argued with the woman. She told me she was going to complain to the cruise director, as though he had some control over me.

Right then the pooch did a silent toot that permeated the office.

"I guess the pineapple didn't agree with him," I said.

"Oh for God's sake, don't blame the dog." Then her eyes started watering.

I didn't know what caused the sulfur smell, but he must have had a lot of it.

I didn't enjoy constant confrontation with the cruise passengers, nor did I want to clean up after them. This one looked like she was going to hurl. Maybe I needed to talk to my boss about how they'd handled the bathroom problem in the past.

"Uh, go ahead and use it." I gave in.

By this point she was getting the dry heaves. I didn't want wet heaves. Too late. While I was watching her, the pooch did a projectile vomit that splashed her espadrilles. It looked a lot like the stuff Liebe had for breakfast. Whatever it was, it didn't seem too healthy to me. She no longer seemed interested in my restroom. In a moment she was gone, slipping and sliding from my office like a Ninja—the mutant turtle kind.

Chapter Four

I called the Harbors Division office in Kahului to speak with my boss. Yake was out. His assistant, a woman formerly known as his secretary, said he was at the doctor's office getting a splinter removed. Seemed like overkill to me, but what did I know. She passed me on to Gil Mangas. I explained the problems I was having with the tourists and the bathroom. He told me to suck it up. Rules are rules, no exceptions, if you can't handle the job, quit. What a *moke*, I thought to myself.

I also needed some supplies and asked if Gil were coming to the Lahaina side, could he deliver. Big negatory on that one too. I ended our conversation with less answers and more frustration than when it started.

My next phone call was to the audiologist. She had time to see me right after lunch, so at least my day wouldn't be a total waste. I tried twirling my pen and instead launched it across the room. I needed a break. So did the dog. He paced by the door looking like he was tired of hearing about other people's bathroom problems.

My job description included walking the harbor, checking the facilities, and noting boats anchored in the Roadstead that needed to pay moorage fees. I snapped a leash onto Wharf's collar and offered him a relief break, while I patrolled my domain. On the door I affixed the "Be Back Soon" sign and let him lead.

We moseyed along the concrete platform where boats had backed into their slips. According to Max, there was a waiting list to get these prize locations. He had said the commercial slips added hundreds of thousands of dollars to the value of a business, but they were non-transferable.

Somebody had to die in order for one to open up. Most of the boats along this side of the harbor reflected that affluence. There were large catamarans and schooner-type sailboats that specialized in whale watches and dinner cruises. In between were a couple of fancy glass-bottom boats. There were some empty slips where the snorkel and dive mooring there had already set out on their three-hour tours. This thought of course left the "Gilligan's Island" theme song ricocheting inside my brain like a pinball.

Little shacks along the dock housed chalkboards and brochures with prices and schedules for each vessel. A few had hard-tanned workers hawking their products to the early rising tourists. Most were empty. I noticed that the workers eyed Wharf as if they knew him and he wagged at a few. He mostly ignored the tourists, but sniffed about half the paper and gum on the concrete walk. No one seemed to need me, so I shuffled along pondering the dog's dead master.

I wondered about Colley's business and his boat. Did he book charters himself? If he had a crew, would they keep the business running or would Zhen? I'd need to look up his file when I went back to the office. Maybe look up Nigel's too. I wasn't being nosey. It was my job. At least that's how I rationalized it.

We got to the mid-harbor concrete boat ramp. It was littered with skiffs. They bobbed up and down like dirty cups in a flooded trash can—all padlocked to something. A few had the gas line to their engines removed. I'd heard from Gil that this was to prevent joy riders and thieves. Seemed like the same thing to me. Used to commute to the boats moored in the Roadstead—some commercial, some private—the dinghies ranged in quality from crappy to okay-in-a-pinch. I knew enough about boats from being an ex-Coastie to know I wouldn't want to count on one in more than two-foot seas.

Wharf remained disinterested in the boating part of my job. When I stopped to look at the skiffs, he sat down, hiked one strapping leg up and scratched his ear. His entire yellow fur coat oscillated. When he finished scratching, his big pink tongue hung out the side of his mouth and his golden eyes had a sleepy look. I could swear he smiled.

Then he hopped up and tugged me over to the park under the gigantic banyan tree. The tree and the Pioneer Inn, side by side along the harbor front, were relics of a bygone day that clung to their perches in Lahainatown like an old hooker on orthopedic stilettos. The banyan tree, said to be well over a hundred years old, spread its branches over an entire block, held up by ground-attached secondary trunks and two-by-four scaffolds.

At the far corner, I could see a long-haired hippy guy preaching at cars driving down Front Street. Japanese office girls were taking turns climbing the tree and shooting photos. Two backpackers on a bench ate papayas, carving out the seeds and flinging them onto the ground. Nice. The dirt below the tree was dry and shady, something Wharf found less than inspirational as he walked us back to the harbor.

Just past the skiffs, I tried to get him to skirt the Dumpsters, but they seemed his destiny. He marked the first three as his own and took a doodle behind the fourth. I tried to look oblivious. Fortunately, the Dumpsters weren't drawing a big crowd. I heard a weird noise I attributed to my hearing aid and tapped it for good measure. It sounded like snoring and the tap didn't make it go away. Wharf too, heard the sound and pulled me via the leash up to the last brown metal bin. Through the space between the two lids, I could see a woman curled up in a blanket, cushioned on trash. She had a face like a Shar-Pei, all wrinkles and skin folds. Her bed smelled of rotting fruit and empty booze bottles mixed with general garbage, stink and sweat. Even with the blanket, I could see her chest move slightly with each snore. Welcome to Paradise. I opted to leave her be, but added to my list of things I needed to ask Max or Gil: What was the policy on Dumpster slumber?

Wharf and I moved onto the catwalk that accessed the south and west sides of the harbor along the jetty breakwater. Huge rocks held the ocean's sometimes choppy waves outside the harbor and protected the little fleet. It wasn't pretty, but effective, according to Max, even in the last hurricane. Apparently, Iniki had skirted Maui and wreaked vengeance on Kauai. He hadn't speculated as to what would have occurred in a direct hit. He also mentioned several tsunami alerts in the past few years, again, neglecting to qualify what might happen. I'd have to ask the policy on hurricanes and tsunamis, too. Yep, Paradise.

The boats on the breakwater side of the harbor were a mix of cabin cruisers, charter boats and sailboats. It looked like some were permanent residences. For a moment, I had a little daydream about living on a boat, sailing the world, with new tropical ports of call on each horizon. Then I remembered that "Joneses don't do disability" and I had to work for a living, especially if I wanted to live on Maui—in something other than a Dumpster. I really needed this job.

Wharf had balked as we entered the catwalk, and the farther we ventured around the harbor's perimeter, the more difficult he became, biting at his leash in resistance as I tried to get to the end of the moorage. Eventually, he somersaulted onto his side while staring at a stick on the rocks a few feet away. I took a look at it and it looked like mesquite. It made me think of barbecue. Maybe the same was happening to the pooch. I tried coaxing, jerking, and threatening him, but he had become Gandhi with fur. Dropping his leash, I kept walking, although I muttered at him as I left, questioning both his heritage and his loyalty. He didn't look upset.

From the end of the breakwater, I had a fabulous view of Lanai, the pineapple island, some ten miles away from Maui. In the foreground, the harbor entrance buoys bobbed a slow rhythm. Then something caught my eye near the closest red nun buoy. There was another body floating just south of the channel. I looked offshore and saw the familiar lines of the *Awiwi* cruising inbound. Holy crap, it was happening all over again!

Then the body lifted its head, took a breath and kicked down into a free dive. I started breathing again and turned away from the channel to face Lahaina. Where I stood was only a few hundred feet from my office by water and right above the place where I'd recovered Colley's body. I wondered if this was the reason the dog didn't want to come any closer. Was he having some kind of post-traumatic stress reaction? He didn't seem the type to hold in his feelings.

Gee, could I anthropomorphize any more?

As I walked the harbor, I'd turned my hearing aid down with the thought that I'd turn it up if I wanted to speak with someone. I still wasn't comfortable with the way things sounded when it was on. Perhaps that was why I felt, rather than heard, footsteps behind me on the catwalk. They were so light I thought Wharf might have changed his mind.

When I turned to see if it was, indeed, Wharf, I was surprised instead, to see a tiny Asian woman teetering toward me on five-inch heels. Intermittently, one of her magenta stilettos wedged between the planks on the walkway and she had to bend over and reef the shoe out by hand. When she did, a long brunette ponytail whipped over her shoulder and hung all the way to the dock. Given the length of her skirt, I wondered if the bending over might not violate some kind of public indecency law. When she looked up from the shoe debacle, she gave me a little wave. I hoofed it toward her.

"Why don't you just take them off and go barefoot?" I said.

She turned her head and glared while she pulled on the shoe. "And get splinters? I don't think so. Not to mention my foot-girl would kill me."

"You have a foot-girl?" I had a doctor, a dentist, and an audiologist, but not a foot-girl. "Is that like a . . . ?" Before I could say more, I noticed that her feet were child-sized. "Man, you've got the smallest feet I've ever seen." Plus, each toenail was decorated with some kind of black flourish over the hot pink enamel.

"Eh, not everyone can surf without a board." She pointed at my size sevens, which by any account were average, not large. I tried not to give her a mean squint. I failed. It did give me time to see the rest of her get-up, which included a white, mini tank-dress over a magenta demi-bra that may have been working over its load limit. A swatch of floral gauze belted her ensemble. She made me feel like an Amazon, as though I should carry her on my shoulders to her next destination. It creeped me out. I wondered if she had the same effect on men or the just the opposite.

Then she did something that I'd seen only a few times in my entire life. This was something so shocking, so attention getting, so beyond the pale, that it gave me pause. She apologized.

"Listen, I'm sorry about that last comment. I'm just sensitive about my feet." She stood in front of me and held out her hand. I apologized in return and we shook on it. "I'm Brita Beamer." She looked at me as though I should know something. I didn't. "And you are?" she asked.

"Aloha Jones," I said.

"Just who I was looking for," she said, "Can't beat that with a stick." Then she pulled a narrow journalist's notepad from a small shoulder bag, opened it, and started to question me about finding Colley. I came back with my best "No comment." She stopped writing and looked at me. "This your first interview?"

I nodded.

"I thought so. Let me give you a few tips." She spoke like a humming-bird moves. It was so fast I almost couldn't follow her. "Never say 'no comment' to reporters. It's a cliché. It makes you look guilty." She flitted past me on tippytoes to the end of the walkway and turned.

Apparently she'd found a solution to her high-heeled problem.

"Is this where you found him?"

I nodded in lieu of another 'no comment'.

Out of her bag, she pulled an undersized digital camera. She seemed to have the market on miniature in everything but breasts.

"Don't agree to an interview if you don't have anything to say," she said. The camera didn't p-ching, but I knew she'd just shot a photo of me. Mouth open, about to say something, but stopped by her advice.

"Be prepared." She called this one over her shoulder as she took a shot of the *Awiwi* cruising up the channel. She waved at them and the customers and crew dutifully waved back. "Know your subject matter," she said, then, asked, "Is that your sister at the wheel?"

Yep, that was Liebe. Sadly she was one boob short of a pair. She must have lost one snorkeling. Nigel had his arm around her waist as she steered. He didn't seem put off by her temporary imbalance. In response to Brita's question, I nodded again. What could I say? I saw her adjust a little zoom lens button and focus on Liebe. Was this what they called ambush journalism?

"Conduct an interview on your home turf." She tippytoed back past me and I followed. She shot a photo of Wharf doing Salvador Doggie, one back leg and his fuzzy yellow tail drooped off the catwalk like a watch oozing off a dresser. "Colley's dog?" she asked, but she didn't even wait for an answer. She just grabbed a look at his doggie I.D. and nodded, "Looks sad." He sat up and she shot another photo of him. This time I think he was going for pensive, either that or thirsty. Sometimes I struggled to interpret his vast emotional depth. I followed her like a zombie in "The Night of the Living Dead", mute but without my arms extended. This was completely out of control.

She was making good time for being so short. I was hustling to keep up with her and had turned my hearing aid up to the max to try to hear her. I had grabbed Wharf's lead as she stilted past him and tugged on him to keep up with her. He wanted to check out the crabs scuttling in the rocks. I didn't.

She stopped, stepped next to me, and said, "And above all else. Stay calm." She handed me her card and shot another picture of me looking dazed. Her voice had registered in my head at the amplitude of a tsunami alert and even though I had my hand on the hearing aid, I was too late in turning it down. Then she stepped off the catwalk and clickety-clacked her way along the dock to the *Awiwi* as it backed into the mooring. I looked at her card. Yep, she was a reporter and I was toast.

Chapter Five

By the time I caught up with Brita Beamer, she was interviewing happy tourists disembarking the boat and handing out her business cards for follow-up calls. To the first couple she said, "What's it like chartering a killing machine?" They didn't look happy anymore.

The next group had been waving at friends on the dock as they approached the slip. Brita asked them, "Was there still blood on the bow as you came aboard?" They weren't waving anymore.

Several groups slipped past her unmolested. At one point she said, "Did you know the victim?" The tourists just looked confused.

Brita had handed out more cards than a Texas Hold 'Em dealer, but I doubted she'd gotten the quote she needed. I could see her make the same assessment as she turned to the crew.

Liebe was helping Nigel and the crew bag trash and hose down the decks. The rule was to always leave the boat charter-ready. It took the entire crew about five minutes to disappear while Brita found out what the remaining customers thought of the "accident" the day before. To her credit, she didn't actually make little quote marks with her fingers, but the implication was there. I wondered if she would write this up as an accident or a murder. It seemed to me that Ho thought Colley had been killed on purpose, though not by the *Awiwi.*

Before Brita could capture my sister's attention, Liebe hopped off the boat hidden by an armful of trash bags. Nigel wasn't so lucky.

"How did it feel to run over a man?" Brita queried him, her itty-bitty camera at the ready. He smiled. Even with those obligatory bad English teeth, his smile was killer. Again, he wore a bandana wrapped buccaneer-style over his bald pate. One eyebrow cocked, he held the fine line short of a leer, but strong enough to make Brita blush, something I thought impossible. Then he laid on the accent as if he'd just stepped out of the queen's throne room. Watching them was like watching a British "Pirate's of the Caribbean" meeting Asian "Gidget". I crossed my arms and leaned on a barstool in the dock shack. This was going to be good.

"You said your name is Bright Beams?" He leered at her melon-simile-inducing cleavage.

"Uh, no, uh ... " For a moment, I thought she'd forgotten her name. "Brita, Brita Beamer, like the water filter and the sports car, pure and fast." Then she actually smacked her palm against her forehead. It would have been bad enough but she was still holding the itty-bitty camera. The metal smacking bone noise made me flinch.

He gave her a break, one it looked like she needed, just to catch her breath and answered her first question with a question. "How'd it feel to run over a man?" He gesticulated. "You wonder: Did I sense a tingle in my spine as the hull crushed his skull? Did I sleep last night haunted by dreams of floating ghosts or did I bury myself in a woman's warm embrace?"

His voice rose in volume and pitch. I think he must have done Shakespeare in high school or whatever the Brits called the equivalent of high school. He wasn't good, but he was entertaining. "Did I fill my body's bilge with ale and wallow in seas of despair?" He really had her attention now. She wasn't even taking notes. Then he stopped his soliloquy, slapped her on the ass, and walked off the boat, saying over his shoulder, "I felt bad for the guy."

Bummer, I thought. The show's over, time to get back to work. In reality, it was time for the Second Act. Liebe was running toward Nigel along the concrete dock, coming back from the Dumpster, the human

Shar-Pei in hot pursuit. This piqued Wharf's interest. He pulled the leash loose from my sweaty palm and actually high-tailed it toward the racing women. Then he came to a sliding stop and did his best *Woof.* I could tell he thought this would work like gangbusters. Liebe ran around him and the Shar-Pei barked back.

Wharf cowered.

Still wrapped in some kind of blanket, the Shar-Pei resembled a bad imitation of Superman, not a big "S" in sight—just lots of stinky red cape—yelling what sounded like "obsessed Fred" over and over again.

Liebe ducked behind a storage bin on the dock and the caped-crusader leapt on top of it. Liebe hadn't been screaming for help but she'd thrown every dirty phrase she'd learned in boot camp at the crazed Dumpster sleeper. Nigel tried to block Liebe from an assault. Just as the dog-woman was about to pounce, Brita rushed up and said a few words to her, then helped her down from the storage bin and walked her back to Dumpster-land. Brita carefully removed a stick from her charge's hand and tossed it in the water. The Dumpster wasn't the happiest place on earth, but it seemed to work to calm the agitated woman.

"Aloha, what the hell was that, that, that ... ?" Liebe seemed short on words over four letters. Typical.

"I think she's a street person who lives in the last Dumpster on the right." I don't know why I felt obliged to make it sound like an address or directions you'd give to someone coming to dinner.

"Well, she barked at me. And, and, and ... she chased me." Liebe never stuttered. "And she smelled like ... " Then Liebe got a transcendental look on her face and said, "¼dog poop!"

I looked at Wharf. He looked away. If he could have done an innocent whistle, I think he would have. Liebe sniffed, then lifted one foot and looked at the bottom of her sandal. Nigel handed her a hose.

I checked my watch. "I gotta go. I'm late for my audiology

appointment." I couldn't think of anything else to say, so Wharf and I sauntered over to my truck parked in its special space.

In downtown Lahaina, designated parking was one of the great benefits of the job. In the truck, I reached for the radio tuner, then stopped. Since my accident, listening to the radio had become more annoying than pleasurable. We waited in silence to turn onto Front Street only to be stopped at the first crosswalk where a group of scuba divers schlepped their gear from a dive shop down to the harbor.

Traffic was bad; an island cross-section of motor coaches, low-rider pick-ups bouncing to the bass beat of their stereos, red rental convertibles, shiny SUVs and shinier Harleys edged their way through town.

On one side of Front Street, I could see the Roadstead, the island of Lanai, and the Pacific, on the other, a series of art galleries, T-shirt shops, and timeshare swindlers disguised as activity booking desks. The art visible through the open doors seemed to have a certain uniformity: Ocean, flowers, whales, beaches—in a word—Paradise. I guessed it was what sold to vacationers. I hadn't had a chance to explore the shops yet, but I was sure they were out of my price range. I knew enough to avoid the timeshare scams. Still, Front Street culture was one-of-a-kind and I owed it to myself to explore. Liebe and I would need to tour it before she left town.

Eventually the traffic edged forward and I turned right on Lahainaluna heading toward the Honoapiilani Highway. Ahead of me at the intersection with Wainee, I saw Brita Beamer in a BMW convertible—how ironic—with the woman from the Dumpster. She crossed ahead of me and pulled into the McDonalds' drive thru. Maybe there was more to her than I thought.

It took me a half hour to get to my appointment, which made me fifteen minutes late. I debated what to do with Wharf. Leave him in the truck with the windows open, tie him to a tree, or take him in with me. Heck, this was Hawaii, according to Nigel, things were casual. Maybe I could pass him off as a service dog. I found a spot to park in the shade and rolled down the windows. It was eighty degrees and the afternoon trades had yet to begin. My shirt stuck to my back and my hair drooped: Wharf's hair stuck to his back and his tail drooped.

"Sorry buddy, this is the best I can do." He stretched across the seat and was asleep by the time I had gathered my backpack and keys.

The office was air-conditioned to a level suitable for maintaining permafrost. I had a sweatshirt in my pack and I pulled it on before I became hypothermic. The receptionist seemed unaware she was in the tropics. She wore cords, Birkenstocks, and a sweater. It's possible she was in charge of the thermostat.

A woman and her daughter sat in a "kids' corner" of the waiting room. The girl, who looked about eight, spoke in an auctioneer's voice—loud and fast. Her mother, as though to compensate, whispered. The mom looked like she belonged with the hippy preacher I'd seen proselytizing under the banyan tree. She wore a multi-layered batik skirt with a gauze peasant blouse and flat leather sandals. Like Charlie Brown's Christmas tree, she had ornaments hanging precariously from every branch—baubles, bangles and beads became her.

As I looked closer—some might say I stared—I could see that the jewelry wasn't junk, but instead appeared to be original and expensive. Still, her daughter wore dirty tennis shoes over dirty socks. I could see smudges of red dirt on her skinny white legs, navy blue shorts and stained sky blue shirt. The little girl fiddled with her hair that was pulled back in a sweaty ponytail. I could tell she was trying to style some hair over her ears and hearing aids.

"Aloha Jones?" The doctor, a white-coated woman with matching glow-in-the-dark white teeth smiled at me. "I'm Darcy Kamakana. Nice to meet you." She slipped her palm across mine so lightly that it tickled in what passed for a handshake. Her fingers were cold. I looked at my hand to see if they'd left frost marks. Nothing.

I followed her to a little exam room set up for hearing testing and privacy. Within minutes, she had warmed the room with her exuberance and had my hearing-related medical history documented in her notes. Then she got out what I'd come to know as an otoscope. In the past few months, I'd learned all kinds of terminology that I'd never needed to know before. I braced when the scope touched my ear canal. I felt her breath on my neck, then incredible pain when the scope went in. I flinched so hard we bonked heads. It was like trying to take care of a hangnail with a hammer.

"I won't ask if that hurt." Darcy sat back and grimaced.

"Thanks." What could I say? I didn't like my disability, pain or weakness. So far, she was three for three on examining my dislikes.

"You've really jacked your ear up, ya know?" she dropped her kind doctor persona.

"Uh, yeah, occupational hazard."

"I think we both know better than that." She busted me. "You have no business diving. You're going to screw it up worse at this rate."

I shrugged. Geez, like I really needed a lecture. I wanted to ask her where she learned her bedside manner and if they might want to reconsider her training.

She took on the subject without my saying anything. "So you were a Coastie, huh?" Then she pushed her blouse over to expose wings tattooed on her shoulder. "The Air Guard paid my way through school. You miss it?"

No wonder, she had the same pulse as Liebe, maybe once removed. I thought for a minute about my answer. "Yeah, I do. I miss knowing my future, knowing that everyone I worked with had the same rules and training. Of course, I miss my friends, but hey, now I'm in Paradise." It sounded less authentic than I intended.

"How long you been here—in Paradise—that is?"

"A little over a week."

"Kind of hard to adjust in a week."

"My sister came to help me move. It's been okay."

"When did you re-injure?" She was breaking the sentences down into shorter pieces.

"Uh," I had to think about it. When had I pulled a dead guy out of the water? "Yesterday. I had to do a free-dive."

"Had to?" She'd raised an eyebrow.

I told her about the past twenty-four hours. She ran both hands up from her chin across her face and back through her hair. Then she surprised me. "So you've got Wharf." Of all the things she could comment on, this was not what I thought anyone would choose first.

I nodded.

She made some notes in my file and began what I had learned was a basic balance assessment, moving my head into different positions while watching my eyes for nystagmas or jerky eye movement. It's what the cops use to check drunk drivers. You can't cheat.

"What are you doing about the balance?"

"Surfing."

"Excellent." She smiled. "Have you been up to Honolua Bay yet?"

I laughed. "No, I thought I'd move up to those waves in increments."

"Yeah, I've been through the washing machine there a bunch of times."

"You surf?" She didn't look the type.

"No, but my husband does. I stay inside on a boogie board and still get thrashed." She sat back and crossed her arms. "So you want the prognosis?"

"I think I've got that already. I'm deaf in one ear."

"Well, yeah, but when you put it like that it doesn't sound as good as I was going to make it."

I shrugged.

"I'd like to check your ear again in a couple days. You have fluid in there, that's what's causing the pain. I'm going to give you two prescriptions." She scribbled onto a script pad and handed it to me.

I looked at it. It was for an antibacterial wash. "What's the other one?"

"Hula."

I did my typical hearing aid tap thing.

"You know that doesn't help don't you?" she said. "I'd like you to sign up to take hula lessons or join a *halau.*"

My confusion must have been evident. "*Halau*?"

"A hula group," she said. "I'm sensing that you're missing music, with hula you can dance to the drums' beat even if you can't hear the melody. Hula is great to help with balance." She was ticking these off on her fingers. "And, you'll meet some fun people." She paused. "I just know that when I moved here I felt pretty isolated. This will help you adjust to island life."

So, she was not only a doc, but also a mind-reader.

"Thanks Darcy." I decided not to fight it. She was right. Once Liebe left, I'd be without a pal, except for one. "How do you know about Wharf?"

Her eyes shifted from up to down and then back at me. One side of her mouth tightened and her brows crunched together. "All I can say is that I've worked with him. He's a good boy. He's smart." Then she shook her head. "Don't get attached." She again shook my hand with those cold fingers and showed me to the door.

In the hall, I could hear the loud girl speaking to her mother in the next room. As Darcy walked in, she looked over her shoulder at me. Then I heard her say, "I'm so sorry to hear about Colley." And, the door shut.

Chapter Six

I'd just seen Zhen Blue, Colley's girlfriend. If my boyfriend had just died, I might be a tad bit distraught. In a word, I'd call her nonplussed.

When Darcy commented to the woman and girl about Colley, I realized why the woman's jewelry appeared expensive. I'd surmised from the evening with Koni and Nigel that Zhen's art career was successful. In hindsight—always my best view—she looked a lot more like an artist than a hippy; slightly more upscale, nicer shoes, finer weave in the gauze, stylish hairdo. I glanced in the mirror. I showed plenty of blondish hair but no style, enough crow's feet that you could gauge my age easier than counting the rings on a tree's cross section, and freckles, freckles, freckles.

Wharf's gut interrupted my thoughts with a gurgle. I detoured through Mickey D's and got us each a cheap burger. I added French fries and a Diet Coke to my order and chicken nuggets to his. We drove back to my office and ate lunch while I shuffled more paper. This job was a long ways from my former life, but I reminded myself it was a job. One I needed. The clock seemed like it was broken.

Finally, at five, Liebe showed up. I changed into a swimsuit and locked the door. Wharf sat next to the truck so I rolled down the windows and let him in. From inside the canopy, Liebe and I grabbed our surfboards, which we proceeded to wax with enough Mr. Zogs Sex Wax that we'd never lose our grip. The smell of sandalwood permeated our palms. Then, we did the sunscreen thing, even though the sun was low and the rays long. I had on the same suit I'd worn the day before. Liebe didn't comment on my tattoo. In fact, she was not her usually chatty self.

"What's wrong?" I asked after we'd each successfully outmaneuvered some twelve-year-olds for a wave and had paddled back out to sit in the line-up.

"Thinking about dying," she mumbled.

I don't know what I thought she'd say, but this wasn't it. "Because of Colley or the cancer?"

"Little of both I guess," she said. "I'm not ready. Don't want to be old. Don't want to die. What's that leave?"

She had me there. "Mid-life crisis?" I asked.

"Yeah, I guess that's what I'll do. I'll have a mid-life crisis." She seemed satisfied with the solution.

"Nigel gonna be your boy-toy?" I wondered aloud.

"Little long in the tooth for that I think." She looked around at the local kids hunkered down on their boards wanting to get a wave maybe more than we did. She shuddered. "I guess I'd rather have a midlife-toy than a boy-toy anyway. I'm not into weird stuff like that teacher with her student. Course I don't want someone croaking on me either."

I smiled. Leave it to Liebe to mentally cruise the whole spectrum. I was thinking a mid-life crisis might be in order for me too. I'd always been an early bloomer. My life and career were clearly half over—no more Coast Guard, no marriage, no kids. What did I have? A rental house, a hearing aid, somebody else's dog, and the most sought after restroom in Lahaina. Liebe went flat and paddled fast but a little kid on a big board beat her to the wave. She turned and I could see, if not hear, her smack-talking the little shoulder-hopper.

Past her in the channel, I could see the *Awiwi* heading outbound again. In my mind, I could still visualize Colley, the hull crushing across his back. Then I thought of his head injury. Could it have come from hitting the prop? I know the hull didn't hit his head.

Come to think of it, when I'd walked Wharf around the harbor's catwalk, just before Brita Beamer accosted me, I'd seen what could have been blood on the dock. Maybe he had tripped on the warped boards, bonked his head, fell in and drowned. Of course, how did he get outside the harbor from there? The harbor was like a toilet that didn't flush. Nope, he had to have died on the ocean side of the breakwater or on a boat. So how did he bonk his head?

A little kid yelled at me and interrupted my musings. "Hey, *Tutu*. You gonna surf or what?" Then he flicked me with water, shot into position, and left me sitting on my board. I was pretty sure the little grommet had just called me grandma. If I could catch him, he was going to pay.

Liebe was inside the break again. I didn't know how I'd missed her last ride, but I had and the little kid was right. I was missing the few sets that came through. I watched a little longer, positioned myself for a couple waves that didn't pan out, and finally got one.

I felt the fin grab the water as I shifted forward on the board to keep the speed I needed. The sun was at a low angle so the light on the water was nearly golden. For a moment I felt the warm air caress my skin, felt my body balanced in perfect harmony with the board, and smelled pig roasting at the luau. I shut my eyes to go back in time to the days when the early transoceanic Polynesians settled on the shores.

In that moment, without my sight to compensate, the board shot away from me. I dumped in the water on my back, and my little wave injected saltwater up my nose like a pressure hose. Surfing has a way of taking you to the edge of fantasy and then smacking you in the head. Of course, so does Liebe.

By the time we swam into shore, showered and changed, I could tell she was antsy again. "Liebe, what's up?" I was running my fingers through my hair, trying to get it dry before it went back into the obligatory scrunchie.

She mumbled something, threw her bag over her shoulder and walked away—not toward my truck.

I hustled to catch up as she headed past the front slips toward the Dumpsters. "Geez, Liebe, what now?" I caught up with her and grabbed her hand.

"I told you," she said.

I squinted at her. We both knew I was deaf. This was total B.S. "Okay, what have you gotten us into now?" Someone watching might have seen my shoulders slump in resignation.

"We have a date."

"What?" I looked down at my outfit. The same one I'd worn to work. I ran my hands through my still stringy hair. Then I looked more carefully at her. She'd somehow made time for a little makeup and a fresh sundress. Even her sandals had tiny heel lifts. If my "look" wasn't disturbing enough, I also realized the implication of her statement. "With whom?" I assumed it was a date for each of us, not just me tagging along with my big sister. *Oh, please, don't let it be that.* I remembered something similar when I was in grade school and she in high school. I might have been only a kid, but I still knew when I was a dork. It was a lot like this moment.

"Sorry," I said, "I can't leave Wharf sitting in the truck while we go off and, and, and…" I didn't even know what she had planned.

"We're going to the luau," Liebe said. "And Wharf's at the sitter's."

"What sitter?" I asked, while I again pondered her organizational skills. You'd think she could have at least grabbed me some clean clothes since she had everything else worked out.

"He's with Awiwi's mom."

"Wait a second here, Lib. How do you know Awiwi's mom? Why would she babysit a dog?" Liebe kept us moving the whole time on her trajectory to the beach south of the harbor. She skirted the Dumpsters as an apparent safety precaution, but the Shar-Pei woman was nowhere in sight. Liebe pulled off her cute sandals once we passed the breakwater and walked barefoot along the beach behind King Kamehameha III, the elementary school next to the harbor. It looked desolate without kids in play, the red dirt runways edged by dying grass and naked tetherball poles like sentinels next to frayed swings. They weren't wasting money on outdoor amenities, that's for sure.

"I met his mom when he took me over to the library to ask her to babysit the pooch while we go watch Awiwi at the luau."

The smell of roast pig mixed with the scent of citronella-scented torches drew us up the beach. Ahead of us, I could see people lined up at an open bar where several grass-skirted Tahitian-style dancers handed out some kind of alcohol-laced fruit punch. In front of them, a pair of ginormous bare-chested local boys stood guard at the entrance to the beach. They each held a tiki torch and sported crimson Hawaiian royalty capes and canary yellow helmets. When we approached them, one said, "Hey, Jones girls, thanks for coming. Your comp passes are at the bar." Wow, Awiwi had a second job and six pack abs that made corrugated metal roofing look soft. Before I could say anything, a young tourist couple edged up next to him and asked us to take their picture. Even with the killer six-packs, I still didn't get why it was such a big deal to get a photo with either Awiwi the cop or Awiwi the Hawaiian-bedecked security guard. Whatever.

Liebe led us to a bar, perhaps plucked from the "Gilligan's Island" set, and once again, we had fruity libations served alongside macadamia nuts and pineapple spears. We wandered from table to table, any of which I thought would be a fine place to sit, but Liebe seemed on a mission. Out near a stage built in the sand, the front—and clearly the best—table for four had two empty seats. In the other two seats sat a bald pirate with a soul patch and an Amish Rastafarian with a short-skirted waitress giving him her best smile. It was like *Groundhog's Day* all over again.

Liebe bent and gave them each a wispy kiss on the cheek. Nigel stood up and squeezed her butt in response. Koni refrained. The waitress walked away without an introduction, but her Hawaiian hips spoke a thousand words. If hula was a form of storytelling that gave reverence to a natural phenomenon, this girl's butt had just lionized Koni.

"Let's go check out the pig," Koni said. Nigel and Liebe seemed to need more greeting than we did. We walked around the perimeter of the tables to where a ring of torches lined a hole in the ground. The scent took me back in time to weenie roasts as a child, campfires on the beach as a teenager, and a slew of summertime barbecues as an adult. I took another deep inhalation.

"You didn't call me back," he said.

I snorted. Oops. That's right, he'd left a message. I guess I needed to listen to those. I think I had about twenty, but who's counting?

"They do this every night?" I asked as I watched several guys peeling what looked like layers of huge green leaves off the fire.

"Yep, it takes all day to make *ka lua* pig," Koni said.

"Kalua? Like the drink?"

"No, *ka lua* means "the pit"—the place where the pig is roasted. Lot of people miss the meaning on that one, especially since it then refers to the *imu* or earthen oven where the pig is roasted."

"Nothing's simple I guess," I said. I wished it were. It's hard not to dream a little when living in Paradise. Fortunately, my earlier surfing smack down had reminded me to remain in reality. It was as though he could read my thoughts.

"You look sad. Were you thinking about what it was like living here before the tourists?"

Too tired from work and surfing, I just gave him the sideways look and a shoulder shrug. Koni didn't seem put off. He lightly grasped my shoulder and guided me back to the bar for a refill. Somehow, his touch didn't bother me the way my boss' had the day before. Go figure. Instead, he became my guide to local little known facts.

"Did you know the name Lahaina means land of the merciless sun?" he asked.

"Then what's the deal with that street, Lahainaluna?" I countered, ever the inquisitive little tourist and intrepid fact-seeker. "Does it mean land of the merciless sun-moon?"

Koni laughed. I liked that a lot. He had a deep guffaw and his beautiful white teeth glimmered in the night. My sister Sarang is a self-proclaimed tooth snob and I'd picked up on the nuance over the years. This guy was a tooth-snob's dream. I dreaded her ever meeting Nigel. Sarang was hell on bad British bites.

I guess I was staring a little wide-eyed and nearly missed his next definition.

"*Luna* means boss. Lahainaluna was the road to the sugar mill's boss' house." Koni pattered on about Lahaina only getting an average of nine inches rain a year while the adjacent West Maui Mountains recorded over four hundred inches of rain annually, making them one of the wettest places on earth. There was something soothing and nice about the lecture. I didn't have to participate much and I was learning a lot about my new home.

"In the old days, the Polynesians who sailed here brought little razor-back pigs with them. They lived down along the beach. When the missionaries came over, they brought the huge Farmer John pigs. Then they interbred and the next thing you know there were huge, yellow-tusked porkers rooting through the mosses and lichens up in the mountains, ruining the natural water filtration system that took hundreds of years to build."

No wonder I'd seen notices in the office paperwork about contaminated water a couple weeks earlier because of fecal matter. Paradise, really?

A couple more of the luau staff greeted him with hugs and kisses. Apparently, he was well-known.

We'd circled back to our table with another drink refill on the way when a trio of drummers to the side of the stage increased their beat. An emcee, dressed in white polyester slacks and a Hilo Hattie shirt, announced the buffet was open. The tourists held no quarter for the buffet. They moved en masse like locusts on grasslands.

As Awiwi's comps, we waited until the lines abated and still found an abundance of poi, pork, rice, salads, and fruity desserts. The poi had all the charm of the white paste we were required to sample in kindergarten from the jar with the little brush applicator stuck to the lid. Well, maybe not required, but tell me one person who didn't try it. Anyway, the poi in a word, was yucky and, in fact, went into my mental thesaurus as the opposite of yummy. That's bad. In my mind, I could see an ancient islander smacking his hand against his head after roasting the first pig. You don't have to be very advanced to want barbecue more than paste. On the other end of the mélange, I was wahoo wild about the coconut pudding that Koni called *haupia*.

However, my gustatory exploration came to a near heaving halt when I tried a big bite of *poke*. I'm pretty sure it's the Hawaiian word for "gag me." Both Nigel and Koni ate it as though it was the world's last great invention. Liebe spit hers into her napkin and asked the ingredients.

Koni said, "Fresh *aku,* chopped *limukoho, inamona,* and *alaea*—to taste." Then he picked up another bite—with his fingers no less—and sucked them off. I couldn't believe I'd found him attractive once, even minutes earlier.

Liebe and I stared at him, waiting for a translation. Nigel elucidated in his inimitable manner. "*Aku* is raw tuna, *limukoho* is seaweed, *inamona* is *kukui* nut," he paused and looked at Koni, "is there another word for *kukui*?"

Koni nodded and said, "Candle nut."

Nigel continued, "... and *alaea* is Hawaiian salt that's non-processed, so it has trace minerals in it and then it's mixed with a little bit of red clay." Then he switched from his fork to his fingers and joined Koni's feast.

All I could think of was the red clay dirt of the schoolyard where sweaty little kids had scuffed their shoes, spit, and played. This had to be the worst dish known to man and our dates were licking it off their hands. Liebe and I got up simultaneously and headed to the bar. There wasn't enough alcohol in the punch to drop Liebe or me tonight—too bad.

We looked for Awiwi to thank him for the luau tickets, but he had left his security post. Probably off to a third job. Again, the drums beat louder to gain everyone's attention. We hurried back to our table. I had lost my concern for looking like a ragamuffin since my date was eating raw fish and seaweed rolled in red dirt. Funny how little things can change a moment. Kind of like the difference between a gynecologic exam and foreplay. Same Bat time, same Bat station, totally different show. I had really spent too much time in front of the TV as a kid. And, believe me this evening was all about *Gilligan's Island* and not at all about *Batman*. There would be no trips to the Bat Cave tonight. Of course, no one seemed to be clamoring at the door.

Chapter Seven

The drums brought the emcee back out onstage like teasing a cat with a string. He did the obligatory "*Aloooo-ha*", told a couple lame jokes, and then introduced the first dancers; a group of men and women dressed in muted swaths of what resembled *tapa* cloth. Their rhythm was slow feet in perpetual motion; their waving hands told stories while the emcee interpreted. They did everything from the ubiquitous *Hukilau* to my personal favorite *Aloha 'Oe.* Either melody I would now have stuck in my head for weeks.

I was surprised when the emcee took the time to introduce Koni and asked him to sit in with the other musicians. My date, ever the entertainer, obliged and I reconciled myself to sitting alone the rest of the show. Liebe and Nigel had gone for a walk on the beach. I didn't want to know why.

As the next song began, the dancers fanned out into the audience looking for victims—they called them volunteers. I tried to disappear. Apparently sitting alone at the center, front row table wasn't the epitome of stealth. A big paw latched onto my shoulder. When I looked up and saw Awiwi I knew there was no point trying to resist. I schlepped up and onto the stage in my shorts, Vans, and white wife-beater. The troupe recruited other dancers, who though more suitably attired, were a hodgepodge of ages and body types ranging from preteens to geriatrics and from stickman thin to Jaba the Hut wannabes. Talk about a melting pot.

As soon as we got on stage, the lesson began as they taught us to do a figure eight with our hips. The oldest, fattest guy broke into a sweat. The youngest girl just giggled. The audience cheered. Then we practiced hand movements that were like trying to get chewing gum off our fingers. I could feel the beat of the drums so I thought I was doing well; maybe I was a natural. I looked up from the stage to see that Liebe and Nigel were back at the table. Both looked embarrassed. *Jerks.*

Thankfully, the lesson ended and we filed off stage to go back to our tables. My face was red from a combination of blushing and exertion. Koni winked as I went by. His pals in the band made lip-smacking noises and teased him about me. Saying things like "*ono*-licious" and "hotty *haole.*" I wasn't sure what I thought of that. My face got redder.

The show transitioned through various other dance styles until they got to the super fast Tahitian dancers who wore coconut bustiers and grass skirts. The audience was cheering and I thought it must be the show's finale until the lights turned low and just the perimeter tiki torches remained lit. The drums beat louder and the emcee announced the star of the show—the fire dancer—Awiwi. He burst onto the stage in a series of jumps as he lit torches while flipping and spinning them in the air.

I was hypnotized.

Every once in awhile Awiwi would drop one for show and then flip it back into the air with his foot. The audience went wild—clapping, whistling and yelling by the time he was done. Liebe stuck two fingers in her mouth and wolf whistled as though she'd just seen a Chippendale's show. I now realized why everyone wanted pictures taken with Awiwi—he might be a cop by day—but by night he was definitely a star on fire.

After the show ended, we tried to seek him out to thank him but he was the center of a minor mob. I was surprised when one of the female dancers wearing a grass skirt and coconut bustier came up to me. She looked familiar but I couldn't place her.

"Aloha," she said, using my name rather than a greeting, "You looked like a natural."

I cocked my head a little to the side. Man, she looked familiar.

"Darcy," she said, "Your ear doctor."

"I didn't recognize you," I stammered. "You dance in the show?" Nothing like asking the obvious.

"Everybody has two jobs," she smiled. "I'm lucky to have two I love."

Koni came over, wrapped an arm around her and gave her a kiss on the temple. Was this ministerial or what? My face—as usual—betrayed my every thought.

"Koni and my husband say they are some kind of cousins. Like everybody else here." Darcy rolled her eyes. "Anyway," she said, "I was surprised to see you guys here tonight. Especially to see you dancing, Aloha. Way to take my prescription to heart."

I blushed some more. Koni raised a brow.

"Darcy said I needed to learn to hula to help with my balance."

"Cool, she can learn from Auntie Mele," he said to Darcy. Apparently, my invisibility came on a little too late. I hate it when people talk about me as though I'm not there. He saw my discomfort. "Auntie Mele is Awiwi's mom. She teaches hula."

"I thought she worked at the library," I said. Then I remembered—everybody has two jobs. I was starting to feel like a piker with my one little old harbormaster gig. Of course, I had no other skills, at least none that had civilian applications. I doubted that anyone needed expertise in underwater demolition or knot tying. What else did I know how to do? I could bake up a storm, I spoke passable French, and I won every Easter egg hunt I'd ever entered as a child. Granted that wasn't much in adulthood, but I was generally good at finding things hidden or lost. So, if there was a job on Maui that involved finding eggs, using them to bake French pastries and then blowing them to smithereens, I was gold. I didn't hold my breath. Best to do well with the Harbors Division.

We said farewell, or actually, *aloha* to Darcy and the rest of the luau gang. Nigel and Koni offered to walk Liebe and me back to the harbor.

The air held the scent of night blooming jasmine and the waves slurped quietly on the beach. The island of Lanai was a distant shadow to the west. The *Au Au* Channel between the islands looked dark, warm, and peaceful. It was romance central and I was the mayor.

Unfortunately, Koni didn't seem to notice the mood and walked along with his hands in his pockets, his thoughts his own. Liebe and Nigel held hands and she giggled occasionally at his quiet murmurings. When we came to the Dumpsters, Liebe tried to veer wide around them, but there was a strange noise coming from one. Liebe and I stood back while Nigel and Koni closed in to inspect.

"Do you think it's rats?" Liebe whispered and grabbed my hand.

"I don't know," I whispered back.

Our dates edged up to the huge metal bin and looked in. Nigel hooted and Koni grimaced. Then they shook their heads and both hotfooted it back to us.

"What?" Liebe asked.

Koni just shook his head again. He wasn't talking. Nigel whispered something to Liebe.

"Eeewww!"

"What?" I asked.

"The Shar-Pei and the street preacher were doing the horizontal hula in the Dumpster," she said. "On that old blanket she had wrapped around her yesterday."

"Guess he's just another man of the cloth," Nigel cocked an eyebrow at Koni.

Koni didn't smile. He gave Nigel a look that bordered on disgust. Nigel shrugged and smacked Liebe on the rump. "If you can't beat 'em, join 'em," he said, as he winked at me.

I guess romance was in the air—thick, stinky and slightly creepy air. I shuddered. I assumed we'd never speak of this again. I was wrong.

"Well, if that doesn't speak to your spirit of romance, nothing does," Liebe said.

What was she thinking? We all tried to ignore her and walked faster, even Nigel.

"I mean, really, if you're a street person, and you can still find pleasure with another street person, isn't that great?"

It had to be the Mai Tais talking. A tryst in the trash didn't spell romance, I don't care who you are. I pitied the next crew person who needed to make a Dumpster run.

The various evening charters were wrapping up. Lahaina Divers must have had a night dive, since the crew was unloading scuba tanks and taking on a supply of fresh water at the loading dock. The Windjammer, a sailing schooner, was still piping Hawaiian music over its stereo as the crew helped tourists, three sheets to the wind, off the boat. Tied tight in its berth, the other *Awiwi*—Nigel's boat—looked charter-ready for the next morning. I still had trouble with the man and the boat having the same name, although I shouldn't. I'd seen many boats with women's names: *Shirley B*, *Peggy S*, even *Aloha Oi*.

"Where're you parked?" Nigel asked us. I'd left my Harbors Division truck in the space I'd come to call my own, on the northernmost edge of the loading dock parking area. At least I thought I had. Instead, there it sat—one space in. *Weird, I must be losing it.* Nigel and Liebe made out like a couple of teenagers while Koni and I shuffled our feet.

"Listen, Aloha, I'd like to see you again," he paused and said, "Maybe not on a double date." He glanced at his cell phone, then his watch.

I didn't want to be a charity case. "Sure, stop by the office next time you're down at the harbor," I said.

Koni seemed relieved. "I've gotta go. I have, uh, something to do ..." He reached out and ran his hand down my bare arm. Goose bumps jumped to attention and my toes curled. Yeow! He was so hot the air around him crackled and I thought I smelled smoke. He turned and walked past several severely chopped Harleys parked along the street and into the shadows toward the banyan tree.

Nigel had crossed the street to his car, an old but not vintage Austin Martin. He toot-tooted as he left, Liebe and I followed. Through the truck's open windows, I thought I heard a scream and shouting coming from the Dumpsters. My bum ears were constantly sending me mixed messages, so I mentally tuned out as we drove down the one-way alley between the Pioneer Inn and the library. At Front Street, we turned south to head toward Puamana where Liebe said Auntie Mele lived. As we passed the banyan tree, I looked toward the harbor to where I'd thought I heard screaming.

At the end of the block, I could see the street preacher shaking his fist into the dark as Koni grabbed the Shar-Pei woman by the shoulders and shook her. Behind me, in my side mirror, I saw a Maui cop car flash on his lights and turn into the fray. I resisted the urge to join him, relieved I had no dog in the fight, sad to see Koni in trouble.

We found Auntie Mele's condo after only a few wrong turns. It was near the highway but still in the gated Puamana community on the southern edge of Lahaina. Developed in the 1960s, the little neighborhood had always had a certain cachet. Auntie Mele's unit looked a little shabbier than the neighbors' places, lacking some of the upgrades like dormers, skylights, and new windows others boasted. On her stoop, we rang her doorbell and it played the *Hukilau*. Cute. I heard Wharf bark at the sound and realized I'd missed him.

A woman with a long graying braid called to us through the screen. She was sitting at what looked like a huge fabric table. As we entered the room, I realized she had been stitching on a stretched quilt. The pattern looked like a chain of passionflowers in blood red on a white background. She took off a pair of half-glasses that hung from a shell loop around her neck.

"Liebe, Aloha, how was the luau?" As she walked forward to shake my hand, she moved like a young palm tree swaying in the breeze. Her grasp was strong and firm. I felt small, hard calluses on her fingers. Wharf rooted around my other hand with his face until I scratched his ears and he responded with deep, happy noises in his throat.

"The luau was great," Liebe said. "Awiwi's amazing. Did you teach him to dance?"

Mele nodded. "Our whole family dances," she said. "He's also taken classes from some of the best in the business. But I think mostly it's in his blood." She absently stroked the red quilt fabric. "We would have loved to have him make a living dancing, but there's not enough to live on and, of course, he's always wanted to be a cop. He and Koni live by that sense of justice."

Hmm... had I just seen Koni's ideas about justice?

Liebe and Mele chatted about quilting and fabrics. I looked around the room at shelves of trophies and photos of dance troupes where Mele was either a member or the teacher. I recognized Awiwi in many photos from youth to adulthood. In a recent group photo, I saw Darcy, one of the girls I'd seen at a booking desk for one of the snorkel boats and another dancer from this evening's luau. An older photo featured a very young Koni Ke playing a ukulele. His hair was short and his outfit loud, but his bright eyes and white teeth were unmistakable.

Wharf followed me around the room, seeming to share my nosiness. A gold-edged plaque held Awiwi's degree in law enforcement and next to it were his individual and academy graduation photos. I was surprised to see my co-worker, Gil Mangas, next to him in the group shot. It seemed like Maui was a small island with a whole lot less than seven degrees of separation.

I picked up another small frame that held a school photo of the little girl I'd seen with Zhen Blue at Darcy's office. In it, the child wore the same dirty school uniform and I could tell she'd worked hard to cover her ears and hearing aids with stray sweaty hair. Other than that, she was all big smile and wide eyes with a hint of a scar between her bangs and brow. She looked like mischief personified.

Mele gently took the frame from me and set it back on the shelf. "That's Momi, my son Konala's daughter."

I heard my father's voice in my head for a moment. When in doubt, don't say anything. As usual, I ignored it. "Oh, I thought that was Colley's daughter," I said.

Liebe was making faces at me over Mele's shoulder.

Mele snorted. "I always said that *moke* needed a good swift kick in the *okole,* but a crack across the head is just as good." She paused, then added, "Long as he's dead." She again fingered the blood red fabric on the quilt frame that sat like a large island in the center of the room. Then by explanation she said, "Momi's mother left Konala for Colley when Momi was three." Mele moved us toward the door but didn't say any more about her family.

We thanked her for watching Wharf and drove back to my place. It had a nice ring to it: My place. The good thing about being a military brat was learning to settle in quickly.

Again, Wharf slept on the bed. I didn't. I tossed around for a while but it didn't seem to bother him. Periodically, he'd make sad little barking noises and his paws would twitch in his sleep. I somehow doubted he was chasing bunnies but wondered if, instead, he was recalling Colley's death. It seemed like violence was a part of island life, or at least the sphere I'd been orbiting: Koni roughing up the Shar-Pei, Mele wanting to bash Colley, Ho thinking Colley had been hitting Zhen. These thoughts plagued my mind until sleep finally blanketed me.

Chapter Eight

There's nothing quite like an explosion to replace a four-dollar alarm clock. I'd finally gotten into a deep sleep when a bomb hit the corrugated metal roof of my shanty. His fur standing at attention, Wharf perched on the bed barking at the pre-dawn window while Liebe shouted, "Imawake, Ima wake, I'm awake!" and scrambled around looking for a flight suit. It took us all a moment to realize another mango had simply let go the tenuous bonds of earth in pursuit of gravity's truth. I fell back into bed and crushed my pillow over my head.

After a few minutes, I could still hear Wharf whining at the door to go out, while Liebe bellowed in the shower. She'd always been partial to show tunes, so the long version of "Some Enchanted Evening" shouldn't have surprised me. And it didn't. It just annoyed the bejeebers out of me that she could be so cheerful.

I shoved my feet into a pair of what the locals call *slippahs*—I'd always known them as thongs—which of course now refer to underpants in a style I'd never wear. In my pajama shorts and camisole, I opened the door for Wharf, thinking he'd mosey over to a bush and come back inside after a quick whiz. Instead, snout to the ground, he bayed and headed around the cabin. I followed and caught up with him just as he tried to push through an opening where several cedar boards looked as though they'd been pried loose from the fence.

My landlord was going to be mad. He'd already threatened to put concertina wire along the top rail. A security breach of this level would no doubt solidify the concept. I pushed the boards back into place as best I could. After a little more sniffing on Wharf's part, I followed him back to the house. In the soft earth next to my window, Wharf again sniffed and tinkled. That's when I noticed the bare footprints in the dirt. Someone had gotten through the fence and peeped in my window.

Even though the footprints were smaller than mine, I thought: *Bring on the concertina wire.* Then I noticed a wet spot in the dirt at the toes of the right foot. Spit? Blood? Tinkle? Worse? The choices were bad and I didn't want to do either a scratch or sniff test, so I walked away in disgust, not a solution in sight.

By the time I got to work, I was ready to forget the whole thing. Really, a peeping Tom was probably de rigueur in a town the size and density of Lahaina. Plus, I had a few things I wanted to look up in the files in my office. This thing with Colley was bugging me and nobody else seemed interested. If I were back in the Coast Guard, our whole station would have been pitching theories and combing through information. I smelled an Easter egg hunt coming on.

First, I tried to find a something under the name Colley. That's when I realized I didn't know if Colley was his first or last name. Plus, it looked like all the files were organized by the corporate name for commercial enterprises. I called the Wailuku office and asked to speak to Boo-Boo... I mean my boss, Max Yake. I had a couple questions and I thought I'd casually ask the name of Colley's business. Again, his assistant let me know Yake was out of the office and that her time was precious. Bitch.

I asked her to transfer my call to Gil's cell phone, thinking he'd be out on the water and maybe in a good enough mood that he'd help me—you know a little teamwork?

"Mangas," he said. I don't know why guys do that, answer the phone with their last names instead of hello, but I thought it was dopey.

"Gil, this is Aloha," I said in an effort to personalize our relationship.

"Yeah, Jones, whadaya need now?"

The whole conversation went like that. Every interaction punctuated with little kickers that implied he was busy and my brain one cell short of an amoeba.

I didn't care. What was he going to do? Get me fired, dislike me, not invite me to his Christmas party? Blah, blah, blah. I made little chomping motions with my hands as I listened whenever he said something I didn't need to know.

"What are you doing?" he asked.

I was sitting with my feet on my desk, speakerphone on and doing the hand puppet thing. I frowned. "Why?"

"Because I'm standing outside your window," he said.

I looked up, saw him, rolled my eyes back, and lost my balance. Just as he walked in the door, I flipped over the back of my chair and landed on my face with my ass in the air. Wharf opened his eyes and looked at me as though he'd expected as much.

I hopped up with my heels together, threw my arms in the air palms out, smiled, and said, "Ta-dah!" I don't care how much of a hard ass you are, when you see someone flip an office chair and stick the landing in a face plant—it's funny.

Mangas flipped his phone shut and belly laughed. Then he said, "Mind if I use your head?" Being a former Coastie, I knew he was referring to the office bathroom.

"Nope, but it's gonna cost you."

He unbuckled his Sam Browne belt that held his holster, gun, and other law toys and left it on my desk, along with his ball cap. I'd never seen him without a hat before. I don't know if Yogi was bald, but Gil Mangas—my personal version of Jellystone's most famous resident—had not yet made the transition to shaving his head, although it was time. There was little pattern left to his male pattern baldness.

I raised my eyebrows as his gear dropped on my desk. Great, just what

I needed was a forty-caliber paperweight.

"Gotta go number two," he said by way of reply as he grabbed a women's magazine from my desk and disappeared into the bathroom. "I like the quizzes," he said by way of explanation.

Right, that and the article on guaranteed orgasms probably didn't hurt his interest level either. Maybe I was better off when he found me annoying more than amusing. Goodness, we'd become too close for *my* comfort. Through the door I could hear him whistling "Some Enchanted Evening." Maybe I needed to introduce him to Liebe.

When he came out, I capitalized on our new camaraderie and even offered to share my cookies with him. I'd baked my signature chocolate chippers, plus I'd added macadamia nuts. And, although hard to imagine, they were even better than my regular recipe. I was beginning to think mac nuts were the answer to all things good. Mangas seemed to agree.

He dusted the cookie crumbs off his marine patrol uniform shirt and onto a paper towel. Then, he folded the towel and used it like a funnel into his mouth. "So, Jones, whaddya think of the job so far?"

I had a mouth full of cookie. "Imph gomph," I nodded, again showing off my language skills.

"Did finding Colley freak you out?" The crumbs were gone and he was all business. Leaning forward, hands on his knees, eyes looking so deep into mine that I felt compelled to blink.

I answered with a question. "Have you heard what happened to him?"

"Yep, the coroner said he drowned."

I tilted my head and raised one brow. It was my only trick.

"After he was smacked on the head with a hunk of wood," Mangas added.

I pursed my lips, squinted and nodded.

"You don't seem surprised." Mangas held his position.

I rolled back a little, being careful not to tip back too far. That stunt was only funny once. The second time I'd just look like a hotdogger.

"I've seen a few drownings in my day," I said.

"Right, the whole Coast Guard officer thing, *again*," Mangas threw a hand up.

"What?" I didn't get his attitude. My cell phone rang. I looked at the number. It was Koni. I flipped it to message and looked back at Mangas.

Gil looked away. I could fairly see the wheels turning. He didn't have a poker face. "You know why you were hired?" he asked.

I nodded: Qualified, qualified, qualified. Then I began to shake my head. "Come to think of it, I really don't."

He began ticking the reasons off on his fingers. "You short-listed because of Civil Service points, minority points, and disability points. Then you got top ranking because Yake loves officers and he figured with a name like Aloha you'd be so local you'd bleed poi." Mangas laughed. "Boy was he surprised."

"Are you suggesting I'm not qualified?"

"Nope, I'm suggesting Yake was looking for a little honey and he got milk." Mangas laughed again. "Anyway, I was a Coastie too, out of high school, not an officer. Guess I'm jealous."

Then Liebe walked into the office.

"Speaking of honey," he muttered.

Wharf jumped up and gave Liebe the full treatment: Tail wags, kisses, big toothy grin, and then flopped to the floor for a belly rub. She knew how to greet males in a way I had yet to master.

Liebe was in her tall, blonde, Über tourist mode. She could have been the poster child for Euro trash: long, lean, tan legs, short little tropical skirt, and a halter-top featuring her biggest bazoombas. She was still searching for what she called her "optimum" size. She had some kind of crazy scarf, shawl, rag thing wrapped around her shoulders that added a certain *je ne c'est quoi*. Really, I don't know why, but it worked.

"Gil," I said, "This is my sister, Liebe Jones. Liebe, Gil is my . . . ," Hmm, not friend, not boss . . . "colleague."

She peered at his name tag. "M-A-N-G-A-S," she spelled it out in her phony German accent.

I scrunched my eyes shut and willed her to not say anything. It didn't work.

"Do you pronounce that 'Mange-Ass' or 'Man-Gas'?" she asked, looking all cute and confused, still a tiny touch of accent in place.

He wasn't insulted. "It's Mangas," he said, smoothing the pronunciation out, "But you can call me Gil." He put one big paw on her shoulder as he shook her hand with the other.

I think he wanted to flop on the floor belly-up next to the dog.

She gave Gil a wink and a little wave and blew her bimbo image as soon as she spoke to me. "Aloha," she said in commander voice, "1600 at the truck, good to go, ready to launch." Then she changed personalities again, pointed her finger at Mangas like a gun, did the little winky-click thing and in a Marlene Dietrich voice she said, "Auf Wiedersehen, Man-Gas," and whirled out. I thought the actress impersonation was over the top.

"*Your* sister?" He asked.

"Uh-huh."

"She married?"

"Unh-uh."

"She got a job?"

"Yup." This guy was too cheap to make a date anything other than Dutch. During training, he'd only get a Coke at the place that charged cops a quarter for a refill, and sandwiches where he could see his food prepared. I was never sure if he had a bubble butt, or if he carried two wallets.

"Hook me up?" He had the same smile on his face that Wharf did when he saw Liebe.

I shrugged.

"Why not?"

"I didn't say no. I just didn't say yes. Besides, you still owe me one for the facility usage. If I set you up with my sister, you'll owe me twice."

He looked longingly at the door as though he could still see the skirt twirl. "Whadya wanna know?"

I had him show me how to make sense out of the files, what the policy was on tourists using the head, and give me more details on Colley and Nigel than I really had a right to know. I didn't tell him Nigel had already hooked up with Liebe. No point in confusing the issue. He wouldn't tell me squat about Koni or Awiwi—some kind of academy brother loyalty. Of course, I didn't exactly tell him why I was asking. Overall, we had a nice chat. For a guy of few words he talked like a wrung-out sponge. I figured we were square, even though it meant I'd now have to pimp out my sister. Oh well, you do what you gotta do.

I walked Gil out to his patrol boat, freed his lines tied to the cleats on the concrete dock, and watched as he motored out of the harbor. Wharf stood with me, wagging absently. For once, there were no cruise ships at anchor, leaving the loading dock empty. This allowed us to do our daily walk without incident and afterwards settle back into the office routine. Anxious to get into the files for answers, I was frustrated when my office phone rang.

"A-lo-ha, this is Zhen Blue," she said with a pidgin lilt. Did she mean Aloha my name or *aloha* as in howdy?

"This is Aloha Jones, Ms. Blue," I said, "My condolences for your loss."

"Oh, thank you so much," she said. "We've just had some bad vibes around here lately. I don't know what it is. Maybe it's the Republicans in power."

Hmm, that was one thought. But I didn't think they'd killed her boyfriend. "What can I do for you?"

"I understand you have our little puppy," she said.

I looked at Wharf snoozing at my feet. What little puppy? He had to weigh two hundred pounds if he weighed an ounce.

"Un-hunh," I said, while my inner voice begged to keep the dog, promising to feed him, walk him, clean up any messes, *please, please, please!* Aloud I said, "When would you like to pick him up? Or do you want me to drop him off?" I'd kind of like to see where Colley lived, maybe find out about what led to his death, and for sure, check to see what Wharf's place looked like. I had no business being proprietary about him, but I already loved him.

"Would you mind bringing him to our place? I'm just so swamped. I can't get down there," she asked without waiting for a reply, giving me her address.

Before I could respond, she said, "*Mahalo* for your *kukui,*" in her sing-song voice.

What could I do? With Wharf around, I didn't feel so alone. I didn't want to let him go, but what choice did I have? He wasn't really my dog. Liebe was leaving in a few days. I'd be relieved in a way, but I also knew I'd miss her companionship.

Then Zhen said, "Oh, I gotta go. That Filipino cop is here again… He's got such a strong aura." Then she added another *mahalo* and hung up.

I thought of Ho Killingsworth. I think it was more aftershave than aura, but what did I know? Before I could ponder it further, the phone rang again.

"Aloha, this is Brita Beamer." She paused, "The reporter. Short, uh… nice nails, uh… " She again paused in describing herself. It sounded to me like she was insecure. Maybe normal for a writer, who knows… ?

"I remember you Brita. What can I do for you?"

"I'm running an article today on Dan Colley's murder and I hoped to get a comment from you about the increasing crime rate around the harbor."

"What increasing crime rate?"

"Can I quote you on that?" she asked. I had my hearing aid turned up to the max. I could hear her nails clicking away on her keyboard. I wondered what the Kanji characters meant that she painted on them.

"No, you can't quote me." Then I remembered the rules she'd given me, especially the one about never saying, "No comment." My little amoeba-like brain scrambled as fast as it could and I said, "The Lahaina Harbor is as safe today as it's always been. The commercial and recreational users have a great resource and access to the marine environment from this harbor."

That sounded good to me. But never one to leave well enough alone, I added, "This was an isolated incident and I know the police will catch the person responsible." I felt like I'd painted the organization that I worked for, and the harbor, in a nice light without really saying anything.

"Sounds great. Thanks Aloha," Brita said. "How about lunch tomorrow? With you being new in town, maybe I can show you one of our great places to eat." I thought about seeing her drive the Shar-Pei through McDonalds. My stomach gurgled.

"Sure, be at my office at noon and we'll take off from here." If I was losing Wharf, I was going to need new friends. Brita seemed sincere and hard working. I'd had more unlikely friends over the years and I missed them all.

Chapter Nine

My afternoon cruised along at a pace that could only be called Hawaiian time. I made phone calls, left messages, got no responses. I sent letters, second letters, and final warnings to people behind in their moorage fees. It was getting to where a tourist wanting to use the bathroom might be welcome. Then Ho Killingsworth blew back into my office, the smell of Old Spice preceding him like a purple haze that reminded me of my dad. I made a mental note to call him—my dad that is.

"Heard you were at Zhen Blue's," I said, thinking it would be funny to beat him at his own game. Perhaps I should change my middle name to detective. Aloha Detective Jones. Nope, not smooth at all. I guess I'd have to stick with Hickam.

Ho didn't bother responding. He just grabbed the same magazine Gil had perused and headed to the John. At least he kept his gun with him. Honestly, this bathroom was getting more face time than I was. Wharf got up and repositioned himself at my feet, his back to me, facing the counter. He didn't seem to like Ho.

Ho was drying his hands with a wad of paper towels when he returned, careful not to touch the door handles with his bare hands. Must have germ issues, I thought. He slid through the opening in the counter and sat down in the spare chair. Oh yes, it's a glorious, luxury office; it has a spare chair.

"What have you found out?" He sat back with his legs splayed and his arms crossed. I was getting a mixed message.

I crossed my legs and let one hand slide down to stroke Wharf's head, telegraphing back his body language with a reverse twist. Then I said,

"Whadya mean?"

He squinted, rotated one shoulder while he rubbed it, and sat up. "Come on Aloha, I've been looking into your history. You were military police in the Coast Guard. You've done drug busts, been tossed over at sea, and had your ear blown out. You know some shit and you're not the type to ignore some hinky murder in Lahaina Harbor. So why don't you tell me what you've found out?" It was a rhetorical question. The problem was that I didn't know as much about him as he knew about me. And I didn't know where he'd gotten his info. It wasn't all public knowledge. Yet in fact, it was correct.

Ho pulled out his cell phone, punched in enough numbers to make it long distance, and then handed it to me. "Jones," my dad said by way of an answer.

"Dad? Hi, it's Aloha."

"Aloha Who?"

"Funny, Dad."

"Yeah, I like to think so. Your mom's vote is still out, though."

"You know a guy named Ho Killingsworth?" I asked.

"You're calling me on his phone. 'Course I know him. Stationed together in Nellis. Punk ass kid." I looked at Ho, all middle-aged and staid. I guessed they hadn't seen each other in awhile.

"Well, Dad, I'm wondering if he's a good guy or a bad guy since he's asking me for my thoughts on a murder we had here."

"He's a good guy, Aloha. He's also a bad guy." Then my dad started in on one of his existential rants on the nature of man.

"Uh, Dad," I interrupted him, "Scale of one to ten, can I trust him?"

"Aloha, the Eastern German judges give him a solid seven, but I think the French have been manipulating them. The Americans gave him a nine. Call your mother sometime. And tell your sister to stop using that goddamned fake German accent." Then he hung up. Oh, the life of a Jones girl.

Time to spill my guts to Ho. "Colley was behind on his moorage fees, but he wasn't getting dinged. I don't know why. He owns the boat himself, although Zhen's name is on the insurance. He and Nigel had a dust-up a couple months ago at the loading dock. He's had the same action with half a dozen other harbor users in the last five years. In fact, no one's got a nice thing to say about him, well, except my boss, who wrote him a recommendation to be on some harbor advisory board." I paused, felt my voice get all funky and said, "He's got a great dog." Then, like a big baby, I started crying.

"He *had* a great dog, not has. Now you have a great dog. And stop crying or I'll punch you and it will look bad on my otherwise stellar record of not participating in police brutality, no matter how much someone deserves it."

I hiccupped a little sob and wiped my eyes with the back of my hand. I didn't think he'd really punch me. Then I looked at him. This was a guy who didn't like crying. As my dad would say, "If you're gonna cry, I'll give you something to cry about."

Ho cracked his knuckles.

"Okay, I showed you mine," I said. "Now you show me yours."

He raised his eyebrows.

"About the murder," I said. Pervert.

"Colley was conked on the head, but it didn't kill him. He drowned." I rolled my eyes. Everyone knew this much.

"Do you want to hear or not?" Ho asked.

I nodded.

He continued, "Like you said, there're probably a dozen people who disliked him with a white hot rage. People who might kill him if the circumstances were right."

"Really? Who?" I had my pen ready to take notes.

Then Ho's phone rang. He answered with a "Howzit?" The little bit of his conversation I heard was in pidgin. I needed to learn that stuff if I was going to survive here. As it was, I caught the words *kolohe, maki,* and *haole* as he got up and walked out of my office while still on the phone.

I logged on to the Internet and found out these words meant trouble-maker, dead, and white. Sounded like Colley to me. I wondered who was on the other end of the conversation. Since Ho didn't come back, I was left to wonder.

By closing time I was ready to surf. I finished changing into my swim suit and rash guard just as Liebe came in. I unloaded our boards and saw another gal at the shower behind my office where the surfers rinsed off the saltwater. Cool, there was someone else my age and gender who surfed here. It might be nice to have someone to chat with in the line-up who had life experience beyond elementary school.

The afternoon tradewinds were picking up and I hoped the waves wouldn't flatten before we paddled out. I was waxing like crazy on Liebe's board when the other woman quit showering. I knew better than to ask her about the surf. Surfers might talk in the line-up, but it was considered 'gay' to chat on the beach. Just as well, since when she turned around I recognized her—the Shar Pei had been surfing. I stared. She walked by and said, "Howzit?" I said, "Howzit" back at her. She didn't look crazy today.

Liebe came out of my office and did a double take, then backed up a few steps. The Shar Pei didn't seem to recognize her. Wharf was lying next to my truck. She stopped to rub his belly, said something to him that sounded like "absent bed" and toodle-ooed down the dock toward the Dumpsters.

Liebe shuddered, chucked her board off the dock, and dove in after it. I followed her out to the break. Her paddling was getting better, stronger, more like someone who hadn't had the muscles in her chest unzipped.

The kid who'd called me grandma was sitting on his board, a small fiberglass number with lots of scratches over a dated yellow gel coat. He crossed his eyes at me. I took that as a 'howdy' and returned the salutation. He caught the next wave and slid by us, his skinny frame bent at the waist, one arm slung behind like a speed skater.

"So, I know why Nigel and Colley weren't buds," Liebe said, absently swishing her hands around in the water like little rudders to keep her board lined up the way she wanted.

"Really?" I said, trying not to seem too eager, while inside I was doing a little dance that involved a couple of high kicks. Then I smiled, which was like tripping and landing on my mental ass. My inner dancer still needed work.

"Nigel said he was coming in one day on a charter on the *Awiwi*. He passed a couple boats in the fairway and then slid into the channel. As he passed Colley's boat—making no wake mind you—Colley went wahoo nuts and started swearing at him and basically being a big jerk in front of Nigel's customers." Liebe rolled her eyes. "Well, it was one of those days when Nigel had been in the water snorkeling, so once the customers were gone, he was rinsing off his gear when Colley ran down to the boat threatening to kick his ass."

I could see it in my mind, Nigel having forgotten the whole thing and Colley—a guy I'd never met alive—acting like a monkey in a stress test.

"Nigel pulled out his dive knife and told Colley he'd gut him from stem to stern if he wanted to bring it." Liebe paused, "And I could tell by the way he told the story, he really meant it. Just one of those days, I guess."

There'd be a pile of empty people outside my office if I gutted every jerk I'd run into. Yikes! I *guess* it was one of those days for me too.

Then I saw my wave—the one I'd been waiting to ride for days. It swelled up three sets out. I paddled to it, spun my board around, and paddled until my speed matched the wave. In a hop I was on my toes and then rose to a crouch, shuffling my feet to the sweet spot of balance. I adjusted into it as I hung one arm back. I kept my eyes open and focused on the water ahead. This was the Hawaii I'd been wanting.

When the wave finally slowed down and dropped out from under me, I slid off my board and floated on my back for a second. Just long enough to savor the moment as though it were the first sip of a tall icy drink.

When I scrambled back onto my board, I could see Liebe still out with the boys. No one was talking and the sun was setting on the horizon. They were desperate for waves and running out of daylight. I watched for the green flash on the horizon, but didn't see it and wondered again if it was real or a legend, like Colley. I'd never met him, but I was beginning to hear one tale after the other about his violent temper, unpredictable rages, and basically poor behavior. I wondered why Wharf stayed with him. He seemed like too sensible a dog for that treatment. Moreover, how did Colley treat Zhen? And what about the kid? Did he scream at her too? Could she hear him if he did?

Back at the loading dock, I rinsed myself and my board. I glanced around to find Wharf and didn't see him. I looked in the truck. I unlocked the office and checked both rooms. Then I circled the building and eye-balled the park between the library and the Pioneer Inn. Wearing flip-flops and a towel wrapped around my waist to cover my swimsuit, I started hoofing it along the front of the slips, looking behind storage bins and inside booking kiosks. He was gone.

By the time I got back to my office, I was crying. When I looked at Liebe I could see she was doing the same. We loaded our gear and drove home. I'd felt the best and the worst of my time in Hawaii in less than fifteen minutes.

It didn't look like I'd be meeting Zhen and quizzing her about Colley. I somehow thought she'd wait to pick up Wharf until I was there for the handoff. It would probably have hurt the same—something like wanting to not breathe anymore. I could feel each beat of my heart. It seemed too slow. My mouth watered like I was about to throw up and my jaw ached. The Technicolor sky, tropical plants, and riotous flowers had dulled. All I could smell was rotting mangos. An oppressive wind was blowing from the south and the air was starting to sweat.

I saw my landlord battening down the lawn furniture as we unloaded our gear. "Feels like a Kona," he commented. I'd heard about Kona storms from the boaters. The strong winds and swells could really wreak havoc in the harbor, so I showered, changed, and headed back to work, leaving Liebe at home. This was my job, not hers, and my life, not hers. Just like it was my pain, not hers. I knew she had enough of her own. It was like being mad at Zhen about the dog. Her pain had to trump mine.

Chapter Ten

Darkness crept in as the wind scuttled around the harbor. Sailboat rigging clanged on aluminum masts, boat crews tied off extra lines and bumpers, other boats headed in from the Roadstead. The air felt like a wet dog's lick. The loading dock was already full. Plus, there were boats rafted off to others moored along the front slips. Harbor-wise, it was a nightmare. The normally placid water pulsed with the storm surge, akin to a giant aorta just before a heart attack.

I taped a note to my office door that said I was walking the docks. Then I took off. Every few vessels I stopped to help; holding floats, battening down trash cans and calming nerves. Strong gusty winds are at best unsettling, at worst threatening. They make you feel out of control, nature's victim. My defenses were on alert. The wind was whipping at about thirty-five knots and periodically, fronds would shoot like spears out of nearby palm trees.

As I moved from boat to boat, I looked for the Shar-Pei. I wondered how street people weathered the storms. I even checked the Dumpsters, finding cockroaches galore, but no Shar-Pei.

"Aloha!" I heard my name shouted from above. When I looked up, I saw Nigel high atop the *Awiwi's* mast. In the dark and at this distance I couldn't see if he was traveling commando again or not. Just as well. I'd seen enough already.

"Nigel," I yelled, "What are you doing up there?"

He had one leg hooked on a mast rung while he flung an arm out to grasp what I assumed was an errant rigging line. Thunder crackled in the sky and I mentally pictured him like a kabob on a skewer. In an instant, he scrabbled down the mast, took one last look up at his work, and hopped off the boat to walk toward me. He wore a faded yellow slicker over his shorts, the hood tied tight around his face like Kenny on *South Park*. His topsiders made squishy noises with each step. He had no stealth. It made me wonder how someone had sneaked up on Colley in order to bash him in the head. Where had Wharf been? And, where was he now? I hoped he was safely tucked into bed, in a dry, secure home filled with love.

Nigel surprised me with a hug. "Liebe told me about the pooch," he whispered into my ear. I held him for a moment, even though I'm not much of a hugger. I needed the comfort. Then I felt another arm around me. A group hug was more consolation than I could bear. I squirmed out of it to see Koni fake-punch Nigel while he held Nigel's hooded head under one armpit. *Boys!*

Koni was wearing black rubber boots with faded Levis tucked in at the knees. He too had on a slicker with his hood pulled tight. Clearly these guys weren't used to foul weather mainland style, but they were outfitted to the max for Hawaii.

"Got the boat all tied up?" Koni quizzed Nigel.

"Yep, let 'er blow."

"Insurance paid?" Koni teased.

Nigel shot him a look, saw his boots and said, "What's with the rubbers?"

"I figured I'd get cold in this Kona, so I wanted to wear jeans."

Nigel and I were silent, waiting for the rest of the story.

"Well, I couldn't find my belt and I got no butt so I put on the boots to hold my pants up."

I rolled my eyes. "I don't want to hear about your butt handicap. I could give you a transplant and still have some to spare," I said. I turned and gave myself a little smack on the ass just to prove my point. I might have stuck it out just a little bit for emphasis.

When I looked back, Koni had one brow raised and Nigel licked his lips. Uh-oh… I think I meant to say all that in my head. I really needed to work on my inner voice. I needed inner voice lessons more than hula lessons. Well, maybe both. Liebe had said that my hula looked more like burlesque. Apparently I needed less bump with my grind. Ha-ha! I didn't say it out loud.

Koni and Nigel were looking past me anyway. I turned to follow their gaze and saw Wharf towing Zhen down the dock like a waterskier. Behind Zhen ran the little girl I'd seen at the audiologist's office. This time she was wearing pink rubber boots under an adult-sized foul weather jacket that hung to her knees with the sleeves all wadded up and the armpits hitting at about waist level.

As she scampered along, she tried to fix an umbrella that had inverted. With all those distractions, she didn't see the hose snaked across the concrete dock. She tripped and fell face first onto the wet concrete deck with a noise that sounded like a watermelon landing after being shot from a cannon. I mentally cringed and waited for the obligatory screams. Instead, Zhen looked at her, signaled her to get up, and then grabbed her hand so tight I saw the little girl wince. Wharf ran over and licked the tears from her face. He's such a great dog, a great person. Through it all, the little girl didn't make a sound. She swiped a wet hand across her brow where blood oozed from an abrasion. Zhen gripped her hand and plowed toward us. Wharf wagged his greeting, but stayed with the little girl. I understood.

"Koni," Zhen said in her soft voice, "Where's Tan?"

Nigel and I backed away, not wanting to eavesdrop, so we missed Koni's response. It didn't matter, since Zhen started whining loud enough that on a calm day everyone in the harbor could hear her. In the current conditions, only those within about fifty feet could catch the whole show. I don't know where her Earth Mother persona had gone, but I missed her.

"I don't care if he's got a gig! Somebody's got to get that boat into this harbor and I want it done now!" She marched over to me. "You're the harbormaster. You make this happen." Then she poked me in the chest with her pointy bejeweled finger.

That pissed me off. I thought of Nigel threatening Colley with a knife.

I took a breath and said, "I'm sorry. I don't know what you're talking about."

"The boat, goddamnit! Colley's goddamn boat. I need to get that god-damn boat into the harbor before it breaks loose from the goddamned mooring," Zhen swung her arms as she shouted, missing Nigel and Koni by a hair.

Koni didn't look happy. As a chaplain, I'm sure he didn't appreciate the "goddamned" everything. As a person, he probably didn't like the abuse. I hoped he'd punch her. I'd seen him lose it with the street preacher the night before. Then I willed him to punch her. Wow, my hostility level had pegged out on the red-line. I needed to work on the love, here. My mom's mantra—the woman who had named us all love—was, "You've got to give love to get love."

I tried. I briefly closed my eyes and thought happy thoughts. Then Zhen shoved me in the chest again with her abusive index finger. Instinctively, I grabbed her bony little paw and gave it a twist, something cops call the wrist-lock arm-bar. She squealed and Wharf growled. Then he looked like he had made a mistake and wagged at me again. Koni and Nigel pulled us apart.

"You," I pointed at her, "Tell me what you need—politely—and we'll see what we can do to help." Then I cocked my head and gave her my squintiest-squint, the one I think looks like Dirty Harry, and said, "But if you touch me again, I will break your fucking finger. You got it?"

I think she got it. The problem was that she'd just made her problem my problem. Koni and Nigel, being inherently good guys, agreed to go with me in Colley's dinghy out into the Roadstead and bring his water taxi into the harbor. Guess who didn't have their insurance current according to Zhen? I hadn't remembered seeing that in my files, but whatever... There was a job to do and I'd nominated myself for the team. I didn't like the looks of the ocean. I knew Nigel had all the skills in the world, but I doubted that my guitar-playing-former-rock-star-now-a-chaplain-hunka-hunka would be worth a darn out there. Reluctantly, we grabbed three life jackets from the *Awiwi* and hopped in the dinghy.

"I've seen worse boats in my day," I yelled above the wind, about the condition of the dinghy. Much worse. The fact that this one was an old, and I mean older than dirt old, Boston Whaler, was of little consolation.

"It's a Whaler, they're unsinkable," Nigel yelled as he took another pull on the starter cord.

Sure they're unsinkable, I thought, but that doesn't mean you can't get dumped out and drown anyway.

He had the little outboard motor—undersized by about half—started in only a couple dozen pulls after he'd switched off with Koni's couple dozen pulls.

Koni lifted the gas tank and swirled it in the air. "It's almost empty," he shouted to Nigel.

"No worries," Nigel waved him off, "It's a short trip."

Have I mentioned that "no worries" is easily one of the top ten phrases I hate? No, probably not. First off, it's just a little out of date. Second, it's lame. And third, really, you *should* worry, you dumb shit. We're going into a freaking storm in a piece of Tupperware with a crappy motor! Honestly. Worry.

Just in case things weren't bad enough, Nigel made us all don masks and snorkels. He said there was no way we'd be able to breath through the spray otherwise. I made sure I had the life jacket securely wedged under my butt. I was too macho to wear it, but I wanted it handy anyway. Then

I casually grabbed the strap in my fist. Good times.

Koni untied us and Nigel spun our little ship of fools around. We bounced through the harbor, pushing off rafted boats like a pinball. The other harbor rats stood above us on their vessels in relative safety while offering words of encouragement and advice. At least twelve shouted, "No worries." I think they were placing wagers.

As we neared the breakwater, the winds increased and each choppy little wave wore a white cap. As soon as we rounded the point, the value of the masks and snorkels became apparent. I had my feet wedged under the seat and one of the lines clutched in my hand. Koni had done the same. Nigel had braced his legs outboard and I could see that he still lacked underpants. I didn't want this to be my last sight in the world, so I looked away. I felt a tap on my shoulder. Koni handed me a baling can and we both tried to dump water back into the ocean. By the time we reached the last buoy heading out of the harbor, the boat was submarining, the bow going under with every wave. The gas can was floating along with pretty much everything else—pop cans, candy wrappers, and filth had gone overboard.

Once we made the turn north, the waves were at our stern quarter, so maneuvering was tougher, but we took less water over the bow. Most of the waves were now breaking over the stern.

"Son-of-a-fucking-bitch," Nigel screamed into the sea. Now I really don't hear well, and the sound of the ocean and wind was overwhelming, but I still heard him. Maybe it was because I could no longer hear the engine.

Even in the dark, I could see where he was looking into the water past the transom where bubbles blub, blub, blubbed to the surface. Yep, the engine was still running, right into the bottom. The crappy bolts, probably made of something as non-corrosive as soap, had broken off. No worries my ass.

"What now?" Koni yelled to Nigel.

"You're the chaplain, how about a little divine intervention?" Nigel grinned.

I needed to have Liebe break up with this guy. He clearly lacked the discernment to know when to not make jokes. Then I laughed. Who was I kidding? I'd come on this little cruise voluntarily and not really for Zhen's benefit. This was about the most interesting thing I'd done since I moved to Hawaii. In my former life I'd been in worse situations. Hell, I'd had my eardrum blown out. I'd had to quit the Coast Guard. My long ago husband had turned into some kind of motorcycle-riding drug freak. This was a cake walk. I looked up to see Nigel and Koni staring at me with something akin to shock. I was giggling almost out of control by then.

"What?" I said, shrugging and lifting my palms up into the air, just as we swung broadside to the wind and a wave hit us square on. In an instant, I went from sitting on a soggy life jacket on a filthy bench seat in a crummy little dinghy in the ocean to just in the ocean.

My ears popped immediately and I knew I was sinking. I kicked my boots off and swam to the surface. Then I cleared the snorkel by blowing what was left of the air in my lungs out the top and took a breath. I was still negatively buoyant. I shrugged out of my jacket. In an instant I was back on the surface, where I took a couple more breaths and analyzed my situation. I was in the ocean, at night, with no thermal protection, no light, no fins, no life jacket, since I'd dropped it when I went overboard. No one but Nigel and Koni knew where I was, and they were floating on a dinghy to the next piece of dry land, probably somewhere in Alaska. It's possible this was more of an adventure than I needed. Just about then, the "Pirates of the Caribbean" song started to play in my head. And I didn't think things could get any worse?

I'd like to say that I saw my life flash before my eyes, that I had some profound vision from my dad or words of comfort from my mom, or even that one last great orgasm, but ... nada. Instead, I bobbed up and looked around. Between waves I could see the dinghy pushing north like a ghostly clipper ship, one with no crew and no style. Closer to me, I could see Nigel and Koni bobbing on the surface too. I couldn't hear them, but I knew they were calling for me. I swam their way, and within minutes we were clinging together.

"Aloha!" they yelled and slapped me on the back. Occasionally, we'd kick each other as we treaded water. I noticed they too had shed their boots and jackets. I also felt goose bumps on their arms as we held on to each other. Soon, it seemed like Koni's face was in the water more than in the air.

In another moment, Koni was fully face down and no longer hanging on to my arm. In fact, as I held him, he drifted downward. I tried to spit out my snorkel to tell Nigel to tip Koni's head back, but another wave broke over us. "Nigel!" I shouted to get his attention. Facing north I could see an ominous shape getting closer. The next wave pushed us into the dark hull, slimy with algae and pounding the water like a jackhammer. As the storm pushed, it drove us underwater, and I rammed headfirst into the propeller. It wasn't until we bobbed back to the surface and the air hit me that I felt the sharp pain of a cut on my forehead.

Nigel and I kicked frantically, dragging Koni back into the lee of the menacing boat. Nigel shouted, "Grab the float and climb up!"

Like a monkey on a rope swing, I used everything but my tail to grapple my way up onto the boat. I found a life ring and tossed it back to the guys. Nigel grabbed it, still holding Koni, and I towed them in. That superhuman strength they talk about was still missing, but I did my best. He pushed Koni up while I struggled to pull him on board. Then I helped Nigel up onto the deck before starting CPR on Koni. Breath, breath, compression, compression, compression. I flashed through the various rules, remembering the latest recommendation being sixty compressions to two breaths.

I'd been thinking about getting this guy in a lip lock since I'd met him. This wasn't at all what I had in mind.

Nigel spelled me. I huddled next to the cabin and took stock. Then I took another turn at the CPR, wondering how long we'd do this, how long we'd push air into Koni's lungs.

And then, just like a miracle, on about compression gazillion, he coughed. We rolled him onto his side as he hacked up salty vomit. I guess he'd had a margarita earlier, since the froth on the deck reeked of tequila and strawberries. I doubted I'd ever drink one of those again.

After a few minutes of breathing on his own, Nigel shoved a hand in his pocket, took out a key and jiggled it into the lock on the boat's cabin. The door opened. Sweet tap dancing Jesuits! We'd landed on Colley's water taxi. Now all we had to do was get her started—and from the way she was riding, pump the bilge—then get back into the harbor and then… I thought, we'd have "no worries".

What were the chances, I wondered, that we'd bump into the water taxi in the dark? I guess Koni's prayers had paid off. We got the engine started and I hung over the starboard rail watching filthy bilge water pump into the boiling sea. When it got down to where it pumped in spurts instead of a steady stream, I signaled to Nigel that we were dry. We'd already bundled Koni up in the cabin in a stash of faded beach towels we'd found below.

Clutching the railing, I crept to the bow as Nigel edged the throttle forward. The boat pitched and tumbled from trough to peak while I tried to get enough slack in the anchor line to free us from the mooring. After fighting with it and battling to keep my fingers from being pinched off with each jerk, I signaled to Nigel that I needed a knife. I could hear him put the transmission in neutral before he disappeared into the salon.

After what seemed like hours, he reappeared, shaking his head from side-to-side. No knife in sight, he headed back to the helm. This time he threw it into gear and juiced the RPMs. I was damn-near bucked off the bow when a wave hit at the same time. Somehow I managed to pull the line's braided eye from around the cleat. In an instant we were free from the mooring. In another, we rammed forward, ran over the anchor line, and wound it around the prop. I think the mighty Pacific had just given us the finger.

Chapter Eleven

The boat swung around from being bow-anchored to stern-into-the-wind with the prop acting as our new tether to the seafloor. Nigel kicked her out of gear immediately, hoping not to melt the nylon anchor line onto the shaft. We ransacked the cabin, looking again for a sharp knife. Without one we had no means to free ourselves from the mooring. I wasn't sure if that meant we'd have to ride out the Kona storm, call the Coast Guard, or risk dragging anchor into the beach break where we'd probably all die. None of these were what I'd call good solutions.

We did our search while the boat bucked, the wind howled, and the waves broke over us. I felt as cold as I'd ever been, colder than when I'd worked the deck on an icebreaker in Alaska. Colder than anything. The boat had no heater, nothing hot to drink, and no more dry clothes. I rubbed my hands up and down my arms trying to get warm. Even with Maui's relatively warm air, I could feel my body's core temp dropping, fast. At least we'd gotten out of the water.

In a duffle bag under the console in the pilothouse, I found a flashlight but no knife. I heard Nigel on the radio to the Coasties. Ego's a funny thing. I'd always considered myself above rescuing. I'd been there, done that, got the disability, chucked the hat. Now, I was in the position of calling the Coast Guard for a rescue. I realized this was about Koni, not me. I told my ego to sit down and shut up.

"Maalaea Coast Guard to motor vessel *Polu Ka'a*. We cannot provide assistance at this time." *What!* They went on to explain their response. Their boats were already busy, one midway between Kooholawe and the

Big Island where a sailboat had lost its mast and its engine had conked out, and the other was in dry dock.

My ego saw what was happening before I did. When I heard the Coasties transfer the call to the Harbors Division and ask Gil Mangas to rescue us, I felt something inside me tweak. It was my ego jumping up and down and screaming obscenities.

Koni's shaking preempted those thoughts. The books all say to strip and get next to hypothermic victims to warm them. Tempting, but I didn't want to have to explain it to Nigel. Maybe first aid books in England said that was the act of a pervert. We just needed to get him to shore, to the hospital. I didn't care how we got him in, just as long as it was soon. His breathing was shallow, he felt cold, his skin still wet. I knew he was in shock.

I shifted Koni and crept below decks to find more towels. In the fo'c'sle I thought I'd hit the mother lode when I unzipped an overstuffed duffle and found fluffy new beach towels. I wondered why Nigel hadn't brought them up before. I quickly pulled two out and rammed my hand in for more. Instead of warm fleecy softness I hit cold hard cash. There were bundles of bills, not a lot of bundles, six to be exact, since I counted, but they were big stacks of twenties. I wondered if this was why Who-Tzee-Poo—I blanked on her name—was so fired up to have the boat brought in. No time now, but my curiosity was piqued. Especially since I knew Nigel had checked earlier for a knife down here. Maybe he was looking to make a buck, or a bundle, on this deal. I grabbed two more towels from the bottom of the bag and made my way back to Koni.

As I wrapped him up in the towels, I squeezed my eyes shut and tried to think of some prayer, some plea for salvation. All I saw in my mind was darkness and I squeezed him tighter.

Nigel startled me when his hand grabbed my arm. "Coasties were tied up," he said.

I nodded.

"Gil couldn't get out of Maalaea either. She's breaking across the channel."

I stopped breathing.

"He's coming out of Lahaina on a jet ski with a sled to get Koni."

I started breathing again.

Nigel dropped into the engine compartment to tinker with something. I hoped he was looking for a knife.

Once Gil arrived, Koni would get a sucky ride, but better than hanging out with us. At least Gil knew what he was doing on a water sled. I'd heard that he towed some of the lesser big wave guys out at Jaws, up north. In terms of surfing, Jaws, if not the Mount Everest of big waves, it was at least K2. I figured he could ride out and grab Koni without breaking a sweat.

While we waited, I pondered the money. I thought back to elementary school where they told us to get the five Ws in a story. Whose money was it? Well, possibly Colley's and then on to what's-her-name, unless Nigel helped himself, in which case I was definitely going to tell on him. But what was the money for? I mean, this had to be about the most unsafe place to store cash. Might as well bury it in the back yard, unless it was something that had to be transported by water or he had been hiding it from... Zhen—that's right, Zhen Blue. The next W was when. When did the money get on board? When was it *supposed* to disembark? I was starting to think of it as a person—a welcome stowaway with bad habits. Maybe I too was becoming hypothermic. And where was the money going? Where did it come from? Where was that damned lifeguard on his zippy little jet ski? I faded for a minute then came back to why. Why did Colley have the cash? Was he getting paid? Was he paying someone off? Why, why, why... ?

I heard the hum of a personal water craft well before I saw the surf rescue lifeguard emblem zip past the boat looking for a place to land, Gil at the helm in a wetsuit, mask, and snorkel like some kind of aquanautic cowboy. I left Koni and headed out on deck with Nigel. The wind driven waves were breaking up and over the stern, leaving the back deck awash. Nigel had left the engines running to power the larger bilge pump. This left us with diesel fumes billowing up around us. I'm not one to get seasick, but this backwards toxic ride was even getting to me. We clung to the railing and hollered back and forth to Mangas.

"Where do you want to grab him?" Nigel shouted into the wind and next to my "good" ear. Between the sounds of the engine, the ski, and the seas, all our rescuer could do was cup his hand to his ear and shake his head. The wind blew away Nigel's question as though it were trivial in the bigger picture. The wind had a persona all its own.

If I were the wind, I'd knock somebody on their ass, just for sport—to prove a point. This was that kind of wind. An angry bitter wind that says stuff like, "Hey, I'm the wind—listen up!" I figured God didn't appreciate the wind's attitude. Maybe he'd smack Wind upside the head, at which point Wind would spin its rage into a twister. If I was the wind, that's what I'd do. I'm a capricious force. Reckon with me... or else. Or else what? I'll huff and I'll puff... No one believes that. Perhaps I'd lie still like a snake sunning on a rock—only bursting to life when you think I'm dead. The wind is a freak of nature, an invisible jokester on meth. Just then it did its wind thing. It paused for another breath.

Chapter Twelve

One of Ike's little idiosyncrasies while deployed was demanding we all memorize some quote. What came to mind as the Jet Ski shot past us—Gil Mangas hollering instructions—was, "The gods love the obscure and hate the obvious," from "The Upanishads." In my mind, I heard it in a slurpy-Indian, versus a woo-woo-Indian voice, Upanishads being Hindu gods. The gods hating me at this moment for oh-so-many reasons, as I formulated that not-so-politically-correct-thought along with, *the problem with being partially deaf is that you can't hear worth a damn.*

Perhaps I am the master of the obvious, yet deafness was still new enough that it came as a surprise almost daily. Sometimes I'd even shake my head as if clearing water out of my ears, just so I could hear better. I'd already done that move a dozen times before I realized I'd lost my hearing aid. And then I voiced the clincher, "What next?"

Nigel looked at me and away from the Jet Ski, just as Gil, taking advantage of the wind's lull, motored up to the railing. *Ker-splat,* a wave sneaked up behind him and flipped Gil right over the bow.

Aw crap, now we needed to rescue our rescuer.

Nigel had followed my horrified stare and looked back to Gil as he hit the water. He grabbed the ring buoy and waited for Gil to surface. Then he pitched it like a horseshoe, hitting Gil with a dead ringer. Gil's big brown Yogi Bear eyes did a loopy swirl as I imagined twinkling stars in a bubble above his head. The Jet Ski pounded its way down the side of the hull nearly running him over. The kill switch had cut the engine. But a several hundred pound water craft could leave a mark or two. I tried to figure a way to grab the ski, but the wind decided to do its thing again, and bounced the machine away on some route other than rescuing Koni.

As Gil threw a leg over the rail to climb aboard the boat, another random wave slapped into him, causing what looked to me like some kind of compression injury in his nether region, or what we sisters liked to call his "happy place". Even I could hear the scream and subsequent thud as he dropped onto the deck and curled into a ball. For a moment I thought of asking him if he was okay, but I elected to check on Koni instead. Sometimes a guy needs alone time, and I think this was Gil's moment. Nigel followed me into the cabin.

As I tucked the towels around Koni, Nigel leaned his back against the forward bulkhead and said, "Anymore ideas?"

I just shook my head.

Nigel slid down the paneled wall and clutched his arms around his knees with his feet braced out to keep from rolling around like Gil. We were out of words. After a few minutes, Gil slumped into the cabin and joined us on the deck. Only then did I notice his forehead was bleeding from his somersault over the bow of his machine. I crawled over with the first aid kit, cleaned up the wound, and bandaged him as best I could. Then I looked him in the eyes and noticed one pupil was dilated while the other wasn't. *Bad sign.* This guy had a concussion to boot.

"Thanks, Jones," he muttered as he touched the bandage and winced.

"You get what you pay for," I said, trying to be cool in kind.

"Just give me a minute and I'll dive down and cut the line," he said, trying to revive his inner tough guy.

Nigel didn't say anything, so I did. "You can't do it Gil, you've got a concussion."

"Well, it ain't gonna cut itself," he said, giving Nigel a look that said, "Hey, how about you volunteering, sailor?"

In his inimitable English accent Nigel said, "Can't swim." Then they both looked at me.

I felt another free dive coming on.

One thing I had going for me was that Gil came aboard wearing a snorkel and mask, an underwater light on a lanyards around his wrist, and a dive knife strapped to his calf. While he and Nigel gave me tips on how to cut the line that had us bass-ackwards and bucking like a bronc, I thought about my life. I'd done dangerous, dumb stuff before, but I was younger then, fitter, and easily more stupid. Now I felt old, cold, and smart enough to know better. Still, I adjusted the mask's silicone strap so it sat snug on my face, then I took a couple breaths through the snorkel and pushed it aside. Probably wouldn't need it where I was going. Wish I had some fins. Funny how you're inherently too buoyant when you need to free dive, and feel like you have the atomic weight of gold when you want to float.

Nigel tied one end of the life ring line to my waist with the idea that he'd reel me in to keep me from drifting away between dives. I began inhaling deeply, trying to super-oxygenate my lungs. Then I walked to the handicap-accessible opening in the rail and stepped off the deck.

The seventy-six degree water was like plunging into a frozen daiquiri. I was already cold, not quite hypothermic, but damn cold. Kicking like a baby pitching a fit, I dove down to the bronze propeller and started sawing back and forth on the line. My heart was going thunk-thunk-thunk, so loudly that my chest hurt. My lungs begged for air. I kicked back to the surface. The guys shouted down instructions, questions, and maybe swore at me, but I couldn't hear a damn thing.

I gulped air, held my breath and dove again. The feeble beam of the light showed that in three tries I'd made about a quarter-inch worth of progress in a three-quarter inch slippery nylon line. It took me four more attempts to break what I figured was the halfway point. I was hoping the boat's bouncing and the wind would finish the job for me as I took increasingly longer surface breaks. I was beginning to cough and swallow water on the surface. Little stars were twinkling in my mind; they looked like the same ones I'd imagined over Gil's noggin. Stupid thoughts plagued me. With a mental kick in the ass, I swam down again and stayed down for a longer count; until I thought I'd just breathe in the water and be done. The boat bucked again and the line snapped, trailing me away like a bobber.

I cried. The guys clapped and cheered and then towed me in. When they reached down to pluck me out of the water, I just shook my head and dove down again. Now I needed to free the buoy end of the line from the shaft. Thankfully, the line hadn't melted together as the engine wrapped it around the propeller. The trailing end was easy to pull around and in just a few seconds we were free. This time I floated to the surface.

The guys pulled mightily and reefed me up onto the deck. I threw up on their feet and felt better. Gil pulled one towel from Koni and threw it to me. Then he ran up to join Nigel in the wheelhouse. I guess the "Good job, Jones," was implied.

Rather than join them, I curled up next to Koni. This was not just a cheap grope, but in fact, the suggested means of dealing with hypothermia, from which both of us were suffering. Really! There was no heat between us, thermal or sexual. I couldn't catch a break.

The ride back to the harbor was as unpleasant as a long driveway with axel-breaking potholes. Every once in a while I'd catch air, hover for a second and then slap back down on the deck. I tried to brace for the waves, partly to protect myself, partly to protect Koni. It didn't help. After about twenty minutes of thrashing, I felt us turn and start taking the waves on the beam.

Just as Koni rolled onto me, Gil came down the steps from the wheelhouse.

"Jesus, Jones, get a room—!" he yelled, as he clung to the cabin's support stanchions, swinging like a monkey on his way to the aft deck.

I struggled to get out from under Koni. I shouldn't have. In the next wave's trough, I rolled on top of him. And, honest-to-God, I was just trying to brace us. I looked up just in time to see Nigel peer down from the wheelhouse and shake his head.

Only two more shots at female-superior and the rollercoaster ride ended. I rolled over and paused for a moment on my hands and knees. When I looked up I could see lights flashing blue and red reflections on the bulkhead. As I stood, I combed my fingers through my hair. Medusa had nothing on me. I looked down and my legs were scraped and pale blue—the goose bumps the most attractive feature. I looked at Koni and he had a smile on his face. Ha!

The boat thudded against the dock and Nigel killed the engine. A team of paramedics came on board. I signaled them to Koni as I slipped out the cabin's aft door. After the cacophony from the engine and the ocean's rage, by comparison, the scene on the dock was frenetic but quiet. Awiwi was keeping people at bay. I saw the Shar Pei and the Street Preacher flanking each end of the minor mob. Between them stood Mele holding Momi on her hip and Wharf by a leash in her other hand.

Zhen was arguing with Awiwi and trying to push past him to get on the boat while Tan Ringo held her back. Another cop had Liebe in a heated debate. As soon as she shook her finger at him, he put her in an arm-bar hold and took her to her knees. Ho Killingsworth stepped forward and helped her up, giving the other cop the nod to back away. Among the other bystanders, I saw the crew from the *Awiwi,* along with a handful of the dancers from the luau. And then I saw Snake—Snake, my ex-husband—all tanned and sinewy, handlebar moustache to rival Sam Elliott's, biker leather and tats galore. Perhaps there was a cure for my chill. I felt my feet step forward as my mind shook itself. Then my boss, Max Yake, pushed Snake aside and climbed on board. My ex faded into the throng.

Max leaned over to me and yelled in my ear. "Go home. You got no business here."

I couldn't agree more. As I stepped up on the cap rail, a bright light flashed in my eyes. Brita Beamer was on scene, recording the event digitally on something with a bright light.

"Aloha, is Koni Ke going to survive?" she shouted.

Ah, this time the light went on *in* my head. This circus was all about Koni the Rock Star, not Aloha the beleaguered harbormaster saving some poor woman's property after her provider died. I moved past Brita, nodded at Ho, and took Liebe's hand. I wanted to go home.

She looked at me and pulled me toward the truck. I felt a warm, wet caress on my other hand and looked down in time to see Wharf nosing back toward the little girl. These warm stimuli were punctuated like exclamation marks in my somnambulant march to rest. Again, I felt a warm touch, this time on my shoulder. I felt Darcy, my audiologist, push my wet hair aside. She looked in my ear, nodded, pulled a hearing aid out of her pocket, and pressed it into service. I immediately heard the sound of a Harley starting that familiar "potato, potato, potato" rumble. What was Snake doing here? Darcy interrupted that thought.

"When I heard you'd gone out to get the boat and were in trouble, I figured you might need a spare," she said and punched me in the shoulder. "I warned you about diving. Don't be stupid again. Come in tomorrow and we'll check you out." Then she turned and signed something to Momi, who smiled and nodded.

Alas, perhaps I'd made some friends—friends who hit.

Before I could bask in my reverie, Liebe did an arm-bar hold on me and yelled, "You ass! What were you thinking?" and she started to cry. As a final punishment she added, "I'm telling Dad."

Damn. I think I'd rather get hit again.

Chapter Thirteen

"Sir..." I interrupted and listened to my dad rant over the cell phone. It was the morning after the night before and I still hurt. This didn't help. Liebe's such a tattletale. My parents had moved to Oahu and what I didn't need was them thinking they needed to rescue me on Maui.

I started pleading, "Ike listen..."

Rant, rant, rant. I could almost see his face getting pale, the lines around his eyes and mouth hardening. He was turning into Mount Rushmore on the phone.

"Da-aad," I tried again to plead my case. Finally, I just shouted, "Colonel! I'm fine. You would have done the same thing!" Then I handed the phone to Liebe and said, "You started it. You finish it. And when I call you Major, I mean major pain in the ass." And I stomped out.

There was no point in slamming the door, it was a funky little screen thing that seemed to let the bugs in but not out. My landlord had skimped on everything about the place except the paint. More like a glorified garage with a bathroom, it's not really a house. Still, it was dressed like its big sister, wrapped in a creamy chartreuse cloak with a lime yellow trim, which looked surprisingly spectacular against the aubergine door and violet foundation. Only the windows were trimmed in a crisp, stark white with a glossy black edge.

My inner Francophile loved the word aubergine, although she would stomp an eggplant on sight. Eve—my mom, not Adam's wife—had started a "gourmet" phase when I was in high school—a phase that continues today, so I don't know if that really made it more of a bad habit than a phrase—but nonetheless, she'd begun camouflaging food back in the day. So when I'd walk in the door and smell... um, spaghetti—which we all called busgetti, since Amoré couldn't pronounce it when she was little, which was ironic what with her being the "Italian" child and all... but I digress.

Anyway, we'd sit down to dinner and it would be eggplant parmesan, which is only a completely vegetated and adulterated version of something I really liked, called busgetti. Or one day I'd come home from school, all hungry and hung over from scholastic excellence and I'd smell fish and chips. I love fish and chips. Then horror of horrors, on my plate she would plop a rather repugnant and aggressive deep-fried eggplant. This always happened when Ike was away on assignment. He didn't go for that gourmet crap. Sure, I'd peel the greasy batter off and eat it dunked in tartar sauce, but I fed that damn eggplant to our dog Jasper.

Liebe interrupted my architecturally-inspired food trance. "Something happened to my phone connection with Ike," she said, with a straight face.

I just rolled my eyes.

"So, are you going to work today?"

I'd been thinking of calling in sick. My ears hurt, my legs were bruised, my fingers were raw, and I had a black eye from the smack-down Liebe and I did after her arm-bar take down on me. I might have been whipped, but I didn't go down without a fight.

"Of course, I'm going to work." I already had on my cutest Roxy T-shirt with an old-school graphic of a girl surfing, over my favorite shorts that hung from my hips and made my belly look flat, not fat, and my beloved Reef flip-flops with the built-in beer bottle opener. Today was all about comfort. Of course, with the beer bottle opening shoes, I was as prepared as a boy scout, too.

"Lib," I said, as I picked up mango splats from my sidewalk, "Did you see Snake last night?"

Her eyebrows scrunched together as she tilted her head to one side. "No." Then she raised her brows and said, "Did you have one of those out-of-body experiences and see your life pass before your eyes? Was there a bright white light? Did you see Jasper?" Jasper was the dog we'd had in Vegas. Eve, our mom, said he'd gone to doggie heaven. I suspected the eggplant. Did this mean Liebe thought I'd been at the portal to doggie heaven?

I just shook my head at her. I guess she hadn't seen Snake. Maybe I hadn't seen him either. Maybe I was a mess. "Do you need a ride to town?" I asked her.

"Nah, Gil's picking me up here and then we're going to go harass tourists."

"Why?"

"'Cause it's fun," she said in her best Valley-girl accent.

I didn't need to ask why Gil would pursue this endeavor. He had the same reason. Plus he had what I would call a one-woman audience with Liebe, were it not for her multiple personas, if not personalities.

On my way to work, downed palm fronds, muddy puddles, and skittering clouds the only evidence of the Kona storm's visit. At the harbor, it was back to business. The boats rafted in the previous evening were back out on their moorages or offshore somewhere showing tourists a good time, at least until Gil and Liebe caught up with them.

The loading dock was empty save for the *Polu Ka'a,* which someone told me translated to "The Blue Bus." I wondered if it was an indirect reference to Zhen's last name or if it simply meant water taxi. I'd have to ask Mele. She seemed to know more about Hawaiiana than anyone I'd met so far.

As I pulled into my spot, I looked across the street to the Pioneer Inn for a Harley. *Nada.*

Before I went into my office, I decided to check out the water taxi in the daylight. In my memory—only a night old—she looked like the *SS Minnow,* when in fact the *Polu Ka'a* was a 43-foot fiberglass-hulled charter boat. While not of epic proportion, she had nice lines with a sweeping rake up to the bow, a tilt-forward wheelhouse window, and a tidy cabin. From a distance, she looked none the worse for the battering she'd taken in the storm. In fact, she looked chipper and perhaps had faired far better than I.

Only when I got close—in the harsh daylight common in "the land of the merciless sun"—was I able to see the neglect that told me we were lucky to be alive. There were dozens of blisters in the top layer of the fiberglass hull, about half of which were oozing an amber liquid. If they were above the water line, I knew there were twice as many below it. I poked one, ran my finger through the ooze, and sniffed it; a bold move on any occasion.

"Styrene," I said. Talking to myself was normal, especially when inspecting a boat. When I stepped onto the deck, it had "give". Not a lot, but enough to tell me that the plywood below the non-skid fiberglass gelcoat was chock full of water, and rotten to the core.

"That ain't right." I muttered, grabbing the rail for support. It had "give" too. Yikes! I gave it a little wiggle just to double check. One of the bolts connecting the stanchion to the cap rail broke, plunked onto the deck and rolled out the scupper. If you're not a "boatie" the translation of this nautical lingo is: "You might want to look for the life jackets and practice treading water."

Then I looked at the lines tying the boat to the dock. They were frayed, pulled tight, and instead of an upward incline from the dock to the boat, they were sloped downward. "Aw, crap, this sucker's sinking." I walked across the deck and looked over the port railing to see if the automatic bilge pump was running. There was a stain on the side of the hull, but no water was pumping out. And something smelled like mongrel cat piss.

I about wet my bottle openers when I heard, “Abscessed head,” spoken right next to me. The Shar-Pei had snuck up and was looking over the rail with me.

“It’s not the head, it’s the bilge,” I said absently, as I started checking the cabin doors. Aft cabin: Locked. Starboard wheelhouse: Locked. Port wheelhouse: Locked.

She followed me like a puppy. I tried not to ponder the implications of that simile, but couldn’t help it as she growled at each door. Again I noticed that she had a body best described at perfect with a tan to match. If you didn’t look at her face, you’d think she was a swimsuit model. Well… if you didn’t look at her face or her swimsuit. It was a string-tied two-piece and a cute design that would have been black were it not faded, snagged, pilled, stained, and capable of smell-a-vision at twenty feet.

As we circled the cabin, I noticed that her feet had left dirty prints on the deck, including a blood splotch on every other step. I looked down and saw blood oozing from a torn toe nail on her right foot. It was a bright violation on worn canvas.

“Come on,” I signaled her to follow me. “I’ve got a first aid kit in my office.” I’m sure it was against policy to provide medical care to the Dumpster girl. No doubt it would be worse to offer her a shower and some clothes.

At my office, I left the “Be Back At… ” clock with the plastic hands, in the window and closed the door behind us. Then I turned on the water in the stall, testing it until it got warm, handed her a bar of soap, and ushered the Shar-Pei into the shower. I closed the door as I left and jogged out to my truck for my duffle bag where I kept a change of clothes. That’s when I remembered the duffle full of money on the boat the night before. The broken bilge pump was just the excuse I needed to get into the V-berth for more investigation.

Back in my office, I rustled through my bag, pulled out clean shorts, a tank top, and a towel and pushed them into the bathroom where I could still here the water running. "Try these on. They're probably too big, but the shorts have a draw-string." I only wished I had her figure. Damn.

Then I punched in the numbers listed on Colley's emergency contact list. I got lucky on my first try.

"Zhen Blue Enterprises, how may I help you?" said a voice with what I can definitely identify as a phony eastern European accent, based on listening to Liebe botch one on a regular basis.

Wow, "enterprises" sounded prosperous. The accent was over the top.

I didn't editorialize and instead asked to speak with Zhen.

"She's 'in studio' right now and not taking calls." This time the accent bounced west to France.

Now she was speaking my language.

Well, hell, I'm "in office" and her boat is sinking, I thought. Then I went ahead and said it in a really snotty tone.

"*Un momento.*"

Sheesh, how was I supposed to know what that meant? I mean really, how worldly were we going to get here before I just gave up and let the scow sink? Sure, there'd be a ton of paperwork, but really, sometimes it's worth it. Before I gave myself the satisfaction of hearing the receiver click into place, Zhen took my call.

"What now?"

I gave her my five W's. "This is Aloha. The boat's still tied up to the loading dock. She's taking on water and the bilge pump's not working. I can fine you, call the Coast Guard, cut her loose, watch her sink, revoke your commercial permit..." I would have kept going but I'd apparently found her motivation.

"Uh... no... wait a sec'... uh..." It sounded like she was fiddling with something. "Can I pay you to go in, fix the pump? Colley said he used to pay Buck to do stuff. I'll send someone down with a key."

I hated to pass on the chance to get in the boat, but really. "Why don't you just hire Buck?" I asked.

"Well, because. You replaced Buck didn't you? Aren't you the new harbormaster?"

"His name was Junior, Junior Pololi," I said, confused.

She giggled.

I was surprised. She didn't seem like a giggler.

"Oh, sorry, I forgot. Colley called him Buck behind his back. I meant to say Junior. So will you do it? Just tell me how much ..." She let the offer float like a bobber with a tiny piece of bait dangling from the hook.

"I don't want money. Just send someone down with the key and I'll take care of it. But you need to get that mooring repaired and get her back to the Roadstead. We've got another cruise ship coming in tomorrow and we'll need the loading dock clear."

Within fifteen minutes a young woman, with Wharf in tow, duck-stepped into my office and dropped a key on the counter. Wharf slipped his collar and kerchief and barreled around my desk. I smooched him. He smooched me. Then he flopped over on his back like a fainting goat, stuck one leg in the air, and gave me the yellow-dog salute. It can best be acknowledged with a tummy rub, which I did, carefully avoiding the speed bump.

"Waf," his Euro handler called in a deep gulag voice. "Waf, you come." She slapped her size zero thigh. "Waf, come now. Then she said something in a language from a country that no doubt ended in –stan or –ia, which I took to mean "I really mean it, you filthy beast." He seemed to get the tone—if not the words. I was impressed. Those I-don't-know-what-istanians knew how to bark orders.

"I must go collect child," she said by way of farewell. Wharf just gave a wag and a wink.

Then we were all startled to hear a growl. Oops! I'd forgotten about the Shar-Pei. She stood in the door to the bathroom, pure malice on her wrinkled face, my clean clothes hanging off of her like a scarecrow minus the straw. The Euro backed out, pulling Wharf along with her, and slammed the office door. The Shar-Pei stopped growling and looked at me.

I don't know when the shower had stopped, but obviously it had. I wondered what she'd been doing in there the whole time.

"Are you buck-hungry?" she asked, looking at me through sly squinty eyes.

Damn, those wrinkles made me nervous. There was no amount of Botox going to fix that kind of sun damage. I needed to do sunscreen more often.

"No," I said, "I'm Aloha. Aloha Jones." I stood up and held my hand out to shake with her.

She wiped her hands on her/my shorts. This was probably one of the few times in her life where both were already clean.

"I know *aloha,*" she said. "Hawaiians have *aloha.*" She studied my blonde hair and freckles. "You're not Hawaiian."

"Aloha's my name. What's your name?"

She nodded to herself and mumbled. Then looked over her shoulder and spoke to an invisible friend who apparently understood gibberish. I'm not fluent in gibberish, though Lord knows I should be. It looked like they were going to fight. The Shar-Pei gestured and pointed her finger to emphasize a point. Then she tried to shrug off and away from her imaginary friend. It didn't look like they were getting along well at the moment.

I hated to interrupt or even eavesdrop, but I was feeling a little left out, so I repeated my question. "What did you say your name is?"

"Layla."

"Layla, that's a beautiful name. What's your last name?" I asked.

She shook her head. "No last name. No number." Then she showed me her wrists. There were scars on them.

I didn't want to ask what happened. I thought I knew.

"Layla," I looked at my watch, "Are you hungry?"

"I'm not buck hungry, you're buck hungry."

I shook my head. "No, I didn't say you're buck hungry. I wanted to know if you wanted something to eat," I said.

Then she jabbered over her shoulder again, grabbed a handful of Hershey kisses from the bowl on my counter and said, "We don't eat. We're fat." Then she made a 'Shush' sign with her finger to her lips, and ghosted out my door.

When she made the 'Shush' sign, she reminded me of that supermodel who used that as her signature move. What was her name? Blink. A light bulb went on in my head. Her name was Layla. No last name, just a first name, like Madonna or Blondie or Cher. I wondered what ever happened to her. And what possessed the Shar-Pei to use her name and nuance? Moreover, what possessed the Shar-Pei altogether?

It didn't matter. I had things to do, people to see. Well, things to do. I picked up the key to the boat, left a note on my office door, and went out to work on the water taxi. I stumbled over the clothes I'd given the Shar-Pei on the ground next to the boat and looked toward the entrance channel to the harbor. She was paddling out toward the break just about where I'd been when I saw Colley get run over by the *Awiwi*. Quite a life she'd carved out for herself.

"Sad, huh?" Brita said, as she clicked off a photo of me stepping onto the boat. "Ready for lunch?"

Oops. I'd forgotten. "Sure, let me just run the boat for a sec to pump the bilge."

Again, she had on an outfit worth note. It was like Dolly Parton meets Barbie at a swap meet, they both get drunk, wash their clothes in hot water, and redress. Brita was wearing a skin tight micro dress in pale pink, a white pop-bead necklace, and red thigh-high go-go boots. Her hair was wound into a chignon with what looked like a vintage Chanel scarf. Instead of the Chinese characters on her nails it looked liked she'd opted for subtle, with inch-long French tips. And of course, she had the figure for the whole get-up.

This being the second time I'd admired another woman's body in the same day, I realized I needed to call and check on Koni. Gloria Steinem might need a man like a fish needs a bicycle, but I need a man like... Well, some things might be better left unsaid. Nonetheless, rolling around the deck with him in a half-coma hadn't been that bad a deal.

After I started the engine and watched the bilge water pump out in steady squirts, I kept thinking of Koni. Yep, I needed a man like a boat needs a bilge pump.

Chapter Fourteen

Brita and I sat in the upper dining area at Cheeseburger in Paradise—the view breathtaking. To the west, Lanai seemed pristine, like an emerald in a bright, blue bowl. Surfers out in droves enjoyed the Kona storm's leftovers, eating waves with their boards. I figured the Shar-Pei was still out there.

"What's with the street—" I didn't want to call her the Shar-Pei, but I didn't know if I should call her a street person, street girl, or street woman. "—um, the gal who lives in the Dumpster?"

A waiter took our order before Brita could answer. Then she flashed him an enigmatic smile. He said, "Nice to see you again, Brita," and trotted to the kitchen.

"She's mental." Brita did the spinning finger by the ear as further explanation.

"Well, yeah, but—." Oh, *I don't know. I saw her in your car. She's got the best body in town. She barks at my sister.* Our drinks arrived. *Dang that's fast service.* Brita thanked the waiter, clasped his hand, and I think palmed him some cash. No wonder she gets good quote.

"What's the word?" she said.

"Same as last week," he glanced past me, "No deal... yet."

Brita shrugged at him and looked back at me.

"Schizophrenia is the most common psychotic illness." She pulled a paper-covered straw from her purse, peeled it and dropped it into her diet Coke. I used the straw they gave me.

"What are the choices?" I asked. Mental illness fascinates me.

"Well, psychosis is different than neurosis. Neurotics know they're ill."

Was she looking at me?

"Psychotics really believe the stuff they're feeling. They're sick and don't know it." She waved at some guys in Hawaiian office-worker uniforms at a nearby table. They wore khaki pants and aloha shirts. Yep, I've even got shirts with my name. That's not crazy.

It was weird, but two of the three guys had on matching shirts. How gay is that? Then I noticed one of the guys—not in a matching shirt—was my boss, Max Yake. He had his back to me so I pretended I was invisible, which worked until one of the other guys waved at Brita. She looked away quickly, but Max turned around and saw me with her. Dang! I hoped that employee manual I hadn't read forgot to say anything about talking to the press. But really, why would it? It's not like I was in charge of some top-secret project. I'm the harbormaster. I keep track of the boats that use Lahaina Harbor, whether they're regulars or just visiting.

"Cruise ship middle management," Brita said, by way of explanation of who Max's lunch dates were. Somehow I wasn't surprised. Maybe he'd set them straight on the absence of public restrooms on the dock while their guests waited for water-taxis back to the floating behemoths.

Our food came. I had ordered a Caesar salad. Brita had the chili-cheese fries. It looked like the heart-stopper special. I was stabbed with jealousy. Then I thought again of the Shar-Pei.

"Aren't there some drugs she can take? I mean really, her existence is pretty bleak." I said, recalling the scene of her with the street preacher in the Dumpster.

"Drugs are the problem," Brita said. "You won't believe this, but she used to be a supermodel. She used drugs to stay skinny, found addiction, became a hooker, got her Botox beat down, and lost her looks." As an afterthought she added, "Some of it could be genetic too."

I assumed she referred to the mental illness. "But she had it all," I said, "and now she lives in a Dumpster." The Shar-Pei's name really was Layla? *The* Layla.

"Like I said, she had to stay skinny, she used meth once, and that's all it took. She was the poster girl for tweaking. Mangas said it's got a ninety-seven percent addiction rate after just one use."

If there was one thing Brita was good at it was storing and regurgitating facts. Maybe that's part of her reporter's bag of tricks. I wasn't sure if I trusted Gil though, even if he was out squiring my sister.

"And that caused the schizophrenia?" I asked, then added, "Did you do a story on that too?"

"My sister had it," she said, this time in a soft voice. Her change in volume from professional info mode to personal tragedy revelation was matched by her change in demeanor. For someone who had to weigh-in at under a hundred pounds and stood less than five feet, in the two times I'd met her previously, she had the stature of a giant or a super star. All of a sudden she looked like she was twelve and wearing her mom's favorite outfit. Then she shook it off.

"You know, Layla had more money than God. She lost it all," Brita told me between French fries two and three, each heaped with chili, cheese, and Maui onions. Fry number three did a touch-and-go on her little pink dress.

"Son-of-a-bitch," she said in voice best saved for sporting events. I could see the tourists at the next table with their three little kids mentally covering big ears—again. The kids tuned in for more. They'd already heard some fun stuff about methamphetamines, delusions, and hallucinations. At one point, I heard the one in the middle ask the mom about hooking—right before the big one said, "How much money *does* God have?"

Brita turned to them, shrugged, and said, "My bad." Then she scooped up another heart-stopping bite. I pushed some lettuce around on my plate, looking for a crouton.

On her fourth fry, she pushed her plate back and said, "I'm stuffed."

What could I say? "Yeah, me too. These salads are so filling." I'd all but licked the plate and chewed my ice cubes.

Before I could ask more or even change the subject, she said, "My sister committed suicide." Then she fiddled around with her wallet for a credit card. "So," she shook back her shoulders and regained her bearing, "Whenever I see Layla, I take her to lunch or bring her a new swimsuit or something. It's not much, but it's what I can manage." Then she dusted her hands together and said, "That's my story, what's yours?"

That was her story? That was a damn short story.

I gave her a slightly longer version of my story while our bill was settled. I left out Snake, said I had sisters, but didn't get into the details, told her I really needed my job, and hoped for the best. I shuffled through my wallet for a tip. As we left the restaurant, I made eye contact with Yake. He just shook his head at me in a way that said I'd made a big mistake.

Brita clicked along in her five-inch heels as we walked south along the seawall. "Oh, by the way, Koni asked about you when I saw him at the hospital this morning." She frowned, "Although I think he was still out of it. He said you'd given him breast compressions last night. I tried to correct him and tell him they were chest compressions, but he fell asleep."

I played it cool and tried not to trip over the memory.

"Of course, he had a loopy grin when he shut his eyes." She shifted her gaze to the side. "Then he sang—and I quote—*'Rock the boat. Let's rock the boat, baby'.*"

Yikes! The bilge pump wanted a boat.

"Must be the drugs," I said.

"It always is." Then, Brita flashed back to our previous conversation. "Of course, that bastard Colley would always ask her if she was gaining weight."

Was she talking about the Shar-Pei or her sister? Before I could ask, she yelled, "The world's a better place with him gone! Gotta go." She waved good-bye, hopped into a blue Beamer, and peeled into bumper-to-bumper Front Street traffic, cutting off a tour bus and barely missing some jaywalkers.

Was that fair and balanced?

Given her driving style, I wondered if passive-aggressive behavior fit into the neurotic or psychotic side of things. Was mental illness indeed based in genetics? And what was the deal with bringing a straw? Wasn't that obsessive-compulsive behavior? Maybe she killed Colley to settle the score for her sister, or for Layla. What was she doing out on the back of the jetty the other day anyway? She couldn't have known I was there. The pooch had played dead doing his Salvador-Doggy when he saw her. Had that saved him before?

My plan was to go back out to the breakwater and look around to see what I could see. But as I neared the library, I saw Mele heading in from what I assumed was her lunch break. I wanted to check on Wharf and she seemed to know him.

Inside the cool, dark space, I found her scanning books returned under a bar-code reader.

"Libraries sure have changed," I said. "I remember card catalogs and the Dewey Decimal System."

"Aloha," she said, with a smile, "*Mahalo* for all you did last night."

Yikes, I wonder what she'd heard. Please not about breast compressions! That Koni was not doing the confidentiality thing well at all. "Zhen seemed panicked. I guess we all responded to that," I said, opting to refer to recovering the boat. "It was a team effort."

"I meant saving Koni," she said. "Saving the boat was foolish. You should all be spanked. But she has that effect on people."

I assumed she was talking about Zhen.

My hunch was confirmed when she said, "It worked in spades on Konala." Then I swear to you, I heard her say, "That hoochie bitch," under her breath.

Zowie! I wondered how you translated that into Hawaiian. I didn't ask. Instead I said, "How's the pooch doing?" I tried to keep it casual, like being in sixth grade and asking your mom, "What boy at the bus stop?" when she says she thinks the twelve-year-old hunka-hunka burning love likes you.

"Wharfie?" Mele asked. "Well, I think he's fine. What did you hear?"

Oops.

"Did she do something to that dog again? Oh for the love of ...," she muttered. "That's just it. I mean it. *That Is Just It!*"

I didn't know what *It* was, but I was pretty sure I'd started something—like a fire. Well, maybe not started it, but I had spritzed it with gas. It took me several minutes to convince Mele that my question was innocuous; I just missed the pooch.

"That dog has done so much for Momi. When her dad died, the dog was there. When she went deaf, the dog was there. And now, even when that bastard Colley's got himself killed, the dog is there."

I guessed Mele wouldn't support me having the dog.

"What made Momi deaf?" I asked.

"Back when Zhen met my Konala," Mele said, "she was already into her save the world crap. She reused stuff she found on the beach to make 'art'." Mele did finger quotes. "She rescued cats from the dump. She generally protested this, that and the other thing. At the time, Konala was into the Hawaiian homelands debate. Nothing wrong with that, other than that's where he met Zhen."

Mele took a break to check out some surf videos to one of the grommets who'd been grabbing my waves. My waves? Well, maybe not, but still... Little beggar had called me Tutu. I would have pinched him—real soft—if I was sure no one would see me. As it was, I just stuck out my tongue. He flipped me the bird. I called it a stalemate.

I tried to catch up with Mele's explanation. I don't think I missed much. Of course, I always thought that since I'd lost so much of my hearing. Increasingly, I discovered my filling in the blanks wasn't always accurate. Go figure.

"... so she wouldn't take the spira ..." she paused, "spira-something." She waved her hand around as if to say, that part doesn't matter, and continued, "... which allowed her to pass the taxo ... taxa ... well, taxi-what-not, on to Momi."

I nodded. I think I'd missed too much this time. Since I'd made an appointment to see Darcy that afternoon anyway, I'd ask her about the spiro-something and taxo-whatever.

Just then a couple tourist ladies pushed through the front door and dodged into the restroom. They had the requisite cruise ship tags dangling around their necks. I tried not to look guilty.

"Awiwi told me you'd been sending them over here," Mele said.

"Ah, I didn't do it this time. I've been at lunch with Brita."

"Really?" This time her look was calculating. "Don't tell me she's still chasing that story about the missing harbormaster?"

I looked down. Nope, I was still there. Not missing at all. "What missing harbormaster?"

Mele shuffled some papers and made sure the edges were aligned. Why, it was almost like she didn't want to answer my question. Then she mumbled something that sounded like "Hoosier Below Me."

"Hunh?"

"Junior Pololi," she repeated. "Brita thinks he's dead."

I rolled my eyes. "Junior Pololi? The guy that had my job? He's not dead. He retired."

Mele emptied pencils from a tin can wrapped in construction paper.

She organized them on the counter in order from long to short and inspected the erasers. Two of the pencils were so close in size that she vacillated back and forth on which was longer. She reorganized them again. Then the tourist ladies waltzed out of the restroom and said, "You're out of T.P." as they slammed through the exit door. Mele snapped the pencils in half and tossed them in the trash.

I left before she reorganized my limbs. As I pushed through the door, my cell phone rang. It was Koni's number again. Yikes! I flipped it to message—again. The last thing I needed was an audio replay of the night before.

Chapter Fifteen

I scuffed along the red dirt path between the library and the loading dock, thinking dark thoughts and humming "Holly Jolly Christmas." Sometimes life's dichotomies are too complex to unwind. My mood to work was gone and my desire to surf strong.

Then I thought about what Mele had said. Why did Brita think Junior was dead? What next, had space aliens landed Upcountry? This was getting me nowhere. Instead, I thought through what I still needed to accomplish at work and couldn't think of anything critical. However, I still had the appointment with Darcy. The hearing aid she'd leant me was uncomfortable and unreliable. Without checking my office, I hopped in my work truck and braved the cross-town commute. I could almost shop as I drove. It took me twenty minutes to go ten blocks. In the transit, time-share hustlers had stuffed twelve brochures in my open passenger side window.

At Darcy's office, I waited another twenty minutes in the walk-in freezer atmosphere before I was moved to an exam room. My pissy mood careened downhill toward crappy.

"Here," Darcy held out her hand, "Give me that one and I'll get your new one installed." The process was like having my tires rotated. Unfortunately, at the tire store they don't usually ream you a new one at the same time.

"So, Aloha," Darcy started examining my ear, "if you keep diving, you're going to lose what's left of this ear entirely. Is that what you want?" Oh my gosh, she was starting to sound like my mother.

She didn't wait for an answer. I guess it was a rhetorical question.

"I mean, you'd think that given your history, you'd take better care of yourself."

"You sound like my mother."

"Well, maybe you need someone to advise you. I mean really, what were you doing with Koni?" She made it sound like a bad thing. Wasn't he the same guy she'd been all jolly with at the luau?

"What's wrong with Koni?"

"Other than he's a heretic, and a player, and a musician ... " she said. "He's got the triple crown of stay-away-if-you-are-looking-for-something-real going for him."

"We're just friends." I responded with the same thing I'd have told my mom. It was much better than saying I wanted to jump him. Then I went for the look-over-there detour. "Darcy, when I was talking to Mele, she said Momi was deaf because of some drug Zhen *didn't* take. Isn't that kind of weird?" I asked.

She fell for it. Must be an only child. "The whole thing sucks. There's this parasite—*toxoplasmosis gondii*—you can get from contact with infected meat or from cleaning the cat's litter box if the cat's infected. If you get pregnant and it's not diagnosed, there's a one in one-thousand chance you pass it on to the baby. Then, once the baby's born there's another slim chance there will be birth defects."

She'd made sure to speak into my "good" ear while tweaking my new ear piece. She stepped around to insert it and turned it on. *Ah, I had stereo again!*

"Well, that sounds like bad luck, rather than bad mothering," I said, thinking of Mele's animosity toward Zhen.

"Yah, well, the thing is, Zhen knew about it. She had the symptoms. But by then she was already into organics, and all that. It was kind of like she checked out on anything traditional, and went for lucky." Darcy paused. "Not to say organics are bad, it was just a militant time for her. She was completely inflexible. Back then her name wasn't Zhen, it was Mary, or Sue, or something not-so-Zen." Darcy did finger quotes. "And of course, the name 'Blue' was an afterthought too. I thought Awiwi would shit a brick when she changed Momi's last name. Of course, Colley was in the picture by then and all for it."

That's right. Awiwi was Momi's uncle, her father's brother. Maybe Mister Famous Fire Dancer had given Colley some pay-back. I'd have to ask Ho if the wound on Colley's head had any burnt residue on it, like he'd been beaten with a fire baton. Hmm, how could I do that without suggesting another cop was on my suspect list?

I wanted to find Colley's killer. It was my harbor, my waves, my dock, that had been defiled by death. Then I realized I was doing something I'd been warned about when I was still a Coastie. The brass had told us about officers who stepped out from the umbrella of authority offered by the agency and took justice onto themselves. Same thing happens to cops. They start thinking people are speeding on "their roads" and not following "their rules." The problem is that when things go wrong in their personal justice system—say beating a bad guy while someone is recording it—to taking the rules home and running the family like a dictatorship, it leaves the "person-in-charge" with no back-up. I shrugged off the thought. I wouldn't let that happen to me. I needed the harbormaster job too much. I'd just investigate until I knew something and pass everything on to Ho. After all, it *was* my harbor.

Then Darcy jerked me out of my reverie. "So what's the deal with your sister and Mangas?"

"Whaddya mean?" Yikes, she'd spent one morning with him. How much damage had she done?

"Well, my hubby called and said he was surfing up north at Honolua Bay when they saw the marine enforcement boat drift by. When they hiked back to the top to their cars, they grabbed the binocs and could see Mangas with his gun drawn—so to speak."

What! "He drew his gun on Liebe?"

"Ah ... no ... Aloha, not his real gun ... his, ah ... proverbial gun." Darcy pointed to the private zone. Yikes!

"Oh for the love ...," I wailed. "She has got to stop this."

"Liebe, what the hell do you think you're doing?" Then I did my sternest look, the one with squinty eyes and scrunched up lips. I looked like a doofus, so I tried again. "Liebe Ramstein Jones!" I tried my shocked look. Gauging by what I looked like in the mirror, my shocked look was something I should keep to myself. So I gave sincere a shot, "Liebe, honey, what were you thinking?" Yep, sincere was what I'd go with. I finished washing my hands and went back to my desk just as one of the gay guys from Cheeseburger In Paradise walked in.

"Hey, I need you to sign some of these." He shoved a clipboard across the counter.

"What are they?"

"Uh ... Yake just said to have you sign them." He pushed a pen across to me.

"You were at lunch with Max. Why didn't he sign them?" Don't even ask me why I wasn't cooperating. I guess I just didn't feel like it. And it wasn't because he was gay. I didn't ask and didn't tell, but I knew a couple of pretty cool gay guys in the Coasties. They weren't what you'd call flamboyant for obvious reasons. This guy was flaming more than Awiwi's torch.

"Listen," he said, "I'm just doing my job here. Gimme a break, would ya?" Then he flipped his hair. Really.

He looked pretty pathetic. I gave in. "Okay, what am I signing?"

"It's just the form authorizing us to anchor here rather than dock at Kahului on our next run to Maui."

"Why can't you dock in Kahului?" I asked. "At least there you don't need to use the tenders."

"Kahului's a joke. The tourists see it as punishment to dock there. It may have *aloha,* but it doesn't have ambiance."

I could understand his point. Kahului is like taking a reality ride at Disneyland. No one wants to go on the ride that's like visiting the dentist.

"Why didn't you guys just schedule your day in port for Lahaina to begin with?" I couldn't believe I was hearing myself say that. Two days a week of cruise ships was enough of a mess for tiny Lahaina harbor. I asked this question as I signed.

He didn't answer, just grabbed the form and said, "*Aloha* sweetie." Then he patted a manila envelope he'd set on the counter.

I tried to ask another question. I even raised my hand waving the pen.

"Ew, thanks, I need that." He grabbed the pen from me and flounced out the door.

I looked at the envelope. It didn't have an address. I figured that was the same as it being addressed to me. I grabbed the scissors from my desk and sliced open the top. Just as I peered inside, the cruise guy opened the door and leaned back in.

"By the way, tell Max again how sorry I was to hear about Colley. I know those guys were tight."

I accidentally did my shocked look.

"Not like that sweetie. Hetero-tight, not homo-tight." He did a little head shake and eye roll.

Before I could ask what he meant, he was gone. I mean, I understood the hetero-homo part. I just didn't get the part about Yake and Colley being friends.

I decided to call Zhen. As I listened to her phone ring I was frustrated that not even the Eur-au-pair answered. I dumped out the envelope on my desk. Hmm, two free passes to the ship for lunch, the spa, and drinks. I thought I might reverse the order, but other than that, it was a nice perk. Yahoo! Finally, I had something good to start my conversation with Liebe. As soon as I put down the phone, it rang again.

"Lahaina Harbor, this is Aloha. How can I help you?" I had perfected my phone etiquette.

"Jones," my boss, Max Yake said, "Meeting. My office. One hour." Then he hung up. What a prick. He had just been in Lahaina. He could have met me here. And, he could have signed the damned cruise ship document himself. I had nothing to say to him. I checked my watch. By the time I got to the other side of the island and through his meeting, my work day would be done. That meant I'd be stuck in traffic on the Pali and too late to surf. This job was definitely getting in the way of my life.

I grabbed my bag and some fancy chocolates one of the transient boaters had dropped off, and headed to my truck. It seemed like everybody had something spare to share with me: Cookies, candy, and cruise ship coupons. The least I could do would be to pass on the rewards. I figured I'd stop off at the Maui Memorial Hospital and visit Koni while I was in Kahului. If I had to miss surfing, at least I'd have something to show for it.

I had left the side windows of the truck open to keep the rig from being too hot. I'd also splurged on one of those funky metal-backed shades for the windshield. What I hadn't done was leave the door open. Yet there it stood. Good thing I didn't have anything of value in there. It looked like I'd been burgled. I immediately went to the canopy, which I had locked. The hatch was popped. Son-of-a-bitch! Someone had stolen our surfboards. Where were the damn cops when you need them? I looked around to see if there were any witnesses, or maybe some big *mokes* walking around with our boards, or even tourists who looked like they wanted their asses kicked. For once, the loading dock was empty. It was like a giant vacuum had sucked all the activity out of the neighborhood. Maybe that's what took our boards. Even the TSA guys had a sign on their table that said they were on a break. Good thing there were no terrorists around. They'd have had a play day.

I was still swearing up a storm as I climbed into the darkened cab and jerked the sunscreen down from the dash. It landed on something soft. I looked down and there was Wharf, curled up on the passenger-side floorboards. He raised his eyebrows and gave a little tip of his tail.

"What are you doing here?" I asked.

As usual he dummied up. Then I noticed the glove box was popped open too. My stash of powdered sugar donuts was missing. I looked back down at the pooch. On the floor next to him was a slimy cellophane wrapper.

"I'm not saying you took the boards, okay? But did you have to eat the donuts?"

He hopped up into the seat. I could swear his look yelled, "Shotgun!"

"I don't have time to drive you home. Besides, there's no one there." I told him, having just called his place. He hunched down, hiked one leg up over his head and started licking himself in a way that demanded privacy. I started the truck, threw it into reverse and backed into the light pole.

"God-damn-it-straight-to-hell!" I banged my forehead against the steering wheel. When I got out and accessed the damage, the light pole looked smug and my truck looked bent. Well great, now I had something to talk to my boss about.

Chapter Sixteen

The drive to Kahului was normal, if normal includes stop, go, and road rage. At one point, Wharf almost got his noggin chopped off when a tour bus passed us on the right through the pullout at the Pali. A black puff of diesel fumes clouded the cab and our lungs, as the driver toot-tooted his appreciation for our slow caution. I called him several names I hadn't used since I left the Coast Guard.

The road's shoulders around the Pali were jammed with cars parked willy-nilly. It was whale season and by-golly these folks were going to see some whales, traffic laws be-damned. Just as we approached the turn off for Maalaea Harbor, I spotted a Humpback whale breach outside the harbor's boulder break wall. The water it splashed had a golden glow in the afternoon light. I could safely do this, since again, we were stopped in traffic. My meager air-conditioner couldn't keep up, so I had the windows down, although not far enough for Wharf to risk decapitation again.

It was almost five and I was late for my meeting with Yake. And I didn't have a good feeling in my gut. The hour he'd given me to arrive had passed. By the time I got to his office, his assistant, the one who couldn't possibly help me on the phone, was locking file cabinets and picking up her purse. She looked me up and down and shook her head as she left. I knocked on Yake's door and entered.

As usual, his desk was heaped with paper. It was a shredder's wet dream. Of the three chairs in the room, his was the only one not under reams of reports and stack of notebooks. Unfortunately, he occupied it. As I slid in, he talked on the phone and ignored me. It sounded like idle chit-chat, two old guys shooting the bull. This left me standing. I tried keeping my hands loose at my side. It made me itch. Then I tried hands in pockets. I knew I looked like a farmer. I swallowed my gum and hooked my hands behind my back. Great. I was at attention. I waited like that for seven minutes. Yes, I counted the seconds in my head. I was starting to get dizzy, so I alternately unlocked my knees. After about the twelfth time Yake hung up.

"You need to use the John?"

That wasn't the look I was going for. "Uh… No, Sir." That old military background had kicked in full force.

"Have you read your employment handbook?" he asked.

This was why I'd been ordered to drive across island—to find out if I'd read my handbook? Moreover, should I basically lie and say I'd skimmed it? Or should I just fess up and admit that I'd used it prop open the refrigerator in the office to air it out after I'd disinfected it. I opted for the middle ground. "I haven't had an opportunity to read it yet, Sir."

He shuffled through the detritus on his desk, licking his fingers every couple of sheets to get a better grip on the papers. Finally he found what he was looking for and handed a sheet across to me. It was just after a lick. I wanted to glove up. Instead, I grabbed it midway up the side hoping that would protect me from bureaucratic cooties. It was the form I'd signed on the first day saying I'd read the manual. I remembered that day. The woman who put the "ass" in assistant had demanded I read the manual during my lunch break and bring the form in before my afternoon training. That was the day I had gone to get my Hawaiian driver's license. Need I say more?

"Well, Sir… " I began.

He cut me off. "So I can add perjury to your file, too?"

Damn, I didn't know I'd perjured myself. I'd like to get a hold of his assistant for a few minutes. Maybe she could explain to him how she browbeat me. Of course, she was like, four-foot-nothing, so it might be a hard sell. Nonetheless she was pretty intimidating.

"Too?" I said. "Sir, you said you'd add that to my file, 'too'." What else is in my file?"

Yake shuffled through more paper, licking and pawing, just like Boo-Boo flipping through a lunch box in Jellystone Park.

I'm such a dope. Why do I ask these things? Why don't I just scuttle out and keep quiet? And why do I use the word scuttle? Because of scuttle-butt? Scuttlebutt was one of the words we'd had to learn the etymology of in officer training school. I guess it was just so rich in sea lore that they felt we needed to know it. I remembered it came from the word scuttle which means "a small opening" and the word butt, which surprisingly means "a large cask" of water. Yake was shaped like a butt.

Hmm, was etymology the right word, or was entomology? Yep, etymology was correct. I think entomology has something to do with bugs. Well, then, what the heck was etiology?

I'd been staring at the wall behind Yake's desk where he had a Wyland painting of a whale. Its koa wood frame gleamed. It looked like an original oil painting. I'd never liked oils. I'm more of a watercolor gal. I realized Yake had stopped his search when he waved another sheet of paper in my face. I gave myself a mental kick in the head. I wondered how long I'd been skipping around in my brain humming. This is what happens when ADD is untreated or when you're bored to tears and standing at attention in the office of a guy who reminds you of a cartoon character.

I took the paper. It was a disciplinary report on me for speaking to the press without authorization.

"What? Is it against the rules to answer questions too?" I said, more mad at myself than anything, but my hostility showed.

"Yes, Jones it is. And if you'd read your handbook... as you stated here," he shook a copy of the manual in my face, "... you'd know that."

More bad words fired around in my brain. I was getting tired of the game.

"So fire me."

He blinked.

Aha! He had another option. I just wasn't sure I'd like it. No doubt my lips would get chapped.

"So what do I need to do to make this go away?" I said. My stomach tried clawing up my esophagus for air but my ego pushed it back down.

"Why don't you tell me what you were doing on the *Polu Ka'a.*"

"When?" I asked, not sure yet, just what he wanted.

"The night you, Ke, and DeBarros, injured my marine enforcement officer."

I cut to the chase. "Is this about the money?"

Yake blinked—again. He had those wide, watery eyes like the kids on the velvet paintings. Frankly, they were creeping me out. It was definitely about the money.

"What money?" he asked, licking his lips.

"In the duffle bag."

"How much?"

"How much was there supposed to be?"

He almost said something. His mouth had opened and a word started to form, and then he blinked again. Damn.

"You stole it." He didn't ask me. He just said it like a fact.

"Nope." I was done with the "Sir" thing. Screw the cooperation thing too, for that matter. I didn't think he was going to fire me. But I didn't know why.

"If you took it, you stole it. Give it back," he said.

"To who?"

"I'll take it and give it to the widow."

Yeah, right.

"I don't have it."

"Where is it?"

"I don't know. In fact, the last time I saw it, it was on the boat. There were a lot of people there that night." I remembered seeing Yake there, and Snake, and Zhen, and the street preacher, and the Shar-Pei. On the other hand there was also Liebe, Gil, Nigel, Darcy, little Momi, and half the harbor.

He nodded.

"By the way," I said, "I need an accident report form for my truck. And I'll need to send it in for repairs."

"Uh, sorry about that," he said.

I cocked my head. What had just happened?

"The other night I borrowed your rig while I was on the other side." He paused to scratch behind his ear. "I was over there on personal business. Then I had to do some Harbors Division business, so I switched cars for a while. Somebody told me you were at the luau."

Aha! That's how the truck got moved. But who knew I was at the luau and would tell my boss? And was it right for him to just take my truck? And ... why did he apologize?

"That's how the front headlight got broken. I hit one of the bollards as I swung in." He did one of those big-eyed watery blinks again. "I thought I left you a note."

Liar, liar, pants-on-fire.

"Do you play poker?" I asked.

"Just get the money."

I didn't want to tell him I hadn't a clue on how to find the money. Instead, I said, "The cruise ship guy said to tell you he was sorry about Colley."

"Why?"

"He said you were friends."

Blink.

"Just find the money."

Out Yake's window I could see Mangas pulling into the fueling station. He had his boat on the trailer behind the truck. My sister was not with him. Bastard.

Yake's cell phone rang. He looked at the number and waved me out. As soon as I got outside I did a little wiggly butt dance. I think I had just dodged a bullet. I didn't know why, but now I had another reason to visit Koni at the hospital. Maybe he'd seen the money too. Maybe he saw who took it. Maybe he'd need some kind of massage.

Just as I started to climb into the truck, Yake stuck his furry little head out the front door of the office and yelled, "Bring it back or... you're fired!"

Maybe my dance had been premature.

Chapter Seventeen

Hospitals are funny places, kind of like heaven. When stuff goes bad, you hope you'll get there. Up until then though, you basically don't want to think about it. And you don't want to visit. I hope heaven doesn't smell like mashed carrots and disinfectant. If it does, I might want to rethink my options. I love the smell of barbecue.

Maui Memorial could have been any hospital anywhere. Rude receptionist, maze-like halls, abandoned wheelchairs, bad smells. By the time I found Koni's room, I had tunnel vision. My bad ear was naturally blocking out sounds, my good ear and my eyes had decided to follow suit. My size nines were the only things keeping me going. Well, maybe my feet and my pitter-pattery heart. I won't talk about any other body parts' involvement.

I knocked softly on the open door and peeked in. Jesus-in-a-jumpsuit, he looked good in bed. I mean, he'd looked good... in bed. My cheeks burned.

Koni looked up from reading a book. "Aloha!" He seemed happy to see me. "Come in."

I'd stopped at the mall and gotten him some magazines: *Christianity Today, Popular Mechanics,* and *Maxim*. It was like missions, pistons, and positions. As I handed them to him I could see that he'd been reading Joseph Campbell's *Occidental Mythology—The Masks of God*. Zowie! I was out of my league.

Koni's bed was closest to the door. His roommate seemed to have a large family meeting in process. Deep voices mumbled. All I could see below the faded green curtain were black boots and flip-flops. There wasn't a spare chair on Koni's side. "Sit," he said, and patted the bed as he made room.

We did the usual pleasantries. How you feeling? Good. Me, too. Sorry about the near-drowning. Blah, blah, blah.

"Thanks for saving me."

Hmm. What do you say to that?

The curtain slashed back. Three bikers and three bimbos nodded as they left the room. Only the one I used to be married to had given me more than a casual look. His bimbo noticed but didn't seem to mind; must be confident. Snake's eyes glanced at Koni, who gave him an almost imperceptible nod. I was watching these nuances like a spectator at Wimbledon. At the door, Snake turned back. I waited. He walked past me and pulled the curtain back around the other guy's bed. Then he left without a word. I just kept watching the door.

"Aloha?" Koni touched my hand.

I yelped.

"Bikers scare you?" he asked in a stage whisper, one brow cocked. He kept his hand on mine.

"No more than Rastafarians," I said. Then I reached out and ran my hand down one of his dreads just in case Snake came back in the room.

Koni took my cue and stroked his hand down my arm. The hairs stood at attention. If this were high school and I were in a backseat of a car, I knew how it would go. Being the time and place I was, I had few hopes.

"The dreads are just for convenience. I'm not into Rasta, though I find their holy trinity interesting."

I didn't have a clue what he was talking about.

"You know, the Father, the Son, and the Holy Spirit. They believe themselves the Holy Spirit."

"You're a chaplain," I said. "Don't differing philosophies bother you?" I pointed to the Campbell book.

"I'm Hawaiian. The word the missionaries chose to use for God is *Akua.* It's a plural term that reveals and expresses the divine in all things. I think they accidentally got it right."

Damn, how had we gone from groping to religion? And if there wasn't going to be any progress in the groping project, we needed to talk about the money. I sighed.

Koni rested back on the pillow and closed his eyes as he said, "*Akua* literally means to stand in the midst of the Spirit," he explained. "That's just one of the things that intrigue me about you."

Okay, now we were back in business.

"It's your name, Aloha. It has the "a" at each end, the same as *Akua,* The "a" is the breath of the Spirit and it's at each end of your name. I feel that in you."

I blinked.

"In *Akua* the "ku" means to stand. It's crucial in Polynesian spirituality as it symbolizes one's recognition as a part of creation. Stand and be recognized, among all God's creation."

"Koni," I said, "There's something I need to ask you."

He looked pleased. Like a teacher with a smart student.

"Did you see any money on the boat that night?"

He pulled his hand back from mine just as Ho Killingsworth came into the room.

"Good question," Ho said. "A better question is why would Colley have a bag of money on the boat?"

I stood.

Ho walked up to Koni and pointed his finger at him, "Ke, we gonna find out what you know. Den we gonna talk story."

Koni gave Ho a raised eyebrow and tilted his head.

"Uh, Ho ... Detective Killingsworth," I said, "Why are you accusing Koni? He's ... he's ... he's ... " I wanted to say, "One of the good guys," but what did I know?

"He's what?" Ho asked, looking at me like I was about to say something stupid. Maybe I was.

"He's rich and famous," I said. Like that kept people from being greedy? What was I thinking?

Ho's look confirmed my thoughts. "Maybe I talk Ike about dis."

"Oh, for the love of… !" I was so frustrated I couldn't think of what to add. "You're going to tell my dad? What next, ground me? Maybe a spanking?" Oops. I looked at Koni. He looked like he'd trade places with Ho in a heartbeat. Ho just shook his head and pushed past the curtain to the other patient's area. I heard him push a chair up next to the bed and then he started talking too low for me to hear. I turned up my hearing aid. What can I say? I'm nosy by nature. Plus, I wondered who it was that Snake had been visiting, and why. I stared at the curtain like a dog looking at a closed door, knowing the mailman's outside, but not sure what he looks like.

"Aloha," Koni jarred me out of my eavesdropping.

I accidentally gave him the look that says, "What now, I'm busy!"

"Uh, sorry Koni," I said. "What were we talking about?" I'd totally lost track of our conversation.

He leaned close and whispered, "You asked me if I'd seen any money on the boat."

I leaned close to hear him. He didn't smell like the hospital. He smelled like cocoa butter and man. I liked those smells. I took a deep breath through my nose. Mmm… I wondered if Snake still smelled like soap and motorcycle oil and man. I dug the scent up out of my olfactory memory. I made me happy. Then I opened my eyes. Koni was about four inches away. I leaned back quickly.

"The money?" he said.

"Right," I said. "Did you see a bag of money?"

"Nope."

"Oh."

"You sound disappointed. Were you hoping I had it?"

"No, I've just been tasked with finding it."

"Tasked? That sounds serious."

"Yeah, I think it is." I thought of Yake telling me he'd fire me if I didn't find it. He couldn't really do that could he? I wasn't sure I wanted to find out.

"Did you see anybody move a duffle bag off the boat that night?" I asked.

Koni shut his eyes. I could tell he was playing a mental movie in his head. Then he nodded. "Yeah, I think I saw someone hand a duffle bag over the rail."

"Who?"

He started to say something, then, stopped himself. "I can't remember."

He was a bad liar. His eyes actually got kind of shifty. To me that meant it was someone he knew and wanted to protect. Who would that be? He'd gone through the academy with Gil and Awiwi. Was the police brotherhood kicking in? He'd already fought to protect the Shar-Pei. Would he be happy to see her get some bucks, maybe get a better life? It seemed like the kind of thing he'd support. Of course, Tan had jumped on board as soon as we docked. Maybe he'd handed the money over to Zhen, and Koni felt it was rightfully hers to begin with. Heck it could have been the paramedic's bag he saw handed over and he just didn't want to accuse anyone. I could tell though, that it bothered him.

"If you remember, would you let me know?" I asked, as I brushed my bangs off my face.

"Yeah. Sure. Of course. No problem."

His four yeses were like a series of double negatives. I was pretty sure he wouldn't tell me. I needed to make some phone calls. And before I could do that, I needed to go buy a new phone since mine had not responded well to swimming the other night. I tried to think of some way to end the visit on a good note; something that would neutralize the discomfort of his lie.

"You said the 'A's in my name translate to spirit, what's the middle mean?"

He shook his head. "I don't know why I said that, it must be the meds. *Alo* means share and *ha* means breath of life. It's still a good name, a good meaning. Your name means you share the breath of life."

Then he looked kind of pensive and said, "It's like *haole.*" He pronounced it how-oh-lee.

I knew this was the word used for whites. I didn't get what he meant.

"It's got *ha* in it," he extended his hand, "the breath of life. But it's also got *ole.*"

I waited. I'd heard everybody use the phrase. I'm a *haole.* Ho looked hapa *haole.* I guessed Koni wasn't *haole* at all.

"*Ole* means lacking," he said. "The Hawaiians thought the whites lacked the breath of life."

Was this what Nigel had been talking about when he'd mentioned an unspoken element of racism? If so, it wasn't so silent. But Koni was. He'd shut his eyes and his head was back against the pillow again. His breaths—those lively breaths of his, versus mine—were long and low. I picked my white ass off the bed and left his room. I didn't think about Ho, or even Snake. I just felt kind of gross, maybe a little invisible, certainly unworthy. When I say racism is a funny thing, I don't mean ha-ha funny. I mean I wish I wasn't a *haole.*

I wondered if being *haole* was what got Colley killed.

Chapter Eighteen

The cellular phone store gave me a headache. The kind of headache you get when a five-year-old tells you what causes aurora borealis. There's a lot of nebulous description and theory and wide-eyed wonder, but ultimately you still don't know how it works. That's me and cellular technology. Tell me how to get a ring-tone with the Star Trek theme and we're good. The various plans, options, and rip-off deals are more than I need to know. It took me an hour and a half to get a new phone with the same number as my old phone. I'd like to say that at least I still had my dignity. Somehow I'd been sucked into a pink leather phone case and unlimited minutes that corresponded to the time I usually slept. My dignity was shot.

As soon as I cleared the store, I dialed Liebe. No answer. I tried calling Zhen's number again to let her know I had Wharf. No answer. I tried calling my parents, just to check in and maybe make sure no one was telling my dad bad things about me. I got an answer, but it was the machine.

"Hi guys, this is Aloha," I said. "Just wanted to say hi and let you know that things are going well." I had to say that. You can't leave someone a message that says your life sucks, you might lose your job, you're mad at your sister, and you've got somebody else's dog riding around in your truck. You *really* don't say stuff about the Hawaiian preacher in the hospital or your biker ex-husband. Then I ended with another little fib. "Hope to see you soon."

The drive back to Lahaina was not nearly as treacherous as the drive to Wailuku. It was dark, the traffic had abated a great deal, no whales in sight at night, and I wasn't in such a hurry. I took a break from the phone as I wheeled through the Pali. It had bad cell coverage and too many curves for distracted driving. Once I hit the straight-away heading toward Oluwalu, I made another call.

"Brita Beamer," she answered.

"It's Aloha," I said. "Any chance you're available to meet me for a drink?" I wasn't sure if she lived on Lahaina-side, Kihei, or Upcountry. Maybe I should have called her sooner.

"Sure," she said. "I'm covering a gallery opening on Front Street since our Art's writer is on maternity leave. I'll be *pau* in twenty minutes or so. Meet me at the P.I." Then she paused. "If you get there first, order me a Mai Tai."

"Okay, same for me. See you there."

I wasn't sure what I wanted to find out from Brita. But she seemed to know stuff... stuff I needed to know. Since the traffic was light and I had a little time to spare, I stopped at Mile Marker 14 to walk Wharf. The moon had risen and cast enough light to see where the sand was soft. I found a firm spot to park and together we set off toward the water. Lanai's silhouette anchored the western horizon. There were a few boats out, so mast lights bobbed intermittently. As we walked out toward the point, the lights of a cruise ship lit the waters off Lahaina. How many were we going to get this week, anyway? It was really getting out of control.

I felt bad for the regular harbor users. They had more and more difficulty finding a spot on the loading dock for fueling. Those who moored on the land side of the harbor could load their supplies from their slips, but those on the breakwater had to juggle a time and place on the loading dock. The harbor hadn't been designed for the ships' tender traffic, the TSA, and the current use level. It wasn't really about the bathrooms at this point. There were simply too many rats in the cage.

I remembered reading about a study where rats lived in overcrowded conditions. They resorted to abhorrent behaviors, like rodent murder.

Maybe I'd been going at this all wrong. Instead of who killed Colley, perhaps I should be thinking of why. Why kill Colley? The usual choices applied. Jealousy, money, an accident, rage, competition, the list seemed endless.

Wharf and I turned and shuffled back to the truck. The moonlight hadn't offered any answers, just more questions. By the time we arrived at the Pioneer Inn, the evening booze cruises were arriving back in the harbor. Stereos competed in the night air. I wondered who was playing on the *Awiwi*, with Koni in the hospital. As I pulled into my designated parking space, I thought of Yake 'borrowing' my truck. I knew it shouldn't bug me. It was a "state vehicle" and he was my boss. What did it matter?

It mattered because it was my responsibility. My mood just kept dropping. A lesser woman might want a drink to ease the pain. I knew that my ambivalence about alcohol in general wouldn't necessarily ease the pain, although it might offer a delay.

Brita was already ensconced at a table in the corner of the bar. Three bikers were playing pool nearby. No one I knew. I needed to deal with that soon. After years of separation, I wondered why Snake had come to Maui. He didn't seem interested in me. Maybe it was just a coincidence.

Wharf hopped up in a chair next to Brita. This was new. It didn't look comfortable either. One back leg kept sliding off the worn vinyl seat. He looked like someone trying to kick-start a bike.

"What's up?" Brita skipped any foreplay.

"Yake reamed me for talking to you."

"Yeah, I thought that might happen." She sipped her Mai Tai. Tonight her nails were aqua blue. They matched the strange aqua and lemon plumeria print on her black dress. I had to glance down at her shoes. Her shoes fascinated me. Again she wore heels tall enough that she might want to consider having oxygen handy. They were lemon yellow sling-backs that picked up the hot yellow accents on the floral of her dress. This girl knew how to accessorize. I just tried to match.

"So now that I've risked my job to talk with you, how about you help me with some info?" I knew she wasn't the type to need schmoozing. It was a yes or no deal.

"Shoot."

"Who killed Colley?"

She pursed her lips and shook her head. "If I knew you'd read it in the paper." Then she did a series of little staccato clicks with her nails on the laminate table top. It was something I'd do constantly if I had long nails.

"Okay," I said. "Who was Colley?"

She smiled. "Now we're talking. I've been wondering that myself. Here's what I know." She started counting off with her fingers. "By all accounts he was an asshole."

Great, she was telling me what I already knew.

"However, he was also a great dad to Momi. How does that work? How does a guy lose his temper at work, but not at home?" she asked the rhetorical questions.

I thought of my dad. He had been hell on wheels at work. But despite all my mom's, "I'm going to tell your dad," threats, he'd always been even-keeled with us girls. His temper was a tool he controlled and used. Truth be told, I wasn't sure he ever got mad at work, and I knew he had been furious with us kids plenty of times.

"It was an act?"

"Bingo."

"Why?"

"Why do we do anything?" she asked.

"To get what we want," I said.

"Right, so here's my question for you. How did he get moved up on the slip list?"

Uh oh. She'd turned the tide on me—again. Plus, she had info I didn't know. I shrugged and evaded, "So nobody liked him. Nobody likes Yake either, but nobody killed him." I stabbed an errant maraschino cherry, expecting the perfect mix of sugar and rum. Instead I got the fire of jalapeno pepper. My mouth burned even after I spit the cherry into my cocktail napkin. I took a swig of the Mai Tai. It didn't help. I needed dairy to quell the fire. I saw a Pina Polada being set up on the cocktail waitress' tray at the bar. I got up and chugged it. The bikers started clapping.

The bartender, who I recognized as the one with the hula hips from the luau who had attached herself to Koni, simply smirked at me. I guess I know how the cherry had been cooked. I flipped her off. She came around the bar and slapped me. It stung like a son-of-a-gun. I grabbed her hair—fortunately tied back in a long braid—and twisted it around my fist with a flip of the wrist. Then I pushed her head forward and buckled her knees from the back with my foot.

The report in the paper said I'd kicked her, but I hadn't. It was more of a tap. Suddenly the bar seemed more crowded. There were bikers and bimbos coming out of the woodwork to watch. The bartender wasn't going down without a fight. Even though I was above her and had her on her knees, she was screaming.

"I'm gonna kick your ass, bitch."

And when I say she spat, she really did. She was hissing like a cat and was twice as wily. Even though I had her head down, she flailed around with her arms, slapping and scratching me every chance she got.

"You're pissing me off," I said through clenched teeth. "Stop fighting and I'll let you go." Why was I fighting a girl over a guy who wasn't into *haoles* anyway? Just as I had that thought, I felt her relax and I let go. Thank goodness.

I really didn't want to fight. I hate girl fights. Apparently I was the only one with the aversion. As soon as I let her go, she stood up and slapped me again. I saw Brita rise from her chair and ruffle around in her purse.

Thank God someone was going to call the cops. Instead, she pulled out her little camera and started shooting. So help me, when I got done whipping this girl's ass, Brita was next. As the bartender tried to open-palm slap me with both hands. I deflected the blows. She was kind of weak in upper body strength and I told her so in my own way.

"Maybe you'd fight better if you exercised something besides your ass," I huffed.

She made a high-pitched gurgling scream that kind of scared me. Perhaps I shouldn't have said that. She tried to ram me, but I blocked her with a chair just as Brita's camera flashed again in my eyes.

The harbor users were now showing up in droves. I was getting tired. I was just about to let her go when someone jumped on my back and started pummeling my head. Whoever it was smelled like a Dumpster. I call that a clue.

"Layla, get off my back," I yelled. "This isn't your fight."

Of course, she'd piled on while barking, which made Wharf join in. Fortunately, one of the bikers was holding onto Wharf's collar. I wish he'd done the same for the Shar-Pei. Then I heard what I should have feared most.

Liebe screamed, "Don't worry Aloha, I got your back!"

As she raced forward, she pushed one of the biker's beers over, spilling it onto the pool table. He grabbed a cue stick. Nigel snatched him from the back and did a choke hold. The guy holding Wharf let go to save his pal. Brita had climbed onto the bar for better viewing. Unfortunately the same could be said for her short skirt, since the smart-mouthed little kid from the surf line-up had run behind the bar to watch the show.

I'd had enough. I punched the bartender in her flat little solar plexus and she dropped like a hundred and fifty pounds of mad cow. Then I heard a siren.

Liebe had successfully pulled Layla off me and was now wrestling around on the floor with her. There were ice cubes and chopped fruit everywhere, since someone had thrown the bar condiments at me early in the melee. Wharf was eating those like it was a doggy buffet. Layla joined him and let go of Liebe, who I grabbed along with my purse. I pushed her over the open rail to the sidewalk just as Awiwi marched into the fight with an asp in hand. Wharf had the good sense to give up a growling match with the Shar-Pei over some sliced fruit and raced out the door past the next cop, who obviously didn't know a suspect when he saw one.

Before we made our getaway, I heard a woman say to Awiwi, "Do you speak English?"

His look spoke volumes. Out loud he said, "No, ma'am, but I'm trying' to learn."

She looked discouraged and spoke to the second cop instead.

The three of us ran across the street to my office, gasping for air and hoping we'd dodged the law. We took turns in the shower, first me with Wharf, then Liebe.

"Liebe," I yelled into the shower, "I've got some bad news."

"What now?"

"Uh, my truck was broken into earlier today and someone stole our boards."

The scream I heard was primeval. I guess it was one of those last straw things. So I went ahead and said, "I heard about you and Mangas."

"What did you hear?"

"Don't you think you should pace yourself?" I said by way of explanation.

"What?"

I had settled behind my desk and was sorting through the paperwork on who had a position on the list for the next slip in the harbor. "You know, maybe take a day between yoo-hoos." I had decided there was no need to be more descriptive. It was like when I was a kid and I'd woken my dad for more antibacterial ointment on a scrape. As he stood there half asleep and buck-naked in the bathroom reapplying the salve, I'd asked him where it had gone.

"It absorbed," he said.

"What's absorbed mean?" I asked.

"It means 'soaked in'," he said.

Then I looked at him and said, "What's another word for penis?"

The look on his face said he knew other words but he wasn't going to tell me. Instead he said, "yoo-hoo" to get my attention back on my wound. I decided 'yoo-hoo' would be the word I'd use for Liebe's latest collecting venture. I fondly remembered when she only wanted to collect matchbooks.

"What yoo-hoos? I don't know any yoo-hoos," she sputtered.

"Hey, I know the cancer and the divorce and the job have got you all screwed up," I said. "I just think you should . . . " What? Act your age? Act like a lady? Save yourself for marriage—again? I guess I could be more of a hypocrite but I wasn't sure how. I'd been lusting after a priest and an ex-husband—not at the same time of course—but within minutes of each other.

Liebe stepped out of the bathroom. Her mood looked somewhere between confused and furious. Her wispy hair was ruffled, like she'd tried to spike it using water as styling gel. She had scratch marks on her shoulder, and one knee was bruised. "Cancer sucks. One day you're struggling with life's ridiculous challenges: Losing weight, burning dinner, regretting some dumb stuff you said, bitching at your husband for not helping in the yard. Then the next day you're learning words like lipoid, hematoma, and cytology. So if I don't act in a way that you like, well screw you, Aloha. I don't need a lecture."

It was then that I noticed she'd lost a boob again. This time it was one of the small ones. It was going to be hard to explain its presence in the Pioneer Inn's bar. Maybe we could find it later. I just hoped the cops didn't find it first.

Awiwi opened the door and stepped in. He didn't look happy. We'd washed off all evidence of the fight. "You," he pointed at me. "You fight?"

I shook my head.

He pointed at Liebe, "How 'bout you?"

She went all wide-eyed and innocent. She did it a lot better than I did.

Wharf walked out of the bathroom with a towel over his back as though to say, "Nope, not me either."

Before Awiwi could say anything else, Liebe said, "But I'm glad you're here. We need to report a theft."

Good call, Libs! I nodded and smiled.

"Really?" Awiwi didn't look amused.

"Yeah," she said, "Someone broke into Aloha's truck earlier and stole our boards."

"Really?"

"Yeah, and that's not all," she said and glanced at me. "Aloha, tell him what else was taken." It sounded a lot like, "Bob, tell them what else they've won."

Before I could add anything, he pulled his gigantic hand from his pocket and held up Liebe's missing mammary.

"That's it!" she smiled and clapped. "That's what else was stolen. Awiwi, you're the best." She skipped across the room and hugged him. Then she filched the silicone prosthesis from him and slipped it back into her bra. "Can we file a police report with you right now?"

I guess the answer was no, since he spun her around and fitted her with a set of metal bracelets.

Chapter Nineteen

Seeing your sister in handcuffs is one of those mixed blessings. Sure, there were times when I would've hocked Grandma's silver to see it, but this wasn't one of them.

"Awiwi," I stomped up to him, "What in the hell are you doing?"

I saw his personal bubble expand. He fumbled around on his Sam Browne belt for another set of cuffs. I backed away and lowered my voice.

"Why are you cuffing her?"

"For her safety and mine," he said. "Turn around."

I wanted to argue, but by the look in his eye, I knew I'd better comply. The metal wasn't cold like I expected, but really, we were in Lahaina. Even the ice cubes hadn't been that cold. I heard Liebe say "Uh-oh" from behind me. Then I heard a growl. I turned and saw Wharf—hackles raised—creeping toward Awiwi.

"Wharf, no!" I shouted.

He stopped, mid-stride, one paw in the air like a pointer.

"Sit."

He sat.

"Awiwi, we can't leave the dog. Let me make a phone call or find someone to take him somewhere."

Awiwi keyed his mike and called for animal control.

"No," I pleaded, "Don't do that. Please." I had to think. What would motivate him to do what I wanted? "Don't lock up Momi's dog."

He cancelled the animal control request on his radio and switched to his cell phone for his next call. "*Makuahi'ne.*"

I was pretty sure he was calling his mom, but I couldn't understand any of what he said as he rattled off a message in Hawaiian. It seemed like all vowels and pauses, with a dearth of consonants.

Just by watching his face, I could tell he was angry. Still, I didn't know what was wrong with him. After all, he'd been our friend a few days earlier. We'd hung out with his mom. He was the famous fire dancer for crying out loud. Sure we'd gotten in a scuffle, but geez, it wasn't the end of the world. We didn't need handcuffs. When he hung up, I said as much. His response shouldn't have been a surprise.

"You no fight?"

"I didn't want to fight. She slapped me."

"She say *haole* bring it."

Liebe started to argue. I shushed her. "Awiwi, I didn't start it. Really. She ... " I thought back. There was no point in having this discussion. It was just a *haole*'s word against a fellow Hawaiian's. My word didn't have the breath of life. I shut my eyes and tried to think of a way out of the situation.

In a moment, I felt the cuffs release from my wrists. I opened my eyes. Apparently, Gil had slipped in like a Ninja while I'd been formulating my plan. He released Liebe too, and pointed us to the chairs. We sat. He tilted his head and signaled Awiwi outside. When the door closed, Liebe said, "I called him from the shower and told him what happened."

"And he came to the rescue?"

"I had to tell him what I was washing first."

I shuddered.

"He's not all bad."

"I guess you'd know," I muttered and dropped my chin onto my thumbs, my index fingers pressed to my eyes, the rest of my digits criss-crossed over my nose.

As her hand came up I flinched. I'd already been slapped so much my face hurt. I didn't need another. Instead she pulled half a squished cherry from my hair, looked it over for a second, and fed it to Wharf.

I sighed and dropped back to my previous contemplative pose. My hands still smelled like jalapeno juice and coconut milk.

I tried to listen to what was being said outside, but the only thing I could hear was my heart pounding. I was screwed if I went to jail. I didn't know what I'd be charged with. Assault? Assault with intent to... to what... keep from getting the ever-living-crap beat out of me? Was a chair considered a deadly weapon? I remembered there was something about causing bodily injury, scars, disfigurement or broken bones. I don't think the chair would have suffered much disfigurement. Did that count? Liebe put her arm around my shoulders and gave me a little squeeze. Then I included her in my assessment of the situation.

"We're screwed."

"Seems like."

"I was looking for some words of hope here. Not agreement."

"Oh."

Gil and Awiwi came back into the office. Gil pulled out a chair and sat down across from us. Awiwi stood. He didn't look at us. I could tell it was deliberate.

Gil leaned forward and said, "Somebody's going to jail. You guys choose."

"That's it," I whispered. "That's the best you can do?"

He shrugged. "I didn't get into a bar fight."

"I'll go," Liebe said, holding her wrists out together.

Mangas slapped cuffs on her, then squirmed like he was fighting an erection.

I looked sideways at her and shook my head. "I'll go."

"No," she said, "It's my fault."

"No it's not. You weren't even there."

"Yes, I was. Well, at least toward the end."

"See?" I said and looked up at Awiwi. He smirked. I looked at Gil. He shook his head and put cuffs back on me, too. I'd just implicated myself. They didn't even have to question me. I didn't stand a prayer in jail. I'm not much for tears, but I could feel a serious crying jag coming on. It was interrupted by Mele entering my office.

She looked from Awiwi, to Wharf, to Liebe, to Gil, and then finally, to me, and shook her head.

"I didn't start it," I argued.

"You didn't stop it either."

"That doesn't mean it's my fault. I didn't have it coming. I didn't ask for it. I didn't deserve having my drink jacked over just because I'm white."

"It's not because you're white," Mele said.

"Really?" I cocked an eyebrow. "Sure seems that way."

"Who fight?" she quizzed Awiwi.

He said some twelve syllable name, again with nary a consonant.

"Koni know?"

Awiwi moved his massive head slightly from side to side.

Then a dim little light bulb flared in my head. "Is that why Colley was killed, because he's *haole*?" I asked. I knew it was a stupid thing to say as soon as the words slipped out. To say I was overwrought was an understatement. I felt like the elephant in the corner had just taken a huge dump and I was it.

"I'm sorry," I said, "That came out wrong." I'd just accused the widow's former brother-in-law and mother-in-law of genocide. I guess that's what happens when you get cornered. You say and do crazy things. I'd seen it happen before, just not to me. Well, maybe to me a little. After all, that's how I'd ended up in Hawaii. I had refused disability and taken a mind-numbing job in what seemed like a foreign country, even though it was actually the 50th state. The same country I'd made an oath to protect.

I said as much and got no response.

That's when Ho Killingsworth schlepped into my office. It was becoming the Harbor Precinct.

"Yo' *Makuakane*'s gonna have your ass," he said to Liebe and me together.

"Only if you tell him," she replied.

"He called me," Ho said, folding his arms and frowning, as if to say, "dumb shit."

Liebe burst into tears. Since that had been my next ploy, she kind of left me with nothing to do, so I checked my nails. We were pathetic. Bar fight, handcuffs, and now our dad knew. *Think. Think. Think.* The voices in my head were running around shrieking and wringing their hands like Arab women at a funeral.

"What did you find out at the autopsy?" I asked Ho, breaking the tension by deflecting the topic.

Everyone else's ears perked up like a pack of Weimaraners, even Wharf's. He did it the best because he added that little head tilt that's so cute. I patted my leg and he trotted over and nuzzled my hand, ignoring the cuffs. I was grateful someone could.

Ho looked around as if to check that the coast was clear. "Unless Colley knocked himself unconscious with a *kiawe* branch while swimming, I'd say he was murdered."

We all pondered the information. Personally, I was imagining Colley smacking himself over and over again. "Multiple hits or just one?" I asked.

"Twice," Ho said, pointing to the back of his head, "Once on each side, probably from the back."

Liebe had stopped crying and was recovering her wits. "What's *kiawe*?" she asked.

In unison, Mele and Awiwi said, "Mesquite." Then Mele added, "It came from Paris."

"Texas?" Liebe asked.

"France."

"When?" I asked, referring to Colley's death. I guess I didn't make myself clear.

Mele responded. "In 1828, Father Bachelot—the first Catholic priest in the islands—planted it at the corner of a church in Honolulu. Now there's 150,000 acres of it throughout the islands. Maybe you can see why we don't always welcome non-native species."

Is that what I was, a non-native species? Should I be eradicated? My fists clinched automatically. Fight or flight, which would it be? I reflected on my situation. It looked like the answer was neither. Then I remembered what I really wanted to know.

"When did Colley die?" I asked Ho, ignoring Mele.

"At least six hours before you found him."

"That would be mid-morning," I said.

"I said, 'At least six hours', but it could also have been as many as sixteen hours."

"Based on what?"

"Rigor mortis and algor mortis."

Liebe giggled. We all stared at her.

"Get it, Al Gore Mortis," she said, spacing each word out separately. "I always knew he was a walking stiff." She giggled to herself some more. I think she was in shock.

I guess we'd all watched enough CSI to know about rigor mortis. So Mele asked about the second half of the equation. "What's Al Gore Mortis?" she asked, repeating Liebe's pronunciation.

"It's post mortem body cooling," Awiwi said to his mom. Then he looked at Ho and said, "Should we be discussing this with civilians?"

I'd been thinking the same thing, wondering why Ho was answering my questions at all. Was it because he knew I'd been an investigator in the Coast Guard? Maybe it was because we had found the body. Or perhaps he saw this as some kind favor to my father, his former commander. Whatever, I'd had no intention of asking him. Now Awiwi had broken the spell.

"It's in the paper," Ho said.

Good enough for me. "Doesn't the fact that his body was in the water change the nature of the numbers?"

"We accounted for that, which is why it's such a big window. It's my guess that it happened sometime in the night, just because I'd think we'd have a witness otherwise."

"How do you know he was hit with *kiawe*? Did you test DNA?" I asked.

Ho smirked. "We no have DNA lab on Maui. We pull out sticker."

"A sticker?"

Gil finally chimed in. "Hurts like a sonuvabitch. Got one last year when I was hunting pigs Upcountry. It festered for a week before I could squeeze it out. Yellow-green pus squirted out and hit the mirror."

We did a collective gag at his colorful description. What did women see in this guy? I sneaked a glance at Liebe. She looked like she might blow, but not in a good way.

Then I looked around at the rest of the room's inhabitants. Awiwi was back to being the stoic cop who'd pulled the body out of the water. At the time, I didn't know he was the dead guy's girlfriend's former brother-in-law. I couldn't resist.

"Why didn't you say something about who he was?"

Awiwi shook his head.

"When we brought Colley's body to the dock? You didn't even say you knew him, that he was practically a relative."

"I didn't 'know him' know him," Awiwi said, emphasizing the first set of words with finger quotes. It was cute. How did this guy go from cop to cute in an instant? It was just like he'd gone from dumb to sly the first day I'd met him.

"Well, you're Momi's uncle. Didn't you keep an eye on the person she and Zhen were living with?"

Mele interrupted his answer. "Zhen kept us away from their place. Whenever we saw Momi it was at school, or practice, or when she visited."

I looked again at Awiwi. He hadn't had to lie. But I could tell by the way he let his mother answer, that he'd been keeping an eye on Colley and that he didn't like the dead man. In fact, in retrospect, he hadn't looked surprised when I'd towed Colley to the loading dock. I thought of the fire sticks Awiwi twirled and threw when he danced. I wondered if they were *kiawe* sticks. It made sense that mesquite would burn perfectly for something like that. I glanced at his meaty hands looking for infected pustules. He held them together in what's known in police jargon as "interview position." It kept me from seeing his fingers or palms.

I had a brainstorm. I'd fake an appendix attack and when he reached to help me I'd grab his hands and give them the once-over. While I tried to decide if my appendix was on my left side or my right, the door to my office opened.

Brita Beamer held the door while she lied to someone about me. "She's usually here in her office. Works day and night. Never takes a break." She looked up at me and winked, just as my parents squeezed into my already crowded office with Nigel in tow. It was the last straw for Liebe. She got up from her chair—hands still cuffed—and ran to the head. We all listened to her barfing for about a minute. Nobody said anything, but Wharf's nose wrinkled at the smell and he started to pant kind of loud. After the toilet flushed she stood in the doorway. Wharf pushed past her and we could all hear him drinking from the toilet bowl.

I think that about summarized my night.

Chapter Twenty

If you want to have a bad day to an exponential degree, it's important to cap it off with your parents seeing you handcuffed. If you can have your sister alongside you in the same position, well, that's just the cherry on the sundae.

"Aloha Hickam Jones! Liebe Ramstein Jones!" My mother, never for lack of enthusiasm, gushed as she edged through the crowd to give us each a hug. In contrast, Ike strong-armed his way to Ho and struck a salute.

Brita shot a photo.

"What're the charges?" Ike intoned.

Ho shrugged. "Not my beef."

My mother, all five-foot-nothing of her, turned to Awiwi, squinted at his name tag, and said, "Officer Lono, you give me that key." She poked him in the chest with her pointy little index finger. "And, release my daughters this instant!"

Bright Beams captured that moment too.

It took him about a second and a half to grab my mom's hand, squeeze it, and drop her to her knees. Well, if you've ever seen geriatric roller derby gone bad or a pack of wild hyenas crossed with K-Mart shoppers on a blue-light gazelle, or maybe a combination of both, that's the scene that ensued.

Mele, appalled by Awiwi's disregard of an elderly woman, my mom—tried to help Eve back to her feet.

P-ching went the shutter on Brita's little digital camera.

"Back off, Mom," Awiwi said, in a voice loud enough to be called shouting, but a distinction he'd later deny. Then he gave her a little shove.

I think Brita switched to some kind of video mode for that because the sound changed. I could almost hear some tourist in his cheap-ass hotel say, "Turn up the tee-vee Bertha, there's gonna be another poe-leece beatin'."

Ike, who had stood by quite stoically while Awiwi put the grab on Mom, came to Mele's rescue. "Hey there son, you might have a reason to drop my wife, but you got no right to push your mother." And he bulled into the fray.

Gil, the consummate cop, simultaneously decided to cover his brother-in-arms, and grabbed Ike by the shoulder, repeating and modifying his salutation. "Hey, there ol' feller, let's not get your heart rate up."

Well, that tore it for my dad. He sees himself as ten-feet tall and bullet-proof, therefore, not having aged since he was forty.

"You'd best take your hand off me boy, or I'll knock you to kingdom come," Ike boomed.

Liebe and I glanced at each other. We'd long debated where exactly kingdom come was, but we knew for sure that it was on the shortcut to Dad losing it. Fortunately, Ho, having served with my dad in the Air Force, also knew the kingdom come code. He put his hand on Gil. Apparently Mangas was getting a little testy with all the physical contact in front of him—without sex being involved. He didn't look back and slapped away Ho's hand.

There were about twelve more photo-taking noises through all this.

I'd been told there's some kind of racial hierarchy you learn when you grow up in the islands. The Chinese are above the Japanese. The Japanese are above the Portuguese. The Portuguese outrank the Samoans and Tongans. The Filipinos mix in the middle somewhere. I don't know where. And sadly, all those groups dominate the Hawaiians. The reason being that the other groups didn't lose their islands to some honky missionaries.

I never heard where the whites ranked, but I had a hunch.

Anyway, Ho took the attitude that a Filipino-Chinese mix trumped Gil's Port-a-gee—the local pronunciation—heritage. So, he did some crazy Kung Fu choppy thing and yelled what sounded like "Hi-Ya!" right before he knocked Gil to the ground.

It was another Kodak moment.

This freed Mele to rejoin the fight. At five-foot-nothing and wearing a billowy muu muu, her response seemed a trifle aggressive. For no particular reason that I could understand, she said, "I don't need your help old man," and, hiked a knee into my dad's groin. I have to give him credit, he didn't scream. I would have. Instead, he made a deep gurgling noise and crumpled to his knees.

For once, Brita let her victim maintain a shred of dignity. I watched her turn around and survey the scene.

For a mid-game recap, we had Liebe and me still in our chairs in our handcuffs. Gil, my dad, and my mom, were in various positions and dispositions on the floor. Ho was still in his martial arts' stance, just looking for a taker. Awiwi, having seen what his mom did to my dad, had her up against the wall with one arm behind her back. He was talking to her real quiet like, but I could tell he was still fired up, since his breathing was fast and there were sweat stains under his arms.

Nigel had put the grab on the dog and was holding him back, while he did some kind of Cujo impersonation—Nigel, not the dog. I thought I saw some foam at the corner of his mouth, but I could have been wrong. Wharf, on the other hand, was indeed struggling to get free, but purely because my mom had dropped two bags of homemade cookies on the floor, and he wanted them. Even from where I sat, I could see the criss-crosses of a fork imprint, so I knew they were peanut butter.

Wharf looked up from the cookies and met my gaze. We both dove for them at the same time. Nigel lost his hold and went face first on top of my dad as Wharf jumped him to reach the cookies. I figured worst case scenario, I'd get a bag and so would the dog. Liebe, as usual, was a split second ahead of me.

I either completely lost my limited sense of hearing during the fray, or it was just too disturbing for Brita to keep shooting. I heard nothing but the increasing beat of my heart and a strange growling noise emanating from my own throat as I grabbed for something to eat. I lost.

By the time I regained my feet, not easy considering the layer of humanity—or lack thereof—on the floor, Liebe and Wharf had each chewed their way into a bag of cookies. That was just *it* for me. I wanted to send somebody to kingdom come and back again. I had just pulled my leg back to give Awiwi a swift kick in the ass on behalf of the entire Jones family, when the door opened again. I couldn't help but think, "What could be worse than this?"

"Ah—ten—shun!" You could tell who in the group had been in the military. We all hopped to our feet and popped a salute ... to Boo-Boo Bear. That's right, my beleaguered boss, Max Yake, had come to call. Ten o'clock at night, my office, bodies everywhere, cookies gone, mini-reporter on the loose. It looked bad. Real bad. I stole a glance at him. He looked mad.

The only ones not at attention were Wharf, my mom, and Mele. Hmm, I didn't know Nigel and Brita were former military too. They, along with Gil, Awiwi, Liebe, Dad, Ho, and I held our positions. Wharf stayed on the floor, Hoovering for remains from his cookie heist. Mom and Mele brushed each other off and made nice.

In some ways, I missed the carnage. At least in the heat of the moment, I hadn't been thinking about the repercussions. In contrast, the consequences of the evening's activities were looming like an ominous radioactive cloud over an innocent Polynesian village.

"Gimme the camera," Yake held out his hand to Brita.

We all did a collective intake of breath. Had we been betting people—and not at attention—I think the odds on Yake would have been slim. Granted, I'd heard he wielded a lot of power, but really, there was this thing called freedom of the press.

He cocked a furry brow at her.

She handed him the camera.

He pulled out his glasses. Then he punched some buttons and handed the tiny camera back to her. "Thanks for letting me see your photos Miss Beamer. I tried to organize them for you, but now they're gone. Format means organize doesn't it?"

She squeaked but didn't say anything.

"Out," he barked.

She left.

He turned to Awiwi. "Code-Four, then Code-Whatever-Leaving-Here is, then Code-Go-To-Dinner." And he nodded toward Awiwi's mike.

Awiwi immediately spoke codes to his dispatcher.

Yake signaled him to the door and said, "See you next week."

Awiwi looked at Mele.

Yake splayed his hands, as if to say, "What?"

"She's my mom."

Yake signaled her to go.

"Wait a sec," he said to Awiwi, "Gimme your keys." Then he released Liebe and me from the cuffs. Awiwi held his hand out to take them. Yake just shook his head and said, "Finder's fee."

Then he looked at my mom and dad. "Cruisers?" He assumed they were harbor users, new in town on a sailboat. Not a bad guess, but wrong nonetheless.

I started to answer for them, but he shot me a look that made me stop.

Apparently, Yake was a man my dad understood, because all Ike said was, "parents" and shot a look at Liebe and me.

Yake rolled his head back, lifted his pork-pie hat, and shoved his fingers through his comb-over.

"You take the old one and I'll keep this one," Yake muttered to my dad.

I thought Liebe would punch him right then. Me, on the other hand, I was starting to appreciate his observational skills.

Then he said, "For now."

For now? He'd keep me for now? Liebe could go for now? My loyal family hit the trail so fast he didn't have a chance to change his mind.

Next was Nigel. I glanced around. Seemed he had already hit the bricks. Didn't need an invitation to leave. Lucky duck.

That left me, Mangas, and Wharf, who right then slipped out the door and into the night. I thought dogs were more loyal than that. I could tell by the look in Gil's eyes that he'd do the same as soon as he had a chance.

Yake gave it to him.

"Heard there was a boat sinking in Maalaea Harbor, might want to check it out." Yake dismissed Mangas with a wave.

It was like Obi-Wan Kenobi telling the storm troopers they had the wrong droids. A wave of the hand, a few words, and bingo, bango, bongo, the party was over.

As soon as Mangas baled it was just me… and Yake.

"Find the money?" he asked.

"I… uh…" I shook my head.

"Find the money," he repeated himself. This time without the question.

Well, this was one of those moments. You know, like when the girl in the scary movie opens the door to the monster 'cause he says he has a cookie or has to go to the bathroom, but you know that's not it at all? The monster is really going to eat her. Maybe burp her up later like a bad pizza, take a Tums, and then look for the next idiot who will open the door. Anyway, I'm that smart.

"Whose money is it?" I responded, as I mentally smelled the monster's breath through the metaphorical key hole. I think he'd been eating something made from sulfur or curry. They smelled about the same to me.

Yake gave me a look. I could see why everyone else bailed. It was like looking at cold sweat.

"Really," I said, shuffling papers on my desk. "Whose money? Is it yours? His? The Harbors Division's?" Were there a movie audience watching, they'd have a huge kernel of salty popcorn stuck right in their collective windpipe. It was tense.

He glanced out the window.

The monster morphed back into Boo-Boo. Yake laughed. "Money belongs to Zhen. I just want to make sure nobody rips her off."

I smiled. "I thought so."

"Good work Jones, on checking it out though. I wouldn't want you to think otherwise." Then he laughed some more. "Funny seeing you in cuffs. Bet you're glad I showed up?"

I nodded.

"Well, let's get this place locked up and you can head home and see your folks," he said as he walked around and checked the windows.

I'd heard he was thorough.

"But let's find that money tomorrow. Then bring it to my office."

I admired the use of the word "let's." It was like we were on the same team. Well, other than the part that implied I'd better take care of it—stat. It seemed to me that the monster had spotted an easier meal. Grateful, I decided not to ask any more questions.

Chapter Twenty-one

The thing I like about shopping for surfboards is the smell. Surf shops reek of neoprene. To me neoprene smells fresh. Sometimes, I still missed being a diver.

Credit cards, on the other hand, don't have a smell. But if they did they'd probably smell like fried liver or Brussels sprouts or cat doody. Credit cards are bad. Mine was about to have the numbers ground off with the expense of all new surf gear. Liebe had a wad of twenties filling in the cup of her halter top. For balance, she had said, since she was wearing the one jumbo prosthetic, shotgun. I assumed she'd be getting change in singles rather than coins or she'd have a serious droop.

"Eh," the surfer guy at the counter said as we walked in.

I rolled my eyes. I could tell he thought we were too old to surf, or worse, tourists.

Liebe ignored him and walked up to the display of boards with a handwritten paper signed attached that said, "Don't touch." She rubbed her hands together, cupped them to her lips, blew on them, and then stroked the polished balsa face on the biggest board in a way that made me want to suggest they get a room.

The surfer guy grabbed his telephone handset and called for backup.

What a pussy.

"That's one big-ass board." Liebe moved her fingers from the deck to the rails. "What do you think, twenty-four, twenty-five?" she asked me, referring to its width.

"At least." I couldn't help myself. I traced my fingers across the abalone inlay. The board was a piece of art.

She laid her face against it and looked to the tip. "Hardly any rocker to it though."

She was right. Even if you were crazy enough to take this board into the water, knowing it would be ruined, you'd not enjoy the paddle. No rocker meant no lift at the nose. Of course you'd look like a million bucks right up until the ocean held your head back and forced water down your throat.

Someone bumped me from behind. I figured it was the kid. Liebe glanced over my shoulder. I didn't like her look, so I turned. Zhen's nanny was in my personal bubble.

I frowned. "What do you want now?"

"Can you not read?"

Her Euro accent and flipped words annoyed me for no apparent reason. Maybe I'd seen one too many girl fights lately. I decided to walk away. Liebe didn't.

My beloved sister licked the board.

Euro trash about popped her cork. "You, you, you ... " She seemed at a loss for words, at least English words. She switched to German and called Liebe guttural names I'd never heard before. They didn't sound flattering. If body language counted for anything, there was a real risk she'd bust out of her crocheted halter dress as she puffed like a peacock. A metallic bikini with T-back bottoms winked provocatively through the dress's woven hemp.

Liebe smiled. "Now I guess you know how it feels."

I was confused on an exponential level. It was like trying to figure out the square root of a gazillion in a story problem. I hate story problems.

Then the blonde—tall enough to match Liebe inch for inch—but a tad younger, said to me, "Vere's da hound?"

Well, that was a problem. I'd spent half the night looking for him. I walked the harbor calling his name. I'd searched around Lahaina Banyan Court Park. I walked from King Kam School to the Methodist church on Front Street hollering his name and asking people if they'd seen a big yellow dog. I'd had no luck. Surf board shopping on my lunch break was supposed to get my mind off losing Wharf—again. It wasn't working.

"I'm sorry," I tried not to blather. "He was with me last night, but he got away, and I haven't been able to find him." I looked down. "Yet," I added.

"Maybe he fear she bite," the big blond Amazon said as she snapped her teeth at Liebe.

"I've just about had it with you ... you ... " Liebe took a step forward, " ... you man-eating ... " She seemed at a loss for words.

Her antagonist simply rolled her eyes. "No more touch boards."

"Or what?" Liebe put her hands on her hips.

Great. It was just like second grade.

"I call police."

"Yeah, well, bigger bitches than you've had me in cuffs before and I still got out."

Oh, *my God*! My sister was going all ghetto-prison on me. Had she forgotten she was a forty-year-old divorcee with breast cancer? Being in those handcuffs had totally gone to her head, but in a bad way. The little time I'd spent with her when I got home the night before had been the same. She made it sound like she'd been a lifer at Folsom.

"Liebe! What next? Are you going to sharpen your toothbrush into a shiv? Come on, let's go." I pulled on her elbow.

She flicked me away.

"I'm not doing this again, Liebe. The third time's *not* the charm. We are *not* tough. We're middle class, middle-aged ... " I tried to think of the next best word.

The look she gave me spoke volumes.

"... chicks," I ad-libbed, thinking that would appease her. It worked. Well, almost. It worked until Miss Pissy-Pants, Uber-bitch muttered "middle-aged" under her breath.

Liebe flung her arm out for a round-house swing that I stepped into to keep us from going to jail. It hurt like a son-of-a-gun, again, right to my bad ear. The phrase "cleaned my clock" came to mind. At least there was a definite chiming involved.

"Aloha!" Liebe grabbed me as my eyes rolled back. "I'm so sorry," was the last thing I heard her say as I slumped to the floor.

Again, the smell of neoprene was a comfort. However, having a zipper embedded in my cheek was not. I woke up on a wetsuit, on the floor. A price tag hung from the zipper. My eye was approximately an inch from it but I couldn't focus enough to read the numbers.

"She works here?" Liebe asked. "I thought she worked as a nanny... or a hooker."

I watched the sales guy who had said "eh" when we walked in do a tiny intake of breath and look over his shoulder. "Just like everybody else, she works two jobs in order to live here. And if you want that discount, you need to stop calling her names."

Great. Liebe had turned bad behavior into a reason for a deal. You gotta love her.

I pushed up from the floor. "Maybe we can shop for new boards some other time. I'm not feeling so good."

"Oh you'll be fine," Liebe said. "Don't be a pussy."

So help me...

"Listen, Miss, I can give you a discount today. But I don't want to have to tell my boss what happened, so if you want the deal you need to get it together."

Man, he was awfully preppy proper for a surfer dude. In fact, he looked kind of wimpy. I bet he didn't even surf. Dang, that didn't seem right. "Do you surf?"

"I can't tell you how much I love to surf." His eyes shifted up and to the right. He'd never surfed a day in his life. He just knew the lingo and how to make a sale.

"But you show up on time and you're honest and your boss loves you, right?"

He gave me a look that said I was right.

I shook my head to clear the cobwebs. It didn't work. Then I told him what I wanted in a board. Without a lot of preamble or flash he showed me what I was looking for. It had turquoise rails, triple fins, and a tongue depressor nose. I loved it. Liebe selected a board slightly longer and narrower in yellow. She'd had trouble paddling her old board because of the mastectomy. So narrow was a better choice. We both grabbed new leashes and he gave us Sex Wax for free. While he rung us up I watched Zhen's nanny make a call on her cell phone. As Liebe paid for her board, she stuffed her change in wadded up bills and a receipt in one bra cup. Suffice to say it was no substitute for the real thing. I was thinking of getting a set of spares to carry for her myself.

I walked to the nanny for a chat. "What was Colley like?"

"A dog," she said, as she hung up the phone and started folding T-shirts. She stacked them just so. I could see why they hired her. Order. Order. Order.

"What?"

"Snobbery...?" she searched for the right phrase, "...you know wet-mouth."

"You mean slobbery?"

"Yes. He kiss everyone," she said, making kissy noises.

"Did he kiss you?"

"He kiss everyone except Zhen."

"What about Momi?"

The nanny just cocked a brow, shrugged, and marched away. "What the hell kind of nanny are you?" I muttered. "Weren't you supposed to keep Momi safe?"

"She's a liar." Liebe had sneaked up behind me.

"How do you know?"

"She's lied about everything else. It's just who she is. She's a liar." Then Liebe walked back and grabbed her new board.

I shook my head and did the same. I didn't know if the nanny was a liar or not, but she sure was a jerk. Of course, so was Colley. If he was abusing Momi, no wonder he was dead. Had I known, I'd have been tempted to kill him myself. And what about Zhen, didn't she pay attention? It was time for her and me to have a conversation. Somewhere in there I guess I'd have to tell her I'd lost her dog, too.

At the truck, Liebe was still muttering about the nanny. I couldn't help myself and said, "You jealous?"

"Of what?"

"Her." I tossed my head back toward the shop.

Liebe looked me square in the eye and said, "Yes. Are you happy?"

"Why?"

She rolled her eyes and sighed. "Because Man-gas—that worthless piece of Port-a-gee sausage—showed me the door, or the dock as it may be, when she showed up."

I shook my head, confused.

"I didn't go boating with him. As we were getting the gear loaded, she showed up, trumped my German accent, hopped aboard, and ran her tongue up his neck. He made some lame-ass excuse and left me high and dry. And she took my beach bag with my spares."

"So it wasn't you on the boat?"

"Doing what?"

"*Him.*"

"Ugh! No, he's disgusting. He's got more hair on his back than most dogs."

Liebe had always liked a smoother look. Maybe that was Nigel's appeal. He was smooth to a whole new level. "Then why'd you get a date with him?"

"So I could see if he killed Colley," she said, as though I was the dipshit of the year and she was helping hand out the awards.

"Why'd you think that?"

"'Cause when you guys came in that night with Colley's boat, Mangas made sure he unloaded a duffle bag full of money before he got checked out by the paramedics."

"How'd you know about the money?"

"Duh, I looked in the bag," she said in her best Valley-girl accent.

"Why didn't you tell me?"

"If I was wrong I didn't want to ruin your ability to have a good working relationship with him."

What could I say? She was doing my work for me.

"I wonder why Darcy thought it was you on the boat." Might as well see how far she went.

"I put my name on my 'spares'." Liebe finger-quoted the word as she referred to her breast prosthetics. "When Mangas was schtuping that German yahoo, she threw my boobs at some surfer like they were water balloons. Since I'd been losing them so fast, I'd put my name on the ones that were left."

As though they'd get confused with someone else's boobs? Maybe there'd be a whole flotilla of them and it would be tricky to find the right ones. The mental picture was something it might take me years to get over. I tried to find my brain's control-alt-delete to no avail. "Uh, Libs, how many of those did you bring?"

She looked down at her chest with its one remaining filler and the wad of cash in the other cup. "Not enough."

Time to change subjects. "Did you see what happened to the duffle?"

"Yep," she said. Then she looked at me with those piercing blue eyes and tilted her head just a tad to the right. "How did you know about the money? Why should I tell you where it went? And ..." she smiled, "Why do you want to find it now?"

I thought we were on the same team there for a minute. Maybe I was wrong.

I answered her anyway, holding up three fingers to represent each answer. "One, I found it on Colley's boat when I was looking for a knife to cut away the line around the prop." I folded down my ring finger. "Two, you should tell me because I'm your sister. I'm the harbormaster and I asked nicely." I folded down my index finger leaving her with my bird finger up. "And three, if I don't find it, my boss is going to fire me. So, if it's not too much trouble, just answer my damned questions!" Okay, I guess I was losing it a little. Why not? I'd lost everything else: The money, the dog, our boards, and perhaps my tenuous grasp on sanity.

Liebe didn't even flinch at me flipping her off. Instead, she said, "It's in the harbor."

"What?"

"I zipped it shut and it ... it kind of fell into the harbor."

"It fell?" I remembered the story about when she was little and had had a fight with our next oldest sister Amoré. Our mom had seen Liebe rap Amoré on the head with her knuckles and said, "Don't hit your sister."

"I didn't," Liebe had argued, despite live visual evidence to the contrary. "What do you call this?" Mom had asked as she demonstrated the action back on Liebe's head.

"I call that a tap." And she walked away from the screaming toddler with a clear conscience. Liebe was the queen of semantics.

So I repeated my question. "It fell?"

"Well, yes. It did." She looked away. "Right after I kicked it off the dock."

Chapter Twenty-two

People don't change. They get older, better educated, married, or even duped, but deep down, they stay the same. Liebe was and always has been... what's the word I'm looking for? Not sneaky... contrary. Me, I'm all about justice. Things need to work out right—or else. Or else what, I asked myself? I knew the answer, or else I'd make it right.

Then I thought about the other players in this little melodrama. Colley—although a victim in this case—seemed like a bad guy. To quote Liebe, he was basically an ass. It was even hard for me, Little Miss Justice, to get all that worked up about his death, other than the fact that I liked things tidy. It simply bothered me to have a dead body floating in *my* harbor without knowing how it got there.

And then there was Zhen, who had "FOLLOWER" written all over her. It sounded like there hadn't been a cause, phase, or trend she'd missed. Rescue cats. Create a Hawaiian homeland. Eat organic. All great ideas, but I wondered if following was enough for her. Did she truly believe in each cause? Or did she need to clear the deck for a new leader? With Colley gone she was free to pursue Tan. Granted, even his name was a shade of beige. He made poi seem spicy. Koni said Tan was a great drummer because he always played the music the same each time. He never once varied. It allowed the rest of the band to improvise at will. They'd never had a drum solo. It just wasn't done.

This thought of course, led me to think of Koni. I blushed and glanced across the truck's front seat to where Liebe had her head leaned back and her eyes shut. Good, I could go back to thinking about the singer. I was sure he was interested in me, but I wasn't sure why. On one level he seemed too Hawaiian to settle for a *haole.* On another, he seemed fascinated with females—all females. He was like an avid bird watcher on vacation in the tropics. It looked like he was garnering quite a "life list." And some of his finds weren't taking to the idea of him gazing elsewhere.

I ran my fingers through my hair in an absent-minded check for more bar condiments. When I'd showered this morning I'd found half a macadamia nut in the drain. But my question remained: Who was he in his heart? I suspected he was a fellow seeker of justice. He'd rousted the street preacher for doing the boom-boom with Layla. He did the whole police chaplain volunteering thing. These were two dichotomous stands, however. In one he took justice upon himself. In the other he supported those who had to enforce the laws, not write them.

As I drove, I continued to look for Wharf, thinking "Wharf, Wharf, Wharf, where are you?" The surf shop we'd visited was north of Kaanapali. At the intersection of Honoapiilani Highway and Front Street, right where the Chart House used to be, I swung my truck to the right to check Mala Wharf. Maybe he'd gone to his namesake. The quick turn jarred Liebe awake. I decided to take advantage of her disorientation.

"If you've got nothing going with Mangas, what's up with you and Nigel?" The Englishman remained a "person of interest" on my list, despite Ho's assurance to the contrary.

"No future there," she said, disappointment evident in her voice.

"Why not?"

"He thinks I have freckles."

I didn't look at her. I knew she had freckles. It was the one feature we shared more than the other sisters. I also knew she chose not to believe she had freckles because she finds them "creepy"—an opinion I find disturbing, considering my similar plight.

"Um, Liebe... does he like freckles?"

"Well, duh." She rolled her eyes. "I just don't want someone to look at me and see ... those," she said, waving her hands around and toward my face.

"He's seen you with practically no hair and he likes how you look."

"Sure, but the hair will grow back, eventually."

"He's seen you in a swimsuit. Most women think that's the worst."

"Oh he's seen me in less than a swimsuit," she said, nodding in the affirmative.

I gulped. "Then he's seen you without boobs."

She nodded.

"Some women," I said, distancing myself from the statement, "... might think that's more difficult to show a man than her freckles."

"Oh, sure, but I know I don't have boobs anymore, other than this." She lifted out her lone prosthetic. "But, I don't have freckles. So I don't know why he'd say he likes them. He might as well say he likes ... " She seemed to search in her mind for an equally ludicrous attribute. "... horns."

I pulled into the Mala Wharf boat launch parking lot. It was a good time to change the subject.

"Colley had a commercial permit for Kaanapali. I wonder what he was doing at Mala Wharf," I said, thinking of how Wharf got his name. I still preferred the Klingon version.

"Nigel said he picked up passengers here."

"That's crazy. The old wharf's too decrepit, and the launch and dock are only for those with Mala Wharf permits." We had parked where we could see the old wharf. There were a handful of surfers working a left hand reef break. We watched each of them find a wave from the line-up.

Liebe spoke first. "Ready?"

I looked at my watch. It was a quarter to one. I was supposed to be back at work. I looked back at the break. There was a slight northeasterly offshore wind and a long groundswell. I'd heard this was a capricious break. It seemed on its best behavior. "I read that there were lots of urchins here." Maybe I could dissuade Liebe.

"Sharks, too" she added.

"Somebody told me the locals get nasty here." I thought this would do it for her. They called all non-locals *kooks*. It didn't mean wacky like I'd first thought. It translated to "shit" in Hawaiian.

"Good enough for me," she nodded. "Let's go."

She had the new boards out and was waxing hers in less time that it took me to justify surfing during work hours. I'd work late tonight. There was a cruise ship arriving in the afternoon, and chances were there would be problems I'd need to handle. There always were. I grabbed my suit and ran over to the public restrooms to change. I wondered why Mala warranted public restrooms and Lahaina didn't. I totally lost any thoughts of Colley, and sadly, Wharf for that matter. By the time I got back to the truck, Liebe had my board ready for me. We walked down one of the launch ramps, paddled out through the channel to avoid the spiny reef dwellers, and got into the line-up.

And there we sat on our mid-sized boards, while the old farts on their long boards snaked us on wave after wave, making catcalls and high-fiving each other as they paddled back into the line-up after each ride. We'd made a tactical and technical error. Our boards weren't suited to the waves at hand. The break was just too fast and jacked up for us to catch. And wiping out on a pincushion was another limiting factor in our desire to "just give it a try," as the reef was a scant foot beneath our boards. As it was, we kept our feet kicked up to keep from getting pricked while we sat on our boards and watched the old guys get waves. One had on a floppy hat and every time he got a wave it rode up in the air above his head, and he looked like Yosemite Sam.

"Bad call." I said to Liebe, by way of giving up.

"Could be worse," she said.

"Yeah? How?"

Life is funny. Not ha-ha funny, but more like "If you're going to cry, I'll give you something to cry about," funny.

"You could be a turtle," Liebe said, pointing at a turtle on the surface, not fifty feet from us.

I glanced to where she pointed. The Green Sea turtle was exhibiting strange behavior. It looked like it wanted to walk on water. When I turned back to Liebe, she was paddling like mad toward the rock jetty that protects the boat ramps and piers from the ocean. She was waving me toward her, but I couldn't quite hear what she was saying. The damn hearing aid was on the fritz again. Guess they weren't really meant for saltwater. Then she took one hand and put it on her head wiggling her fingers in the air with her thumb pointed toward the back of head. It was the international symbol for shark.

I looked back toward the turtle. It looked like about a two-hundred-pounder. I could tell because it was held above the surface, being shaken like a dog toy, in the mouth of what had to be a fifteen-foot tiger shark. Had I had the presence of mind, I would have wet myself right then. Instead I gulped a lung-full of water over the tip of my board and spun it around to paddle after Liebe. It felt like I was paddling in syrup—cold, sticky syrup. I didn't want my hands and feet in the water, but I didn't want to stay where I was either.

People were starting to climb out onto the rocks. I guess we weren't the first to see the shark.

As a compromise, I crossed my legs at my ankles and held them above my knees. I flung my hands and arms through the water in what I was sure looked like a cartoon character running in place. Every couple of strokes I'd look back for a telltale fin following me. Instead, I saw the turtle, now bloodied and dissected, floating on the surface. A swirl of whitewater and a huge splash were the only signs that its killer was near. I wondered if the blood would bring in other sharks. How long did that take? Was it like the Internet? A gazillion messages sent and received in a moment?

The people on the rocks were shouting and waving us in. I could see, if not hear, them offering encouragement with their words, while their faces betrayed them. They too, thought we were going to get chomped.

The other surfers who had been with us in the line-up had unceremoniously grabbed waves and surfed to shore, faster and safer, than Liebe and me. Ahead, I could see that Liebe was tiring. Up until this point in our surfing forays, we'd paddled to and from the beach in a rhythm that we both found comfortable, one she could sustain with the massive damage inflicted on her by the surgeons. Those wounds seemed to pale in comparison to the shark's incising potential.

In my core, I could feel malice in the water. Why didn't I feel it before? Perhaps my imagination was on overdrive, much like my hands, continuing to flail, while inch by inch bringing me closer to shore.

Suddenly the offshore wind was my enemy. It held me back, where before it had been my friend, lifting and holding each wave in place. How naïve I had been. We'd even scoffed about sharks. I'd been thinking of little white tips, lazing about the old wharf's pilings looking for snacks in the sand.

I felt my board bump. Oh my God, it was just like in *Jaws*. It was bumping me! I started screaming. Then I looked back—there was nothing behind me. I looked down. I'd hit a rock, an errant straggler meant for the jetty. The board tipped. I slipped into the water and stepped on an urchin. I screamed some more. People had clamored down to the water's edge, eager to help me up, yet not eager enough to wade in. I respected them for that. I scrambled up the rocks, putting nicks, gouges, and dings in my brand new board. I didn't care.

By the time Brita Beamer showed up, camera and journalist's notepad in hand, Liebe had used pliers to pull urchin spines from my right foot. We declined comment. As usual, Brita wore a skimpy skirt with paint-by-number matching ultra-high heels.

"You see the shark?" she asked.

We nodded.

She glanced at the bloody towel under my foot.

"You get bit?"

I shook my head. Liebe held up the pliers with a tiny chunk of bloody spine still stuck in there.

"Piss on that." Brita spat.

We both nodded.

"No really," she said. "You piss on the wound it'll counteract the effects of the toxin."

I gave her a look that I hoped said, "Buzz off."

"Really," she said, "The sea urchin is made of calcium carbonate. If you look at it under a microscope, its spine looks like Chinamen's hats stacked on top of each other. They're barbed all around."

I guess if you're Chinese you can say stuff about Chinamen's hats.

"So when the spine goes in, it's brittle and it breaks off immediately. It crumbles. It's like trying to grab hold of chalk."

Maybe that's why Liebe's attempt with the pliers had produced such poor results.

Brita continued her report. "What makes it painful is the exterior surface's protein sheathing. So there're two parts that are bad. The first's the obstruction, the second's the poison. If you open up the wound and can get a weak acid in there it will neutralize the calcium carbonate."

She looked like she was waiting for applause. Then she said, "Vinegar, hydrogen peroxide, or uric acid will do the job. What have you got on you?"

At this point I wasn't sure if I had any uric acid left in me. Between the shark and the urchin I might have released all my uric acid. She didn't wait for a response.

"Once the spine's dissolved, your body will metabolize the protein poison."

I felt hopeful for a moment.

"It takes a while, though," she added.

So much for hopeful, I thought.

"By the way, did you know your dog's in jail?"

Hopeful returned, but I knew better than to say anything she could use in an article. She'd tricked me ten ways from Tuesday already. So I just shook my head.

"They said some guy from Harbors Division dropped him off as a stray."

I looked at Liebe. We were thinking the same thing. Only she's the one that said it first.

"Mangas is a flaming asshole."

Brita smiled. I guess she got her quote after all.

Chapter Twenty-three

It was time for my conversation with Zhen. At the least, I needed to tell her about Wharf. At the most, I was hoping for some answers. I cloaked the visit under the auspices of Harbors Division business. I needed to see how they wanted to handle *Polu Ka'a*'s disposition. Sure, naming Colley's boat the Blue Bus was probably cute on some level, but keeping these Hawaiian words, along with their spellings and meanings, straight in my head was getting tough.

First, I dropped Liebe off at Baby Beach where my parents said they'd be sunbathing. She was going to take them for a late lunch at Kimo's. I was jealous. Kimo's grilled tuna sandwich with Thousand Island dressing was about my all-time favorite food in the world. Well, after lobster, raspberries, and chilled lemon soufflé—not together—I guess the sandwich was my favorite grilled food. And if I could follow it with their mud pie, well, it would be a good day. Of course, it didn't really matter, since I wasn't getting any. Not getting any seemed to be the story of my life at this point. Instead, I stopped at my office and picked up the necessary paperwork to make Zhen the person responsible for Colley's boat.

Again, driving through Lahaina was a pain. The traffic putted along like a parade without a band. I briefly thought of diving into the harbor for the money-filled gear bag and taking it directly to Zhen's. However, the idea of further damaging my ears on top of the still healing urchin spine wounds seemed like just one too many pains to inflict on myself. Besides, I got the feeling that Yake wanted to be the hero on this one. No point in confusing the issues. I checked the file to make sure I had the correct address and headed for Zhen's house on the hill above Puamana Park.

Funny that she lived so near to Mele but didn't let her see Momi at home.

As I drove up the hill, I was surprised to see papaya groves in many of the yards. These houses looked like they were each on about two acre lots. I guessed by having "orchards" there was some agricultural tax break on the land. I'd heard the billionaires were pushing the millionaires out of town. Perhaps this was how the lowly millionaires survived.

I pulled my truck into a long paved drive. The house, a two-story hacienda, seemed to enjoy its perch. The view across the Au Au Channel to Lanai took my breath away. A halo of clouds clung to the highest point of the pineapple island. I wanted to get over there to explore at some point. Today wasn't the day. I walked to the massive *koa* wood door and pushed the doorbell button. "What's New Pussycat?" chimed through the courtyard.

Zhen answered the door wearing an iridescent mango-striped sari tied around her chest over deep green tights with Pepto Bismo-colored ballet slippers. Her hair was held back in a jeweled clip. She wore no makeup, but she looked lovely. Relaxed even and… happy. She held a fat Siamese cat in her arms like a baby, making little rocking motions. There was little small talk. Maybe she remembered me twisting her arm at the harbor. Maybe she was thinking her own thoughts.

I followed her through a horseshoe-shaped courtyard and into the main part of the house. At the door to the entry, I slipped off my shoes. It is considered poor form to enter a Hawaiian home while wearing shoes. Red Mexican Saltillo tile floors extended from the entry into the kitchen, dining, and living rooms. They were cool on my feet. They must have cost a fortune. I tried not to limp.

Zhen pulled a chair out for me at the dining table. I accepted her offer of ice water. She put down the cat while she prepared our drinks. I scanned the living room. There were cardboard T-shirt boxes stacked in the corner. It looked like she'd been packing. There was another cat on top of one. It looked like a Manx.

"Are you moving?" I asked as she placed a tall glass with a blue rim in front of me.

"No, why?" She fiddled with a tray of glass beads on the table. In fact, trays of beads were on many of the tables. I guessed she designed jewelry wherever she sat. She moved a fat black and white cat aside so she could put down her drink. It looked like it had just eaten a basketball. It was the Anaconda of cats.

"The boxes," I said by reference.

"Oh, no, those are ... " she paused. "I'm packing Colley's things."

"So soon?"

She smiled, but it wasn't a happy smile. She stroked the furball.

"How long since you've loved him?"

"What year is it?" She laughed.

The cat looked at Zhen as though it were assessing how full it would get by eating her.

"What?" I asked, thinking I'd heard her wrong.

She didn't answer for a moment.

The cat seemed put-off by her caftan, like it might have to bite off more than it could chew. Then it eye-balled me. I gave it a look that said I'd put up a fight. It started licking its behind.

Zhen regrouped. "We've been together since Konala died. Take that year, subtract this year, and whatever's left is how long I haven't loved him."

Even a dim bulb like me, who didn't know the square root of a gazillion or my times tables past ten, could figure the math on this one. She'd never loved him. I said as much.

"Well, that's not really true." She fiddled with organizing some beads by color. "I loved him at first." She tilted her head back and shut her eyes. "I loved him because he seemed to love me. I loved him because I hated myself so much that I hoped he loved me. That was about the last hope I had."

When she opened her eyes, they were welling up.

"I'm sorry," I said.

"I loved him because I thought he was 'the one'. You know; the one who could look into my soul and see something good, someone special, something… worthwhile." She shook her head. "But it turns out you need to reflect that back to a man. I didn't understand. I didn't know how to fake that look of complete trust and adoration. I screwed up. He found it somewhere else."

Zhen started lining the beads up in rows. It seemed that just organizing by colors wasn't enough, now they needed to be arranged by size too, largest to smallest. Heaven forbid those crazy beads be out of order while you talk about the man you'd lived with but not loved for seven years.

"Who do you think killed him?" I asked.

"He did."

"Who?"

"Colley," she said, as though I was slow. "Colley killed himself. It didn't surprise me. He'd been depressed."

"Zhen?"

She looked up from bead sorting and right into my eyes. I could see what she was talking about. I saw a glimpse of her soul. It was tragic.

The cat walked over and lapped a drink from my glass, perhaps to get the nasty taste out of its mouth. I hadn't been that thirsty anyway. It gave me a look that said, "Touché," and skittered away to wherever cats go once they defile a drink.

"Zhen, he drowned."

"You have to admit. That takes a lot of effort, but if anyone could do it, he could." She nodded. Then she slid open a window behind her. This prompted a cat race. The basketball could barely squeeze through.

"People don't commit suicide by drowning," I said, "At least not without jumping off a bridge or something. Zhen, he was hit in the head, knocked into the water unconscious, and he drowned." I paused. "Colley was murdered."

She looked at me again. This time the shutters were closed. It scared me, but not enough.

"Did you kill him?" I had to ask.

She shook her head. "Why would I kill him? I told you. I didn't even love him."

Somehow that made sense. Behind her, through the window, I watched the three cats tripping in a huge patch of what had to be catnip. They were high as kites and twice as capricious—jumping, biting, clawing and generally beating the bejeebers out of what had to be their imaginary friends. They reminded me of the Shar-Pei.

Zhen paused from sorting beads for a moment and signed the papers transferring the boat into her name.

I slipped on my shoes and walked out.

My mind gave a little jolt as I realized there were days I still felt like killing Snake. I hoped that didn't mean I still loved him. The little tripped-out twelve-year-old twerp in my head danced around for a minute singing the K-I-S-S-I-N-G song. I told her to shut up. I'd already had love—I thought—and marriage. Thank goodness there hadn't been a baby carriage in the picture or I would have killed him.

He'd had too many secrets. It seemed like he still did. Seeing him in Koni's room at the hospital was beyond weird. Some people would call it a coincidence. Suffice to say I'm not one of them. Oh, no, he was up to something. As soon as I solved Colley's murder I was going to find out what Snake was doing on Maui. Then I'd send him packing.

My cell phone rang. I checked the caller ID. It was Koni. The 'tween in my head screamed, "I'll get it!" I knew better than to let her answer the phone. She always answers in a happy sing-song voice. "Hello-o!" she said. She's fast, too, faster than my middle-aged me.

"Hey, Aloha! You sound great." Koni apparently liked the 'tween me. What a shock.

I mentally punched her and grabbed the phone. "Hi, Koni. You outta the hospital yet?" *Keep it light. Keep it light. Keep it light.*

"No, I'm ... um ... " he stumbled for words. "I can't talk right now. Can I call you back?"

Before I could answer, he hung up. My 'tween, kidney-punched me, I guess we were even.

As I drove away, I realized I hadn't told Zhen about Wharf. Of course, she hadn't asked. I stopped at the bottom of the hill and turned around. Despite my violent inner dialogue and penchant for surfing during work, I really am a decent person. Step. Limp. Step. Limp. I hobbled to the gate and through the courtyard to the door. Again, an instrumental version of Englebert's hit echoed through the yard.

This time Momi answered the door.

I signed "hi." She signed back. That was pretty much my whole sign language vocabulary. Well, other than making little pointy horns with my thumb and pinky, followed by a flick of all digits. I didn't think it was appropriate to sign "bullshit" to a kid. Instead I said, "IS YOUR MOM HOME?" in a really loud voice, moving my mouth too much for each word.

She rolled her eyes.

Maybe that was *her* version of B.S. She signaled me to follow her into the house. Zhen was on the floor picking up beads. They were everywhere. I'd like to say it looked like she'd dropped some, but I'd be lying. It looked like she'd swept them off the table in a rage.

"What?" she cried.

The Zhen I'd met at the docks, the one with the pokey finger and bad attitude was back. I wasn't sure which persona was better or worse. It didn't matter.

"I need to talk to you about ... " I switched to a whisper and shot a glance at Momi " ... Wharf."

"She's deaf, not dumb. You don't need to whisper." Zhen signed Momi to leave the room.

"Wharf's in jail." No point it getting into the details I figured. Deliver the message. Take a hike.

"You do that?"

"No!" I said, shocked at the accusation. "I love that dog. I'd keep him if you'd let me." Oops. I might have said too much. No wonder I sucked at poker. If I had two aces, I'd always smile like I had two aces. If I had three aces, well, I'd do a little chair dance of happiness. This dog was like having four aces.

"I'd let you have him except for Momi." Zhen said, casually, as though he was a disposable part of the family. "How'd you find out he was at the pound?" She asked, figuring out what I meant by doggy jail.

"I heard someone from the Harbors Division dropped him off there." Might as well tell her that much, no point in busting Mangas.

"Only you, Mangas and Yake work on this side," she said.

I nodded.

"It must've been Mangas. Max would've known to bring him home."

"Max?" I said, surprised to find her on a first name basis with my boss.

"Max is a family friend," she said. "He and Dan knew each other from the mainland." By way of explanation she added, "Same hometown."

Dan? I puzzled. Oh, right, that was Colley's first name. "They stayed in touch?"

Zhen grabbed a broom from the pantry and slowly swept up beads. "Dan idolized Max, especially his financial security. He would have done anything to take care of Momi and me the way Max takes care of his family."

Was this the same Dan Colley who started fights with just about everyone he met? The guy who the nanny had said was slobbery?

"He must have worked hard," I said, of Dan, not Max. I knew better on that one.

Zhen rolled her eyes. I guess I knew where Momi had picked up the gesture. "He wanted money, but he wouldn't work for it. He hired all the dirty work done." Then she added, "You don't know what it's like to have a rich friend when you're not rich."

I looked around the house. They seemed rich enough to me. How much money do you need?

"So was money a problem?"

"Yes and no." She kept sweeping. Swish, clatter, swish, the beads danced away laughing. She didn't seem to notice. "He was all about grand gestures, being the big shot. He wanted to be 'The Hero'.

"Was he?" I asked.

She didn't seem to mind the questions, although she ignored the last one.

Her eyes welled and a tear dripped along the side of her face and off her chin onto the tile. "It doesn't have to be all about me," she said. "Just sometimes, I'd like it not to be all about him."

It seemed as though, even in death, Colley held everyone's attention. Poor Zhen, she was an underdog with a complex. As I left, I realized I'd fallen for her victim persona again. She was that good.

Chapter Twenty-Four

"Sure, I take advantage of people, but at least I'm honest about it." Mangas said, with what he seemed to think was his boyish look. He was again in my office preparing to defile the bathroom. It was the second time today. I'd also been turning down cruise ship guests at what seemed like every eight minutes, which roughly corresponded to my attention span.

"Would you at least lift the lid and flush?" I muttered, remembering the mess he'd left the last time he'd used *my* facilities. He left it like the splash zone at Sea World. Forget the Harbors Division, this office was officially *mine* at this point. I wasn't in the mood for cleaning after a Mangas visit.

"In that order?" he smirked.

Although he found himself charming, I did not. If he took off his duty belt I'd grab the gun and give him something to cry about. I'd already sat in tinkle once. I wouldn't do it again. I gave him a hard stare.

He took his duty belt with him into the John. I think he got my message.

I couldn't bear to hear the sounds that usually accompanied his visit, so I turned down my hearing aid. Mangas did more oohing and aahing over a whiz than a crowd watching aerials at a fireworks display.

In blessed silence I refocused on my job. I'd made this the day I would reorganize the entire filing system, both for myself and for my successor, since my interactions with Yake were getting bleaker by the day. Again, I was knee-deep in paperwork, trying to figure out Junior Pololi's filing system. He had things like parking permits filed under "C" for car. I found the mileage trip logs for my truck filed under "T". Was it trip or truck? I looked and saw the file labeled tax deductions. Interesting, I thought. How'd he manage to deduct something that was a state expense?

So basically, I really was knee-deep in files. They were stacked everywhere. When someone grabbed my shoulder I knocked over the tallest pile, almost leaving a puddle on my chair.

"DAD!" I gave a little scream, toning it down in time to say, "Mom!"

Ike gave her a little punch in the shoulder. "Told you we could scare the piss out of her," he laughed. Then he started picking up the stack of files I'd toppled.

Good times, Dad, I thought. There's not much funnier than scaring your daughter. How about faking a heart attack now? That would really be a hoot. I looked at my mom. She was laughing too, but it didn't seem sincere. She deserved a medal for putting up with him sometimes.

"Where's Liebe?" I asked, thinking I could deflect attention away from myself as I turned up my hearing aid.

"With that pirate," Mom said. "I think he's kind of sexy, what with no underwear and all."

Dad growled. "You won't let me go commando. How come it's okay for the pirate?"

Where were they getting this "pirate" business? Nigel wasn't a pirate. Then I thought about it some. That accent of his was a pretty good Johnny Depp impersonation. Hmm…

"'Cause you're not…," my mom paused.

As she searched for the right word, my mind began mentally filling in the blank…young, good-looking, able to fulfill every woman's fantasy. Of course, I thought to myself, none of those things defined Nigel either. Why did Mom think it was okay for him to flaunt convention *and* equipment.

"…shaved." She'd found a word I hadn't thought of, especially in regard to my dad. I felt queasy.

He looked up, gave her the same funky smile Mangas had given me earlier, and said, "You could shave me."

I was definitely going to hurl. I needed to Lysol my mind.

"Honey, I'm flushing," Mangas sang from the commode. Both my parents looked at me as if to ask, "Who's that?"

"Co-worker," I said.

"Darling, I'm putting the seat down so your delicate white hiney doesn't get da-amp." Then he did a big toot. "Oopsie, Dearest, I think you'll need a new air freshener." His voice had crept higher with each statement. He was speaking in a raspy falsetto when he opened the door. "You might want to buy some of that ultra-soft tissue next time. I'm feeling chafed." When he looked up and saw my parents his voice resumed its normal tone, "Uh … I can explain … " Then he didn't, he just gathered up his gear and busted it out of the office.

Ike and Eve pretended they didn't hear anything. I went along with them. Sometimes that's the best way to handle things. Besides, what I really wanted to know was what they were doing on Maui. They lived on Oahu. I knew I'd see them more when I'd moved back to Hawaii, I just didn't think it would be this week.

I needed a delicate way to ask. After I pondered it a moment I said, "Whatcha doin' here?" I didn't do delicate well.

"Brought you a present," Ike said.

"A little something to make you more comfortable here in the islands," Eve added. Then she did something I hadn't seen in awhile. It was two quick blinks and a slight smile. This look was one of her quirks. Until now I hadn't figured out what it meant. Then the dim little light bulb went on in my head. She was lying. Two blinks and a smile revealed Mom's "tell."

My dad rubbed his hands together and smiled. "I've been working on it for months."

I watched Mom. No response. Did this mean he was telling the truth?

"Don't you want to know what it is?" he asked.

I nodded.

"Well then ask him, Love." Mom smiled her little Mona Lisa smile. I didn't know what it meant. Maybe was just a smile.

I fell for Ike's tricks every time. "What is it?"

"If I told you it would ruin the surprise," he laughed and slapped his knee.

He wasn't going to need to fake a heart attack when I got done with him.

The sound of a loud engine rumbled past my office. I ignored it. Ike however, registered the noise. He tipped his huge bald head to my mom and said, "Gotta see a man about a horse." She seemed to get his drift. I on the other hand remained clueless. I didn't bother asking any more about the gift. They weren't known as great gift givers. One Christmas they gave my youngest sister, Viva, all their old kitchen utensils, boxed and wrapped with Santa paper. Later Viva described it as a box of tetanus. God knows what they had in store for me.

"Don't do anything I wouldn't do," I called after them, using one of Dad's favorite phrases. Mom turned and waved, smiled, and blinked twice.

I sat for a moment surrounded by my sea of paperwork. I was the good ship organization. I thought about that and decided even making myself a ship wouldn't turn the project into fun. A handful of the preteen surf grommets swaggered into the office. Five twelve-year olds wearing baggies, rash guards, and slippahs created a communal smell like a locker room. Maybe my nose was overcompensating for my hearing loss. Or maybe they just reeked.

"Shouldn't you be in school?"

"No, Brah. Holiday."

"What holiday?"

They ignored the question. "Gotta use the bat'room," the littlest one said. He was the one who'd been giving me the most trouble in the lineup. The one who'd called me Tutu.

"These aren't public restrooms." I don't know why I was hard-timing them, maybe because it looked like they were on their way to surf while I shuffled forms.

"Dude, he gotta go or he gonna 'splode."

They looked serious, especially the 'sploding kid.

"Nope, it's the rule."

"Junior let us use it."

"Junior's gone."

They got all shifty eyed and began scratching around in their pockets. Then they huddled and conferred. It was like watching stock traders on the floor of the exchange. The biggest one opened his palm and held out a handful of cash. "Four fifty-three," he said. "It's all we got."

"I don't want your money." I waved them off.

They huddled again. When he turned back he held a bigger wad. "Okay, ten bucks, but now we gotta skip McDonald's."

"Listen boys, I don't want your money." I saw the 'sploding kid grab his gut. "Go!" I said. He didn't even smile or say "thanks." He just bolted for the head. The other guys relaxed, scratching themselves and adjusting things. Boys.

"Why you no take money?" The big kid asked.

I might not have the wits to out-quiz my dad but I figured I could handle a twelve-year-old. "Why'd you offer me money?"

"'Cuz a dah Golden Rule."

I shook my head. Do onto others?

"Junior told us, 'He who got da gold, he make da rules.'"

Oh, *that* golden rule.

"You not so smart if you don't know the rules," he observed.

I didn't hear a flush, but the little kid with the bad gut swaggered out doing a fair Mangas impersonation.

"Did you flush?"

He shrugged.

"Go flush." I pointed at the bathroom.

He went back to the bathroom and I heard the toilet cycle. Phew!

When he shuffled out the little kid said something odd, "Boss go nuts, no money."

While I wondered if I'd ever understand the nuances of Pidgin, the boys rattled out. I decided it was time to walk the docks. This paperwork shuffling was a pain in the rump. Really. My butt hurt from sitting. I forwarded my office phone to my mobile, locked the door, and was assaulted by the heat. You couldn't fry an egg on the sidewalk, but you could definitely poach one, it was so steamy.

In just a few minutes I was missing my air-conditioned office. I also missed Wharf. I'd enjoyed having him with me on my harbor patrol. He knew everyone. He smelled stuff I wouldn't want to smell, but I envied the stories they told him. I had the feeling he knew more than I did when we walked. Three slips up, I saw the *Awiwi*'s crew getting ready for a charter. Nigel carried cases of soda on board, his arms loaded in a way that he couldn't see me as he watched his footing. He chattered with the other crew as he worked.

I leaned against the loading ramp of the glass bottom boat and turned up my hearing aid. I could hear my heart going thump, thump, thump. I could also hear Nigel directing his crew on their various activities—without an accent.

I walked over. "Hey Nigel," I waved.

"Aloha!" He smiled.

"You seem to be missing something."

He patted his pockets, checked for his sunglasses hanging on his back attached to a braided nylon cord around his neck, and then looked at me.

"Your accent," I said, "It's missing."

He pursed his lips, smiled, and blinked. "Ah, that."

"Yeah, that."

"Here's the deal," he crossed his arms, tilted his head back and looked to the sky, as though his thoughts might be written on its infinite screen. "You had to know I wasn't really British, since you have to be a U.S. citizen to have a Coast Guard license."

I guess I'd been a little slow on the uptake. I did know that, I just hadn't been thinking. It made me wonder what other obvious clues I'd missed. I mean, this was just about a funny accent, but what had I missed about other people, other things. Between my hearing loss, the new job, new home and new life, I was not as sharp as normal.

"How about we keep this between us, just for a couple days?" Nigel wasn't looking at me as he spoke. Instead, he watched something over my shoulder. Then he frowned and shook his head.

I ignored his denial and said, "Why would you do it?"

Nigel yelled, "Duck!" I felt air swish past my ear. I shivered. Then, he shoved me so hard I tripped on the wood bulwark and toppled hearing aid first into the harbor. Yes, I had fallen for my sister's boyfriend—in the worst way.

Chapter Twenty-Five

"Dude! Why'd you knock me into the harbor?" I sputtered as I doggy-paddled to the dock, thinking an apology was in order.

"Sorry, what's-her-name looked like she was going to hit you."

"So *you* pushed me?" I struggled to keep my head above water. My shoes were a little heavy but I didn't want to kick them off. They were new and I'd paid full price.

"No, I was trying to push you away so she wouldn't hit you."

I rolled my eyes.

"Really," he said. "She looked like she was going to clean your clock."

I looked up at the dock. I couldn't see any what's-her-name. Why would he push me? I tried to find a handhold to climb back up on the bulkhead.

"Chips and ticks," Nigel said, as he grabbed my wrist first, then the belt loops on my shorts, as he heaved me up onto the dock. I was grateful, since from my vantage below in the water I had again—inadvertently—peeked up his shorts where his equipment dangled. I felt squeamish. The guy really needed to opt for undies. Granted I hadn't seen much male anatomy in my personal life lately. If lately is defined in years rather than days, but still ... ew.

"Chips and ticks?" I repeated. With my hearing aid again waterlogged, the words were a little fuzzy.

He shook his head.

I swiped some eel grass off my face and then spit a couple times. Something about Lahaina Harbor water gave me the oogies. I'd seen too many fuel, bilge, and head pumping "errors". Every vessel that used the harbor had had some spillage at one time or another. A crew person had pumped the bilge. A customer leaned against the sewage discharge button. The fuel nozzle had stuck in the on position. I halfway expected to see three-eyed fish every time I looked in the water. Mostly, I hadn't seen any fish at all.

I spit again while I rattled my head like a soggy dog.

"No," he yelled, "Tips and chicks. I did it for chicks and tips."

I heard him this time. Of course, so did every one else in the harbor. For a moment it was like E.F. Hutton had spoken. Everyone was silent, then they looked away. I hoped he hadn't planned on keeping it a secret.

We both lowered the volume. "You faked an accent so you could hit on tourists?"

"Du-ude, have you seen how they go for Johnny Depp in *Pirates*? And he acts gay!"

"Nigel, that's Johnny Depp. He's hot. It's not the accent."

"Yeah, but he's got bad teeth."

Yikes! I didn't want to have the teeth discussion. I had to change the subject quick, quick, quick, to something safe. "I'll bet he doesn't shave his ... " Oh my God, that wasn't safe. That was unsafe. Think of something. Fast. " ... head." I smiled and blinked twice.

Nigel barrel laughed then paused. "Are you going to repeat all this to Liebe?"

I shrugged.

"Do we have to have this talk right here?" He scanned the harbor.

I shook my head and followed his gaze. I still didn't see the mystery woman he had claimed was trying to hit me. "I could use a towel. Want to talk in my office?"

"No, too much bad mojo there," he said. "How about on the boat? I've got tons of towels."

I don't know why, but I had no fear of Nigel. I followed him onto the boat thinking about the bad mojo in my office. It did seem like there'd been some bad vibes there lately. Of course, some of that could be attributed to Mangas' stops. But really, it wasn't that. There was Colley's death and Zhen's crazy behavior. There was the constant hassle over the bathrooms, the Shar-pei, the weird little surfer kids, the TSA, and my truck break-in. That was just the stuff I'd seen this week. What would happen next week?

Nigel handed me a towel. I popped out my hearing aid. I guessed I'd need to see Darcy again. It would give me a chance to clear Liebe's name and reputation. Well, as much as possible. In the meantime, I'd rely on my good ear.

"Okay, so you've been faking an English accent to get dates. What about the tips?"

"You know how people say, 'It's not about the money'?"

I nodded.

"Well, in my opinion, it's always about the money."

I agreed, but I didn't get his point.

"You know what it's like to live here. It's not cheap. That's why everybody has two jobs." He looked at me as though he just remembered I only had the one job. The word 'slacker' hung in the air, unspoken. "Well, most people work two gigs." Then he mumbled something about, "or do something else to make a buck."

Somehow I felt inadequate. *Focus, focus, focus.* "It's about the money?"

"Well, yeah, we figured out that the whole pirate-accent-thing loosened up the wallets. We made so much in tips we didn't have to work the extra job."

"But that's not all, right?" Nigel was still all shifty-eyed. "There's something else you're hiding from Liebe."

I reasoned there was mandatory drug testing to keep a captain's license, so it wasn't drugs. There was a background check for the licensing, so he probably didn't have a prison record. Maybe he had a wife. Or maybe there was more swish in this buckle than swash. Maybe he had a boyfriend and Liebe was just a cover. Of course, nobody but politicians hid being gay anymore.

"I think she's special." He fumbled around tidying up the wheelhouse. "I mean, there are lots of special gals out there. Hey, I love women." He shrugged, then, looked out the cabin window as we heard a deep engine noise rumbling from near the banyan tree.

I guess that answered the gay question, but the wife/girlfriend announcement seemed imminent.

"But Liebe's special." He looked me right in the eyes. "She's beautiful, smart, strong, funny ... " He made it seem like the list was endless as he threw up his hands.

"And ... " I prompted him. The rumbling was getting louder. I was afraid I wouldn't hear his answer.

"And I don't want to tell her that I've got ... "

I'd leaned forward, poised on the edge of the seat. Then a huge boom rocked the boat. We both ducked. I don't know why. I guess if you're being shot at, ducking is instinctive, but probably too late. We crawled out of the cabin and glanced around the harbor. It seemed like everyone else had done the same thing. Other people peered from behind stanchions and scrambled up off the deck looking for the boom's source. In hindsight it hadn't sounded like a gun. And in fact, the rumbling had stopped.

Nigel got a far away look in this eye. His forehead furrowed. He glanced at me with one brow cocked. Was this an unspoken question? I mean, I was still waiting for the rest of his sentence.

"What?"

"You tell me. They're your parents."

I was *so* confused. He didn't want to tell Liebe about our parents? Too late, I think she already knew.

The rumble started again, with another loud boom. This time he didn't flinch. He just pointed down the street to where my parents sat in what looked like Snake's old Mustang convertible. It was factory black. Even then he'd gone for the dark side. What it lacked in color he had made up for in chrome. To say he'd tricked it out was a bit of an understatement. He'd worked on it whenever he hadn't been working on me. Sometimes he'd done both.

For just a moment, I was lost in reverie. Man, if that car could talk. Then I realized it had just spoken. My parents had chugged to a stop in front of my office. Nigel and I walked toward them together, as thought drawn by some magnetic force. I didn't think chrome carried a charge. Apparently I was wrong.

Nigel stroked his hand down the old polished paint. "Sixty-nine?" he asked my father.

"You're not really my type," Ike deadpanned.

Nigel looked like he might have choked on his own vomit right then. Even under his perma-tan he blushed.

"Dad!" People say there is a time and a place for everything, but I couldn't think of one for this conversation.

Ike gave me his best innocent look. "Lighten up, Aloha." Then he stage whispered to my mom, "*Your* daughter need to get a sense of humor."

I felt my face flush. Sometimes my dad thought he was funny, when really he was merely self amused, self-absorbed, or just plain selfish. I was about to tell him so.

"What do you think of your gift?"

I looked from him, to the car, to my mom. She smiled. Her sunglasses hid her eyes.

"This?" I waved my hand along the side of the car, like Vanna White in front of a vowel.

He shook his head and smiled. "I told you. I had to see a man about a horse. Get it, a Mustang?"

"It better have been a man and not a snake." I had that sinking feeling.

My mom piped up, "He's a good man, Aloha."

I don't know if she was referring to Dad or Snake. At this point, either would get an argument from me. I rubbed the tattoo on my back, it was supposed to be my constant reminder. Then I grabbed the edge of the convertible's door, my knuckles in tight, white contrast to the black finish. "Why would you buy a car from my ex-husband?"

"We wouldn't," my dad blustered, turning to my mom for support.

"Of course not, Aloha," she reassured me. "We wouldn't buy you a car. That wouldn't be fair to the other girls."

I shook my head. I didn't think they were getting my point. It wasn't about the car. It was about the man I'd been married to.

"No, Lolo," she said, using my "baby" name, "We leased it for you."

"But we got a really good deal," my dad beamed. "Snake's always been a great son-in-law.

Chapter Twenty-Six

"He.

"Is.

"Not.

"Your.

Son-in-law," I said.

Every once in a while I get so angry that I think my head is going to explode and fly around like a sputtering popped balloon. This was that moment. There was not enough duct tape in the world to hold it on. No amount of counting to ten or deep breathing would help. I clenched my teeth and ran my fingers through my hair. It felt sticky from sweat and harbor yuck. My clothes had stopped dripping but were still wet. My shoes made squishy noises as I shifted my weight from foot to foot. What next? I asked myself. What could possibly happen next? It was the wrong question to ask.

"What do you mean?"

Apparently, I'd actually spoken out loud.

I looked to the right and saw my questioner, Brita, putting her itty-bitty camera back into her teeny-tiny purse. To do so, she had to pull out a teensy-weensy notebook. I was so focused on the miniaturization of her accessories that I almost answered her next question.

"What's Snake's real name?"

My dad started to open his mouth. I shot him a look that said otherwise. "Mom, Dad, you remember Brita Beamer don't you? She works for the paper." Okay if that wasn't a big enough hint to keep quiet, nothing was. Then I wondered why I was protecting Snake.

Brita looked up at me all innocent-like. It was at complete odds with her outfit for the day. She looked like what I imagined Tokyo Rose looked like in the minds of the troops. Brita had on a red silk kimono-style dress covered with a dragon print. It had to be custom-made. It highlighted her tiny waist and non-existent hips in contrast to her planetary breasts. The dress' hem grazed her thighs about twelve inches above her knees. It had a high Fu Manchu collar piped in black satin, with a plunging keyhole neckline below. An innocent look it was not.

I think my head pulsed. "Why do you want to know?" I asked her. I figured I could throw her off guard.

Before she could answer, Nigel said, "Who's Snake?"

No. No. No. No. NO! Nigel needed to be quiet.

"Aloha's husband," my mom, ever helpful, explained.

"Not my husband." My voice rose. "He's my *ex*-husband."

"This is his car," Ike told Nigel.

Brita took notes.

"No, Honey, now it's Aloha's car." My mom corrected Dad.

"Nice ride," Nigel commented as he tilted his head and leaned back as though he was an artist.

"You better be talking about the car there, Fella." Ike glared at Nigel.

My head felt like it was about to spin off. Where was my duct tape?

Nigel shook his head. 'Nah, I'm not into Aloha. Liebe's where it's at." He was still staring at the car so he couldn't see my look that was intended to tell him to suck eggs.

I blew air toward my bangs. They hung in a clump. Brita kept scratching notes into her narrow journalist's tablet.

My dad said, "I don't know if she's into you. She said she was looking to expand her quiver this morning. Most of the time I don't understand what these girls are talking about, but I'm pretty sure that's another word for sex."

"They're not 'girls' anymore Ike." Mom piped in. "They're women. They're allowed to have sex at their age."

Jeez, she made it sound like we each had one foot in bed, the other on a banana peel.

"Maybe she said I made her quiver," Nigel said, filled with hope.

I rolled my eyes. "Dad, it's not another word for sex." Then I looked at Nigel. "Your quiver is what you call your collection of surf boards."

Dad looked at Brita. She nodded.

"Well, there you go." He shrugged.

"Where was she going to board shop?" I asked. And why did she go without me?

Dad looked at Mom. "Didn't she say she was going to beat some German hoochie until she got her quiver back?" He looked at Nigel for support. "Doesn't that sound like some kind of sex thing?"

"No, no, no. Don't tell me she's going to fight the *au pair.*" I put both hands on my head to hold it on. "I've got to stop her." Where were my keys? Where was my truck? Where would she go to find the *au pair*? Zhen's place? I looked at Nigel. "*You've* got to stop her!"

A shadow seemed to block the sun. "Too late, Brah. She in jail." Awiwi stood like a wall behind Brita. A hint of a smile tipped her mouth. I wanted to punch her. I thought she was my friend. Then she took an almost imperceptible step back and Awiwi got the same funny smile. Hmm...

"She told me to give you this." He held her last silicone boob between his thumb and forefinger. He gave it a little shake for emphasis. I guess if he'd been as close to Brita as I suspected, he was well familiar with silicone, though probably in the jumbo size. How fitting. I grabbed it. Then I looked at Awiwi.

"Why?" Was I supposed to glue it to my forehead and go as a Cyclops for Halloween? Maybe use it as an elbow rest while I drank myself senseless at the Pioneer Inn.

"She want you get more," he paused, "… only bigger."

"She want me bust her out jail too, Brah?" Oh, my, gosh, I was breaking into Pidgin.

"Wish *I* could order bigger ones," my dad muttered.

"Don't think you'd look good as a B-cup, Mate." Nigel reverted to his English accent.

"Not for me, for … " my dad thought he stopped himself just before he committed marital *hari kari*. One look at my mom and we all knew he should fall on the sword. Quick. She was beet red and she had her arms folded across her chest, her hands in tight fists.

He hopped out of the car and handed me the keys. "His phone number's on the key ring in case you have any questions about the car … or anything." My mom slid from the passenger seat and started walking toward the P.I. Dad did his old-man-jog after her, skin folds flapping with each step. We watched as he tried to put his arm around her waist. She slapped his hand away. He looked over his shoulder at us and shrugged, like "What's that about?" Then he made the little sign with his pinky finger and thumb out and his hand held up to his ear. He mouthed the words, "Call me." We all looked at each other. Only Brita seemed to bite. "What's his number?"

I knew better than to tell her. "Uh, I'll give it to you later."

"What's your ex's name?"

"Uh, I can't remember."

Awiwi coughed and I thought I heard him mutter "bullshit." I gave him my hard stare. Apparently, it didn't have much effect. He just laughed. I thought some more about what would happen when my head exploded. No doubt it would leave a mess on the concrete.

Brita was not to be deterred. "Have you ever heard the phrase Hungarian muscle hump?"

This time Awiwi choked.

Nigel looked at the prosthetic I still held in my palm and said, "Not with just one."

I tapped my ear. "I've got to go to the doctor." I wished I hadn't heard what I'd just heard.

Darcy's office was still the temperature of a meat locker. My clothes were not dripping wet anymore, just damp at the seams and hems. I sat in the exam room and shivered. My goose bumps were bigger than the prosthetic in my pocket.

"You again?" She stopped inside the door with her hands on her hips, shaking her head from side to side.

I nodded.

"You don't look like you want a lecture today."

"I just need a new hearing aid. Well, and I wanted to tell you that it wasn't Liebe with Mangas that your husband saw doing the nasty."

Darcy tinkered with my hearing aid. "Really?"

"Yeah, it was Zhen's nanny. She and Mangas are ... involved. She was throwing Liebe's prosthetics just to be mean."

Darcy chuckled and then tossed the hearing aid into the trash. "This is beyond help. Let's start fresh. I'll be right back."

I sat there thinking my own thoughts. How cold do you need to get before you're officially hypothermic? Would Koni be willing to return the favor and warm my lifeless body? I needed to call him back. I wondered why he'd called me earlier and then ended the call so quickly. I pulled my phone from my back pocket. I pushed the "On" button. Nothing happened. Looks like I'd need a new phone too. Aloud I said, "What next?"

Why do I keep asking myself that question?

Darcy walked back into the room. In just a few minutes she had me hearing in stereo. "By the way, I thought you could return these for me." She handed me Liebe's autographed breasts. They were the medium-sized ones. I rolled my eyes, thanked her, and headed to the door.

"Have you spoken with Koni yet?" Her words stopped me.

"No. Why?" I blushed.

"Uh, I can't say. But you need to talk to him. It's important."

"Why?"

"Just go find him. He needs to tell you something."

"Come on, Darcy," I begged, "Can't you at least give me a hint?"

She smiled. "Let's say it has something to do with the mouth-to-mouth you gave him the other night."

Yikes! I liked the sound of that. Kind of. I think.

Chapter Twenty-Seven

Once I replaced the cell phone, I called Koni. We agreed to meet for dinner at Kimo's. That gave me two hours to dive back into the harbor to retrieve the gear bag and race home to make myself lovely. I was counting on him making a pass at me. Of course, maybe he wanted to talk about Colley's death. Or maybe he wanted to discuss the Shar-Pei's welfare. Still, the woman in me who hadn't had a romantic interlude in too long was hoping for the best.

I drove back to my office and put my new hearing aid on the desk. Then I dug out my mask, fins and snorkel. I hadn't used them much since I'd renewed my surfing addiction. I didn't bother to change into my swimsuit, as it would mean having to switch back into the damp clothes once I was done. The silicone strap on my mask tended to slide down the back of my head, so I bunched up a pony tail to poke through the strap's opening. I was kind of like stapling on a hat.

My fins were sub-par but they fit and matched the mask and snorkel. I asked the TSA people to keep boats from docking where I was free diving and did a giant stride step off the dock. The water was almost clear enough to see the bottom but it was in shadow from the dock.

I got my bearings on the surface and looked through the mask's face plate at where I thought the gear bag had splashed. There were a few rocks in the muddy bottom just off the rip-rap bulkhead next to a shopping cart on its side embossed with a layer of silt. A barracuda shot after some bait fish in my left peripheral field of vision. I kicked around scanning and just couldn't seem to see the bag.

While I swam around on the surface, I did a series of breaths to increase my lung capacity for a dive. I figured a little depth wouldn't hurt my ears, so I bent into a jackknife, imagined myself a mermaid, and kicked down toward the bottom. I mentally counted my time underwater and estimated that I could stay under for almost a minute, including my exhalation as I came up.

After repeating the process four times I wanted to give up. On the off chance the bag had held air as it sunk, and somehow drifted toward the end of the loading dock, I checked the deeper water. Each time I tried to ignore the pain in my ear. It was probably wise that I didn't tell Darcy what I planned when I had seen her. Especially since so far I'd found the shopping cart, a power drill, an outboard motor, three car batteries, and a small plastic Shetland pony with troll hair, but no duffle bag stuffed with cash.

I heard the rumble of a diesel engine and prayed that the TSA screeners were keeping the tenders from chopping me into shark bait. I gave myself two more dives to find the bag. On the last I saw a shadow cross over me. It was too small to be a boat. As I looked up I could see a tri-fin surfboard skim across the surface. If I were a shark I wouldn't have mistaken it for a seal. I think sharks know they're biting people rather than the attacks being some kind of mistaken identity. Of course, that theory sounded better today than the day I was in the water with the sharks. *Funny how that works.*

I scrambled onto the pier and hot-footed it to the shower. I sloshed past the Shar-Pei as she doused herself and her board with fresh water. I checked to see if she'd gotten a board upgrade that looked like mine, but she was still using the same old stick I'd seen her ride before.

It seemed like she was having a normal conversation, only with herself. In a sing-song voice she said, "I told him no, no, no, absent Dad."

Then in another voice she growled, "Give me the stick." She glanced at my board.

"Ashes to asses," the original voice sang.

Then she started barking and growling as she stuffed an old towel into a filthy duffle bag. "Can't beat that with a stick."

So much for normal conversation, I thought.

"Dad's a tattletale, tattletale, tattletale." The first Layla chanted.

The other one looked at me and said, "I hear things."

The voice in my head said, "I'll bet you do." Rather than jump in and interrupt, I skittered into my office. Really, it would have been rude. I hurried through my work, and by the time I left to go home, she and her second self were gone.

As I walked down Front Street toward Kimo's, I fancied myself as a tourist. The sun edged toward a dip in the sea. The smell of moldering seaweed wafted over the seawall. Afternoon trade winds ruffled my clean hair as I walked along, my aqua halter sundress fluttering ala Marilyn Monroe. Lost in thought, I tripped on the uneven sidewalk.

The strappy sandals that Liebe had once said should have FM stenciled on the sole were not made for street walking. Or were they? They were designed to make women feel sexy. They say men are oblivious to shoes, but in the case of FMs, the message was subliminal, if not sublime.

Liebe had phoned me once Nigel had sprung her from the "hoosegow" saying she'd be home late. They were going to Mama's Fish House for dinner since she said she couldn't bear the "slop they served in the hole." Her two hours of incarceration had somehow morphed into her talking like a lifer. She'd also told me Nigel had said he wanted to "have a talk" with her. Neither of us had a clue what that was about. But somehow I felt it was important and tried to find out more information. Instead, Liebe had focused on my date with Koni. That was when she advised me to wear the FMs.

At Kimo's, the hostess behind the koa wood podium walked me to the table where Koni sat at a table for two, focused on the menu.

"Aloha," he stood and kissed me lightly on the cheek. "I'm so glad you could make it." He picked up a white *pikake* lei from the table and placed it over my head, his fingers adjusting it lightly while lifting my hair over it.

I just smiled, trying to look demure. I thought it was more mysterious than yelling, "Yahoo, I've finally got a date!"

A waitress arrived bedecked in a plumeria lei over a magenta one-piece with a tiny floral skirt that could double as a scarf, with a tray in one hand. "I hope it's okay. I already ordered you a Mai Tai," Koni said.

I knew I couldn't do the silent thing for long, so I said, "It's perfect, thank you." This was truly me on my best behavior. I took a sip, then tried the Mona Lisa smile again.

"Are you feeling okay?" his brows furrowed in concern.

Apparently my seductively mysterious smile needed some work. "I'm fine." I sipped my cocktail and closed my eyes. *Sweet mother of God, I love rum and pineapple juice.* Maybe I'd have a Chi Chi next. Rum and pineapple juice and coconut syrup blended with ice. *Bliss!*

"Aloha, you know you're not alone, right?"

I blinked back into the conversation.

Koni smiled. "You know, at moments like this I get the feeling you're completely self-contained. It's like you're so permanently pleased with yourself that you don't really need anyone else."

I stopped my happy thoughts. Had he been talking to Snake? That was the same kind of crap he used to say. "Where'd you hear that?" I said in my former military voice. It had been an effective tool in the past, though not so much when trying to get a guy in the sack.

Koni looked scared. I smiled. I still had it. Then I realized I'd just proven him correct. Or had I proven it to Snake? "Where *did* you hear that?"

This time I tried the question with a smile and a softer tone.

"That's it? You think you can add a smile and come across all sweet?" Koni laughed, no longer feigning fear. "You're the funniest woman I've ever met." He reached out and patted my hand. That's right, patted. Like a man would do to his grandmother, or the crazy woman next door, right before he called the dog catcher.

Good God Almighty, I was blowing this date! I furrowed my brow and stared at Koni. He was chuckling and reading the menu. Men! I had no idea how to hook them. I lacked the flirtation gene. I needed a special flirtation-handicapped parking place assigned just to me. I'd never get lucky at this rate. Didn't he notice the shoes? Those were supposed to be a big clue. I kicked one leg over the other and flopped my foot up and down provocatively. And what about the halter dress? Didn't he know there were things that desperately needed support? I considered the idea of a wardrobe malfunction. It seemed to work like gold for Liebe. I just didn't have the chutzpa it took to carry it off no matter how "self-contained" I seemed to some people. I kept flapping my crazy-tall strappy-heeled shoe in the air.

The waitress paused as she walked past and whispered, "The bathrooms are down that hall." Oh, for the love of God, my "provocative look" looked like incontinence. Perfect.

Koni closed his menu and looked up. "Do you know what you want?" Was he kidding? I knew exactly what I wanted. As I tried to think of the right verbiage, he said, "I've been trying to hold it back but there's something I've got for you." My foot stopped flopping and my stomach started. Yahoo! Let's skip dinner and go directly to dessert.

He reached into his pocket and pulled out his wallet. Was he reaching for a condom? Right here, right now? I looked around. The restaurant wasn't *that* crowded. And most everyone seemed to be looking at the sunset or a menu or the two guys playing Hawaiian music in the corner or the three tattooed and pony-tailed *mokes* in ball caps yahooing and shooting tequila at the bar. I swear it wouldn't take long for me, but I wasn't sure about him. I looked down the hall that led toward the bathrooms. Too public?

Beyond the hostess station, tourists shuffled down Front Street, some of them with children. No, this would never work. I shook my head and my foot started flopping again as I drummed my fingers against the table. Maybe the wallet was just to pay the bill.

He noticed my virtual seizure. "You look nervous, Aloha. Don't be, you're going to love it." Damn, he was confident. I liked it. I wrapped my lips around my straw and sucked up the Mai Tai like it was cold water on a hot day. The last slurp was straight dark rum. I felt it hit me as though I'd just stepped off a roller coaster. I slid my chair back, thinking we were leaving.

"Where are you going?" Koni seemed puzzled, still fondling his bi-fold.

I looked at it, then at him.

"This is not how I wanted to do this," he shook his head and pulled a guitar pick out of his wallet.

Kind of hard to argue with that logic. Personally, I thought I'd at least get a meal. Then I realized I was losing sight of my goal. Screw the meal. I had to be strong. I thought of phrases I'd heard in the Coast Guard. *Forge on. Eye on the ball. Mission first.* Of course, that last little metaphor made me digress and smile at the thought of missionary first. Kind of ironic, you know with Koni being Hawaiian, and me *haole,* and the history with the missionaries, and... I was doing it again. My crazed brain was off and running leaving my desperate body sitting on a chair in Kimo's. By the time I refocused, Koni was gone. I looked around. He had gone to join the two musicians. They announced his name and everyone clapped.

"I'd like to dedicate this song to my good friend, Aloha." He blew me a kiss. People smiled and stared. I smiled and waved back. Koni signaled me up to sit on a stool next to him. What the hell was happening? When I got there he said, "This woman is the reason I'm leaving the island tonight."

Everyone gasped and gave me dirty looks. I looked at him and said, "Just 'cause I wanted to have sex for the first time in three years?" Unfortunately, he'd just turned me on, well, turned on the mike he'd attached to my lei. As my voice blasted around the room, I knew it was the only lei in my future.

Then one of the tequila shooters yelled, "Hey, Aloha, I'll do ya." I squinted. Ugh. I thought that one tat looked familiar. He slammed down one shot glass, grabbed another, raised it to me and said, "It's been a long three years for me too." As Koni started to strum I damned Snake straight to Hell.

Chapter Twenty-Eight

"I'm so sorry," he said. I could still hear a trace of laughter in his voice even though the light was low and I couldn't see his face. I looked at my feet and shuffled them in the sand. I'd tossed the FMs over the rail at Kimo's when the music started. I'd been barefoot ever since.

"The song was beautiful," I said, trying to shift the focus off me. Hard to do when the song was about me, my actions and my name.

He took my hand. I stepped away. Someone above us on the beach yelled, "Don't pull away, we all know you want it."

I rolled my eyes and headed toward the water. We had walked from Kimo's all the way south to the Lahaina Shores property and had now come back as far as the harbor break wall. I might as well swim toward Lanai and hope for a quick death. The slow burn of embarrassment was too much for me.

"He's right. We all know you want it." Koni pulled me back from the water and kissed my forehead. Then he moved to my lips. I fought it. I swear I did... for several seconds. Maybe it was the Mai Tai, maybe the fact that I knew he was leaving. I don't know what. But the embarrassment faded away and something frantic replaced it.

Still, the part of me that was saying, "Yes, yes, yes!" had to fight the part that longed to lighten the mood. Guess who won? "Hey, you're a chaplain. You can't do this. Not here." I pushed him away.

He stepped forward and held my waist. Then he pushed my hair aside, nuzzled my neck, and said, "I quit." As he ran one hand across my bare back, I felt the calluses on his finger tips from years of playing guitar.

"What do you mean you quit?" I kissed his ear and ran my hand down his Rastafarian dreads. They were softer than I thought they'd be, like braided yarn with beads in a couple sections. I had to open my eyes and look. Those dreadlocks had always fascinated me. As I peered through the darkness, I realized I'd seen one of the beads before, but as an earring. It was distinctive. Where had I seen it? It wasn't even pretty. It looked like crack. I pulled back.

"How do you know Snake?"

Koni started to untie the halter dress strap around my neck. My hearing aid was working perfectly. I heard someone playing bongos in the Lahaina Banyan Court Park. They sounded like the beating of my heart. I didn't hear an answer to my question.

I scrambled across the rubble and up to the pavement along the harbor as I retied the bow on my dress.

"Aloha," Koni ran up behind me with a funky limp and whispered, "I'm not really in a good position to be walking in public." Yikes! I guess he *had* been in the moment. I stopped walking to let "things" relax.

"Sorry," I apologized, as I looked at the rocks next to the pavement. "Think about baseball, or your mom, or, or..." I shrugged. I didn't know what turned a guy off any more than I knew what turned him on. What kind of a loser was I anyway? I just wanted to get back to my office and get some *slippahs* on before I got tetanus, athlete's foot, or drug resistant staff from walking along the pavement barefoot. I wondered how Wharf tolerated having dirty feet all the time. I guess once you start greeting your pals with a good butt sniffing, you don't worry much about dirty feet.

"So tell me again why you quit the chaplaincy." That should cool his jets.

"Because I'm flying to the mainland tonight so we can record the new song. Then we're starting a tour to promote the new album."

"What new album? All you have is a song." I walked a few feet out onto the wooden boardwalk that went to the far side of the harbor. It was a minor detour.

"We've been writing music for years, just waiting for our break again. *Breath of Life* is it."

"How can this be happening so fast?"

"It's been in the works. I just needed a single. You gave it to me."

"When I gave you mouth-to-mouth you came up with a song? It's the craziest thing I've ever heard."

"Well, I'd already written the music. I was just waiting for the words. You, your name, you gave them to me when you resuscitated me." He cocked his brow. "You're my Muse."

Dang. I liked the sound of that. I think every woman wants to do a few things in her life: Christen a boat named after her, be someone's Muse, lose five pounds for no apparent reason. One down, two to go.

"So I booked five tickets and we'll be recording by morning."

"Five tickets? Who else is going?"

"Sandra, Tan, Zhen, and Momi."

"Zhen's going? I guess it's pretty convenient for her to have Colley gone."

Koni frowned and glanced at me. "You don't know everything."

Gee, ya think? "Still seems mighty handy."

"Well, it's not. By the way, Zhen asked if you'd dog-sit Wharf."

"Really? She's going to let me keep Wharf?" Praise all things wonderful! I couldn't have been happier. Then I realized I cared more about the dog than I did about Koni. Not in the same way at all, but still, not a good sign. Plus, he'd never answered my question about my ex-husband. That's when I realized I had no business making out with this guy on the beach or anywhere else. It was like Dr. Seuss might have said, "Not on the sand, not with the band. Not in a car, not under the stars. I will not boom-boom here or there. I will not boom-boom anywhere." Ah, the story of my life.

Then I reviewed his list of travel partners. "Sandra? Who's Sandra?"

"You know her. You met her at the luau and the Pioneer Inn." He had starting walking away, though without the funny limp that had hampered him minutes earlier.

"The 'ho that beat the ever-loving bejesus out of me? That one? I've still got maraschino cherry stains on my favorite shirt." I loved that shirt. It was made by Roxy and had a surfer girl screened on the chest. It was my emblem. At one point, I'd decided to quit wearing it because it's my favorite. Figure that out.

"Yeah, she was in the original band with Tan and me." He got all shifty-eyed.

"With, as in *with* you?" Don't ask me why I was acting all jealous when I didn't care. I guess I was still smarting from her smack down.

We'd reached my office. It was a quiet night on the dock. No cruise ship tenders, no night divers, no booze cruises bobbing in or out. Even the *Awiwi* had been tied up tight as a *ka lua* pig. My phone blinked a message I chose to ignore. I slipped into my spare sandals and walked back out of the office, Koni trailing me the entire way.

"Yeah."

"Yeah?" Yeah, what?

"Yeah, she was with me *with* me. Now she's not. But she's still with the band. She plays bass. Sorry about that. I should've warned you. She's a hellcat."

Then he did one of those smiles that you know means he's talking about in bed. What a hound. I can't believe I almost fell for it.

I grabbed my keys and headed for my truck. Where was my truck? I looked at my keys. Yes, I still had my truck key. I looked at my parking spot. It stayed empty. My truck didn't reappear. I looked up and down the street. No truck. Well, great. First my boards get stolen, and now my truck. What next? I smacked myself on the forehead. If there's one thing

I'd learned, it's to not ask, "What's next?"

A shriek tore through the silence. The hair on my arms jumped to attention. In the darkness I couldn't tell where it had come from. Was there someone in trouble on one of the boats on the opposite side of the harbor? Was it someone struggling in the water? I ran to the edge of the loading dock and scanned the water. With the island of Lanai as a dark backdrop, I had trouble finding the source. The sound of feet pounding down the wooden planks on the opposite boardwalk gave me a clue. Long barefoot strides slapped like a racing heartbeat away from us.

"Son-of-a-bitch!" I heard a male voice growl and the sound of him scrambling up onto the walkway. "I'm going to kill you, you —" He used the word that starts with a "C" and rhymes with runt. I hate that word. Then I heard him beating feet down the dock after his prey.

I stood there for a minute, trying to decide if it would be quicker to jump in, swim across the harbor entrance and climb back on the dock to chase them, or to run back around the paved side of the harbor and intercept them. Koni was a step in front of me. He took off down the loading dock.

We should have called the cops then and there. We didn't.

Instead we ran balls out, right up until I tripped over a hose and fell face first on the concrete. Koni turned, "Aloha, you okay?"

I took a second to assess the damage. I hurt everywhere. Nothing seemed broken. I rolled over on my back and nodded. I wanted to scream, but I didn't. Momi was my role model.

He grabbed my hand and pulled me to my feet. "Good girl. Lose the shoes and let's go." We took off. I no longer heard the other running feet. I hoped we hadn't missed them because of my fall.

Did I mention that everything hurt?

As we ran past the dinghy dock I thought of the night Nigel, Koni, and I had run that stupid dinghy out into the Roadstead. What were we thinking? I remembered giving Koni mouth-to-mouth and how excited I'd been to revive him. Well, and to be close to him. He had that magic something. He really was a shooting star. I knew it'd be a while before he came back to the islands. And that he'd never come back to me. I knew Sandra would prevail, even if he didn't know it yet.

Ahead, I could see the Dumpsters. I wondered if Layla had been asleep there while we had made out, just yards away from her on the beach. My question was answered as I saw her race pell-mell off the boardwalk. She stopped, looked both ways, didn't seem to see us, and ran to the Dumpster. We stopped. I could hear heavy footsteps rounding the corner toward us.

Layla screamed as she hung over the edge of the metal trash bin, her long legs flailing in the air as she chucked rubbish from her den. We could see her pursuer racing closer to what seemed an imminent attack. She must have found what she was looking for, since she hopped back onto the filth-stained pavement. When she turned around we saw that she held a gun. We ducked behind an electrical transformer and peered over the top. Her pursuer stopped when saw the gun, as well.

My boss, Max Yake, stood there gasping for air. He eased toward Layla, one hand behind his back.

Koni had his cell phone out punching numbers. I couldn't hear his whispers, but I hoped he'd called for help and not a pizza.

Then Max pulled a gun from a pancake holster behind his back.

"Put down your gun," he ordered her. "You don't want to get hurt."

The stink from the Dumpsters wafted over us. I don't know how she tolerated it all the time. It seemed she had bigger problems as Max crept toward her.

"We've got to do something." I whispered to Koni.

"I just did," he said.

"What?"

“I called for backup.”

Max edged closer to Layla.

“Stop,” she said with more clarity than I’d ever heard from her. Then she said, “Absent Dad” or “abscessed head”, or “obsessed Fred”. This made me think of Fred Flintstone, which made me think of Yogi and Boo-Boo, which brought me back to Yake. He was only twenty-feet from Layla. I couldn’t hear it, but I saw him chamber a round. Then he raised the gun and lined up his sights.

Koni still held my hand. I pried his fingers off and stood up. Yake saw me and turned with his gun. Layla shot him. Then she turned toward me.

Chapter Twenty-Nine

It had to be a .45. The BOOM-BOOM echoed in my ears and reminded me of the explosion that had blown my former boss into fish food, leaving me deaf and disabled. She had definitely stopped the threat, just like a cop would have done versus us military-types who focus on two to the chest and one to the head. *Pretty good shooting for a homeless chick.*

Since my last boss had been killed in the explosion that made me deaf, I couldn't help but think I was going through bosses kind of fast. A .45 caliber round does a lot of damage, not as much as C-4, but the results are the same. As my undereducated subordinate had said then, "He was D-E-D, dead."

Above the echoing booms I heard sirens. Layla heard them too. She lowered the gun.

I breathed. I guess I'd stopped when I had been in her sights.

Koni walked to her and took the weapon. They said a few words I couldn't hear and she sat down next to the Dumpster. Koni returned and handed me the huge Colt. "I'm not allowed to carry one." I guess he was still a chaplain at heart.

A Maui PD patrol unit skidded to a stop at the sidewalk. Awiwi swung out and stood behind the door with both hands on his service weapon pointed at low ready. Koni walked toward him. Awiwi lowered his pistol and grabbed his radio mike. An unmarked car slid in behind his. Ho got out and sauntered up to Koni and Awiwi. He looked at me holding the .45 between my thumb and forefinger and shook his head.

I did the same back to him.

He rubbed his hands over his face and walked over to Yake's body. As a courtesy he tried to find a pulse, but we all knew it was futile. Then he peeled a glove from his pocket and picked up Yake's gun.

An ambulance eased into position. Those same EMTs that had responded when I'd found Colley floating in the channel, tumbled from the rig like clowns out of a circus car. Clowns scare me and so do EMTs. You really have no idea what they're capable of.

They jogged up to Yake as soon as Ho waved them over. Yake didn't look like Boo-Boo anymore. He just looked empty. Like one of the huge balloons in the Macy's parade after it loses its air and lies on the ground deflated. It took them approximately one second to confirm that he was not a candidate for first aid, resuscitation, or anything but the end of the parade.

The paramedics left him and switched their attention to Layla. Her ass hung over the edge of the Dumpster, her torso hidden, and her legs kicking in the air like a decapitated chicken. In a minute she pulled out her dirty duffle bag, threw it toward Awiwi, and nodded. Then she resumed crazy mode. The EMTs backed away.

"Howzit?" Ho offered me the classic Hawaiian query.

I shook my head. What was there to say?

Ho walked toward me with his hand out. "Gimme da gun."

I held it out.

"Ike's not gonna be happy 'bout this."

Glad to hear it was all about Ike.

Other cops—in uniform and plain clothes—had shuffled onto the scene. Crime scene tape had miraculously appeared, strung from the Dumpster to the dock.

My truck pulled up. Mangas and the *au pair* got out.

Bastard!

I walked over and grabbed the keys from him. "Where did you get these?"

He ignored my question. "Hey, you should thank me. I found your crappy surfboard." He winked at his smirking girlfriend.

"Found my board? You didn't find my board." I pointed at the *au pair* as I tried to think of just the right word. "That little ... " I didn't want to look bad in front of the EMTs, Ho, Koni, or the gathering crowd of bystanders by using the foul language that came to mind in describing her, but I did anyway. " ... 'ho."

Ho gave me a glance, as the *au pair* balled up her fists.

Mangas waved me off and said, "Calm down" as he walked toward the Dumpster crime scene.

I followed him and ignored her. "Calm DOWN? No, I'm not going to calm down. You can't tell me to calm down!" I yelled.

As he walked past Koni he muttered, "Women."

Koni shook his head as warning. Mangas ignored him.

I grabbed Mangas by the arm and spun him around. "Don't you ever do that again!"

"What?" He raised his hands and shrugged with his little boy smile playing to the crowd of cops.

"Don't take my truck. Don't diminish me with your attitude. And don't run your little bimbo around on my dime. That's what." I pulled back my foot to give him a swift kick where it counted. Then I remembered that I didn't have on shoes. Probably best to skip the kick.

From behind me, the lanky blonde *au pair* screamed at Ho, "Arrest her wrinkly white cracker ass." Her German accent replaced with one from somewhere between Brooklyn and the Bronx. She marched over and poked me in the chest. "You and your no-tit-sister can keep your crappy boards. No body wants 'em. They're too damn old and beat up. Just like you."

I should have known the boards would come back once they didn't sell. It kind of bummed me out, but not as much as being called old. And I knew for a fact that my ass wasn't wrinkly. I pulled my elbow back to drop her just like I had Mangas.

Hearing her admission, Ho beat me to the punch as he clicked cuffs on her, faster than she could say "Oi," which she did when he shoved her up against the patrol car and read her her rights. Awiwi was reciting the same words to Layla, with far less force. She sat huddled in the back seat of his car, muttering to herself.

I paced in a circle, taking it all in. I would have laughed at the fact that Mangas had been taken in by a phony German accent—twice—were it not for the carnage of death, the shimmer of the moon on the water, the blood and filth on my knees, the bright lights on the patrol car and my ex-husband standing in the shadows of the banyan tree next to his Harley.

I walked toward him, stopping about ten feet away.

He shook his head and said, "Aloha, I'm sorry."

"Better late than never," I blurted. Then I asked, "For what?"

He just shook his head again, stepped forward and held me. Snot bubbled from my nose as I cried, my face crushed into his black leather vest. Too soon, he released me. A tap on my shoulder told me why.

"We'll need a statement." Ho had reverted to speaking without the Pidgin accent. I wondered why. I followed him back to the chaos surrounding the Dumpster. Yake's body was still there, oozing fluids onto the chipped concrete. Mangas was limping around rubbing his chest while chattering into his cell phone. I heard him say Yake was dead. I assumed he was talking to someone with the Harbors Division. Layla was still in the back of Awiwi's patrol car. Koni knelt outside its open door whispering to her. I hadn't a prayer of hearing what he said.

The questioning started, although Ho didn't ask me much. I told him what I had seen, without any editorializing. Then he opened the filthy duffle bag from the Dumpster. It was chock full of wet cash.

"You know where it came from?"

"I think it's from the cruise ships." I said.

"How do you know?"

I recalled seeing Yake at lunch with the cruise ship guys while I was at Cheeseburger In Paradise with Brita. I wondered if Brita had been following him.

I rolled my eyes. "I'm a good guesser."

"Don't be snippy," he cautioned me. "Just tell me what you *know*."

"What I know or what I think? I think it came from the cruise ships, but I don't *know* it."

"Tell me why." He wasn't taking notes or recording me. He just listened intently, the rest of the world closed out of his focus.

"I *think* Yake was taking payoffs to let more ships anchor off Lahaina. Well, that and skimming from the restroom construction fund."

"How'd she get the cash?" Ho nodded toward Layla.

"We found it on the water taxi. I think somebody dumped it in the harbor when we got back, figuring they could get it later. It's not like the money would melt."

"Who's we? You and your sister?" Ho squinted at me like I had lied to him.

"No, it was when Nigel, Koni and I went out to get Colley's boat during the Kona storm. I found it in the foc'sle."

"Did you all know it was there?"

Hmm... I had to think about that. I knew Koni hadn't seen it. He'd been out cold, at least until I gave him the breath of life. But I wasn't sure about Nigel. I told Ho as much.

"Why didn't you say something then?"

"I went to look for it the next day and it was gone. Then Yake told me to find it or he'd fire me. I need this job. Besides, at the time I hadn't figured out where it came from."

"So he's dead because you were worried about your job?"

Ho sure had a way of looking at things that somehow made me the bad guy.

"Hey, I wasn't the one out here shooting. I wasn't the one who hit Colley on the head and dumped him in the drink. In fact, I'm not the one who's been walking around asking questions right *after* somebody gets killed."

Ho frowned, "So you know who murdered Colley?"

"I think I know, but you should ask Layla. I'm sure she knows."

"You expect me to get a credible witness statement from a schizophrenic meth addict?"

"I'll ask her." Brita Beamer had popped up next to me, listening and taking notes. In a split second she minced to the patrol car. Ho scuttled after her, me in his wake.

Layla ended a solitary conversation with herself as we approached. She glanced at each of us and then at Yake's body, and said, "Obsessed Fred, abscessed head, wet bread, Yogi said, Boo-Boo's dead."

I looked at her and repeated, "Boo-Boo's dead." Recognition crossed her face and she nodded at me satisfied.

Ho looked like her words had verified his earlier statement that she was unreliable of not certifiable. I explained it to him.

"Yake looks like Boo-Boo." By further explanation I said, "From Jellystone Park. Colley looked like Fred Flinstone." I paused to confirm with Layla that I was on track. She nodded and I continued. "Colley was Yake's means of getting the money from the ship to the shore. According to the logs in my office, even when a cruise ship had its own tenders, Colley would make a couple trips between the dock and the ship. I think Colley tried for a bigger percentage to try to keep Zhen from going to the mainland, so Yake killed him over it. Colley was obsessed with money, but got whacked in the head with a *kiawe* branch. Look at Layla's foot. She's got an abscess, probably from a *kiawe* thorn."

I glanced at Yake, but I was thinking of Wharf. He had gone ballistic over the *kiawe* stick in the rocks near the boardwalk. I was willing to bet a milkshake that it was the weapon Yake had used to knock Colley out before he drowned.

Then I thought of Zhen. "Win-win situation for Zhen," I said. Ho, Brita, and Layla nodded in agreement. Maybe Zhen had been dallying with Tan all along. Who knew? Maybe everyone but me.

Again, I glanced around. Mangas stared at me from the other side of the patrol car, like he needed a couple thousand pounds of machinery to protect him.

"Pussy." Oops, I really hadn't meant to say *that* out loud.

"You wish," he countered like a fourth-grader.

"What!" I started around the car. He just didn't know when to shut up.

This time Awiwi stopped me from committing a felony. "We'll let that first one pass, but we can't just let you keep hitting him," he warned.

He was right. It wasn't that Mangas was a criminal. He was simply a serial womanizer and narcissistic lout who thought I was fishing in the same pond.

"You are *so* wrong," I said. As if to prove my point, Snake reappeared, stepped close and gave me the serious full-bodied kiss that I'd been looking for, though not in such a public setting. Before I could respond with more than a groan, he broke free and pulled his wallet from his hip pocket. Like most bikers, his was attached by a chain looped to his belt. He flipped it open, flashed it at Ho, and nodded toward Layla.

A communiqué passed between them that I could only imagine. We all watched in stunned silence as Snake released Layla from the handcuffs and retrieved her .45 from Awiwi's trunk. She walked over to his Harley, grabbed his spare helmet from the sissy-bar and waited.

He started to follow her, then turned back and said to Brita, "You understand?" She nodded, pulled three pages from her journalist's note-book and handed them to him. Then she pressed the little button on her digital camera that said "format". From past experience I knew this meant she had just permanently deleted all the photos from the evening. Every photo of Layla and Snake were gone, though the image of them chugging away on the Harley would remain in my mind forever.

Chapter Thirty

A month later I sat on my new surfboard out in the Lahaina Roadstead. I was on dawn patrol, the first one on the break, waiting for the sun to finish climbing the West Maui Mountains. A fleet of fourth-graders on short boards were paddling out to steal my serenity.

With Yake dead, the little surf groms and I had reached a tentative truce. They quit calling me grandma and I let them use the restroom in my office as long as they kept it clean. I wouldn't say we were friends, but we had an agreement.

When I had to go to Honolulu for meetings, the little one would come to my house to walk and water Wharf. Early on I noticed that he left dusty little footprints inside and out. I wasn't sure why he'd been looking into my house that first week while Liebe was still on island, but some questions were best left unanswered.

A lump on the ocean moved toward me and built into a passable wave. I spun my board around and paddled hard, bouncing a little bit to build speed. I hopped up, my left foot in front of my right and made a swift turn to slow down and hang onto the wave longer, as I totally snaked one of the kids. My new board was the shit. I walked forward until I had ten toes off the nose and grinned as I rode it toward the beach. When there was nothing left but whitewater, I dropped down and paddled back out, glancing at an inbound cruise ship and thinking about my job.

Yake's assistant had been promoted to his position. It turned out her hostility had been due to her animus toward him and the way he ran the office, not me. She was everything I wanted in a boss: Fair, firm, and alive.

She's also the one who figured out that Colley wasn't Yake's first victim. He'd killed my predecessor in a fight over the money set aside for the new restrooms in the harbor. She'd discover Junior Pololi's forwarded mail and checkbook in Yake's desk when she took over. There was no sign of his body, but the tiger sharks at Mala Wharf might have been a clue.

Mangas had closed the waters near the wharf ever since the day Liebe and I had seen them out there. He had also finally gotten the message that I wasn't gay and had proceeded to hit on me for the next two weeks. Eventually, I told him bald guys gave me the willies, but not in a good way. He never came into my office without a hat again, and he always offered a courtesy flush in the potty. Small victories are, indeed, sweet.

For my part, I resisted using a fake German accent on him. I think he was still kind of embarrassed about the sticky-fingered *au pair* using him to protect her side business. She admitted that she used the accent to get the *au pair* gig, since that made her more employable by the upper middle-class *haole* families, than if she were just a girl from New York. Good old discrimination roamed wild and free in the islands, in many different forms.

The little surfer dudes were chattering about feeding Wharf a breakfast sandwich at the loading dock where he waited while I surfed. I smiled. He had become not my only friend, but my best friend. Having such a loyal, kind, and intelligent soul in my world offered me some of the faith and confidence I had lost along with my hearing.

Brita and Darcy too had proven to be smart and funny girls who conned me into hula lessons twice a week with them. At our last after hula "meeting" Brita broke the silence about missing the story of her life as she guzzled her third lemon drop.

"Deep undercover," she muttered. "I've heard of it, but I've never seen it before."

I snorted, not wanting to think about either Snake or Layla. It was still too raw.

While I mused, the boys had been grabbing waves left and right. The little one yelled to me, "Take this one!" It was a generous offer and too good to refuse. I paddled along with it, but it never broke and instead slid under me and on to the shore. Of course, the next one was the set wave and three of the kids caught it. Hmm... I'd have to be sure I didn't fall for that again.

Another guy had paddled into the line-up while I'd dinked around chasing a phantom. He looked to be in his forties, too pale to be local, but too cocky to be a beginner. We sat together watching for the next set. Just as I saw it on the horizon, he started mindlessly whistling the tune I'd been hearing on the radio and from all the booze cruises as they lumbered back into the harbor at night: "Breath of Life."

It gave me just the right combination of adrenaline and power so that I won the wave. As he dumped off and I slid past him I heard him say, "You'll owe me a drink." It was a thought, but it wouldn't be rum. I'd had to give up Mai Tais after the night Yake had been killed. I might have had one too many, only to discover that the tile on my bathroom floor wasn't that comfortable a place to sleep, although it was close to the toilet. Lesson learned.

At that moment, more than ever, I missed Liebe's company. I wanted to turn to her and talk about the board and the wave and the weather. She had left Maui as soon as she got out of jail. Nigel waited a week and followed her. At first she had resisted him because of his "big secret" then relented when the truth wasn't anything we had suspected. He wasn't gay, married, or both—he was going through chemo, hence the hairless commando visual I'd been given the first time I saw him. Underwear made him chafe and the colon cancer made him cautious about a long-term relationship. He and Liebe had a lot in common, with a lust for life right at the top of the list.

The day before, my mailbox had held a few bills, a couple ads, and a postcard showing the break at Rincon. In Liebe's handwriting it read: "Epic surf. High pressure. Clean swells. Long lines. All from your direction. Flawless."